I0417840

Alias Tomorrow
Copyright © 2025 by Anthony Caplan

Cover Art by Eve Caplan

ISBN: 987-0-9815166-8-4

Hope Mountain Press
810 Ray Road
Henniker, NH 03242

Alias Tomorrow

No man* knows how much he is an optimist, even when he calls himself a pessimist, because he has not really measured the depths of his debt to whatever created him and enabled him to call himself anything.

G.K. Chesterton
*(or woman)

One

The dwellers in the glades of blissful freedom made coffee while he searched for words in the shadows. When they came, they would ring with the sound of trumpets and distant harmonies.
Go.

Alpha

Antioch could no longer say with confidence that his conversations with Reid had been kept confidential. Yes, they had taken place in the Zocalo during the recreations of the ancient fire festival. But hidden among the costumed participants there could have been OneWorld plants.

"Look, man. Can you tell me whether Reid will even be here in fifteen minutes?" asked Garcia.

"Wait, give him a chance to show up," said Antioch.

"No time," said Garcia.

"So, you're suggesting that we ditch him. He shows up here and the beach is empty."

Garcia ignored him, shoulders twitching with some memory of insolence or trauma.

"Look at them. They ain't no fishermen," said Garcia.

"Those boys? They're here every day fishing. Snapper, parrot fish. Seen it with my own eyes," said Antioch.

"Parrot fish? They extinct now, like fifty years, brother. You've been set up with some cheap ass special effects."

There was a glitch, a glint of light reflecting off the nets cast by the fishermen from off of the rock. Antioch suddenly thought that Garcia might be right, had probably been right all along. That meant that all the months of stalking and cultivating Reid as an informer, all the notes he carried in his head from their conversations, all the coded entries on the transponder were now worthless. What's more, they were dangerous and would need to be wiped.

"Okay. Say it's all shit, the Reid notes, all his so-called info. We go up to Tijuana. And then what? What's Shoeman going to say? That's gonna be one hell of a conversation," said Antioch.

"Shoeman ain't even real, man. Getcha game on, Antioch," said Garcia.

"How do I know you're real?"

"How do you know anything? Shithead."

Garcia, annoying as he seemed, had a point. Antioch had a hard time knowing anything was real. He'd been raised by Mancie Littell in Tennessee with the perhaps imagined words of his long absent father Don forever in his ears, ringing the alarm of fight. As a runaway teen landing in the streets of Knoxville, he'd come under the influence of a Chomskyite cell that espoused action against the machine as a path to cleansing and personal salvation. Disillusioned with the personal politics of utopia, he'd joined the Democravian military, volunteering to salvage his abused sense of personal honor in what remained of his youth. Years later, battle scarred, part of that defeated army under General Steiner that had surrendered to OneWorld, still searching for redemption, he'd drifted out west. He'd married Winona, and they'd had a daughter, Uvlin, who was the key to their happiness.

He took on freelance work, investigative gigs during those years, and ended up working full-time undercover for Shoeman's foundation, the Anthrog Nosti. He liked reporting to Shoeman because the occasional existential threat gave him direction and a backstop to his own still meandering consciousness.

"Let's go," said Antioch.

"See?" said Garcia.

The two men walked silently, plodding across the waste ground of a parking lot in Cabo San Lucas. In their wake the wind picked up, scattering spouts of dust across the pockmarked asphalt. The Pacific shimmered beyond the break, a silver pool of mystery. In the distance, shrouds of unresolved matter blanketed an army of giant blades. They rotated at a pace dictated by a fragmented logic that was the object of their quest.

Zipping up Carretera Uno, the coast road to La Paz, they stopped at a charging station in the center of a dusty, overheated crossroad. Teenaged girls ate soft synthetic chocolate cones in the shade, sitting cross-legged at the curb. Local boys, rodeo stars, wearing shades and braided rainbow mullets, charged their amphibious vehicles, customized Chinese puddle hoppers, while Garcia and Antioch waited on their bikes. Only their channel blockers, downloaded on the black market, rendered them immune from the wireless, dopamine enhancing blasts from the OneWorld puppet regime in the radius of the station. Once the bikes were fully charged, they looked around, ignoring the local youth, and gunned the electric motors for the road again.

The sun was sinking out on the horizon, torching, eternal fire in and out of sight. At the crest of the hills, buzzards rode the thermals in silent predatory spirals, drifting up and out of the violet dusk. It hadn't rained in 16 months. The desalination plants, running on modular fission, worked overtime to provide the remnant population, descendants of the indigenous Guaycura mixed with a century's refugees from around the globe. The OneWorld north of the border was a sprawling, amnesiac haven amid the wreckage of civilizational collapse. South of the border the lands were running out of water.

Antioch's mind relaxed its fearsome grip on his sympathetic nervous system. He checked the transponder on his wrist with a glance. It was 6:30 Pacific Time. Uvlin was asleep in Atlanta, dreaming her nightly attempts to get unstuck from whatever road she had wandered off on. His cortisol levels were fine but the catecholamines were still in the orange zone. What would Shoeman say? A moment, a breath, a day, and a night at a time. He was on the road, a particularly corrugated stretch of hills, water and sky under the planet's rotational spell of light and gravity. In a few weeks, he would head back East to see Uvlin, settle his mind, see she was okay. They would catch up, eat at her favorite restaurants, hang out with her friends, and try to forget the pain of Winona's long-expected last flight. Whose fault? No-one's fault. Antioch's brain had automated the call and response to that thought.

Two

The phone buzzed on his desk. He hoped it would be Daniel, calling with an update on travel plans. He picked up the phone, thumbing the cracked screen. It was not a known contact, but a 603 area code. He took a chance. A tele-marketer would be an amusing distraction, he thought.

"Hello, is this William Morrow?"

"Yes, who is this?"

"Good morning, William. This is Shelly Patenaud with Sun River Bank in Hanover. I believe you are the executor of the Margaret O'Donnell Cox estate. Is that correct?"

"That's right."

Margaret O'Donnell Cox. Six months gone. Predeceased by second husband Rich Cox, from Covid. Nana's remembrance service in St. Agnes a muddy March morning. Siblings, cousins and long lost acquaintances arrived in waves. Sarah, Mackenzy, and Ellen between, cradling them each with her arms, together in the front row of folding chairs in the community room, facing the table lined with photos and candles. He spoke, tears streaming freely on some of their faces. He couldn't remember now what he had said. Daniel stood in the back with his cousins, dressed in rough weather gear and work boots. The month before, when the old woman had tossed and turned on her final fevered dream, Daniel had called home at midnight on WhatsApp from the depth of the PNW, fuzzy cell phone image of his face, long, black hair covering his eyes, in some darkened Portland street, swaying in the dusk.

Two weeks ago she'd appeared in two dreams. He'd noted them down, as much as he could remember.

"You are aware that the account here is off limits until the probate process has run its course."

"Yes," said Morrow, red flags slowly rising on the tracks of his muddied synapses. He reached for his coffee and

8

waited. The woman cleared her throat and shuffled around in her swivel seat in the Hanover branch office.

"There was an attempted withdrawal several hours ago from that account. The server indicates it came from a computer logged in in your vicinity, William."

"Well, that's impossible."

"In any case, we are obligated by federal regulations to inform you and do some verification. You're saying it wasn't you."

"Yeah, no. Wasn't me. Or anybody here."

Ellen drifted by in her slippers behind him, padding softly on the old, worn pine boards. Mackenzy and Saroj slipped in the back door from the apples. Ellen caught them and directed them to the kitchen table with some commentary on the state of the season and early fall leaf colors.

Shelly Patenaud was going on about "the account has been restored to default status" and "avoiding significant short and long-term financial damage", and "we are prepared to offer you credit monitoring and identity protection services."

"Can I have your social security number, William?" she asked.

"My social security number? Sure," said Morrow, stalling for a second until the numbers appeared in his mind. "Zero five two..."

"No," said Ellen, appearing at his shoulder. "Don't give them..."

"What?" asked Morrow, covering the bottom of the cell phone with his index finger."

"Not your social," said Ellen.

Morrow lifted his index finger and raised the phone to his chin.

"I'm sorry. I guess I prefer to come in in person."

"That's fine," said the woman. "You do understand the account is frozen until then."

"Yes," said Morrow stiffly, putting the phone down on the table. Ellen lifted it and checked it for the details of the call, to make sure it was off. She placed it back on the table.

"Why don't you come and chat for a bit. There's fresh coffee."

"I don't need more distraction right now," he grumbled.

"Oh, come on. It will be good for Mackenzy," said Ellen, her hazel eyes firmly fixed on him. "They're already bored," she whispered.

"Well, that's not..."

"Shh," she admonished.

Morrow rose to his feet, stretching, putting the work aside. The low morning sunlight in the window struck him harshly. He stepped toward the kitchen. Mackenzy and Saroj sat at the table. Mackenzy laughed at something Saroj was saying. Morrow was jealous for an instant. He loved his daughter's laugh possessively.

"Well, I guess I will have a refill," said Morrow, pouring himself a cup of coffee again from the french press on the wood stove. The echinacea flowering outside swayed in a gust of wind, survivor of the tropical storm that had swept through overnight.

"How are you, Dad?" asked Mackenzy.

"I'm all right," said Morrow. "How did you two sleep?"

"Saroj. Allergies," said Mackenzy, holding up her palm, a parodic echo of television show comedians.

"I don't know what it is. Maybe pollen," said Saroj in a sing-song, congested voice, hints of a British colonial past.

"Maybe it's the country," said Mackenzy wryly, screwing up her lips in a comedian's smile, bringing awkward possibilities to the surface in a way that Morrow identified as one of his mother's ancient traits to put people at ease. Sometimes it backfired. It took confidence, a social confidence that Morrow himself had never possessed.

Saroj laughed.

"Could be," he said.

"You'd think the rain would have washed away any pollen in the air. But with the changing climate, the pollen season is getting much longer," said Morrow, leaning against the window in what he hoped was an authoritative yet friendly pose.

"And the growing season," said Saroj. "Possibilities for cash crops, Mr. Morrow?" he added.

"Well," said Morrow. "Maybe."

"Farming is always going to be a hard row to hoe," said Ellen, wiping a counter with a kitchen cloth.

"Especially in today's environment," added Morrow.

"We had the sheep. Remember?" said Ellen.

"I wish we still had them," said Mackenzy wistfully.

"Well, you all decided you were vegetarians at some point in the not too distant past. Made keeping the sheep a difficult proposition to justify," said Morrow.

"We couldn't stand to see them disappear once we figured out we were eating our cute little things, could we," said Mackenzy.

"We always tried to get them loaded and off to the butcher while you were asleep on the weekends," said Ellen.

"Saroj," coughed Morrow seriously. "We had visions of ourselves as homesteaders when we moved here over twenty years ago."

Morrow wanted Saroj, from Punjab and studying in his first year at the college in Maine where his daughter also was matriculated, to see that once they had been appropriately filled with grand ideas about how to live lives of balance and sustainability. Now their field, once humming with an electric fence and mowed by the sheep, was overgrown with ragweed, nettles, thistle and milkweed. At least it qualified as a pollinator friendly, successional ecosystem, if Saroj or anyone were to ask.

"Youthful idealism," said Ellen, smiling at him, tolerant of both their foibles.

"Visions," said Saroj, looking at Mackenzy.

He wasn't smirking, as far as Morrow could tell. But he didn't trust the utterance, and Mackenzy's tight-lipped smile was a new expression. Morrow stored away his thoughts, consigning them in a practiced move to memory.

"We could go for a hike in the woods," said Ellen. "Show Saroj the woods. Our woods."

"It's not our woods anymore, Mom. The ATVs have taken over," said Mackenzy sourly.

"Oh, no. There's still our woods," said Ellen insistently.

Mother and daughter stared at each other, banking their secret accords and disagreements, the shared years that had passed as the children grew into their adult selves in flashes of time. Morrow thought he should say something, but couldn't think what. He gulped a large part of his lukewarm coffee and retreated into thoughts of his book. Where was it headed? Who was the intended audience? He needed to develop the elevator pitch for a phone call he had scheduled with Mitch Epp, his agent in Los Angeles in the coming week. He could feel his throat tighten with the thought.

The buzzing in the kitchen rose in pitch. Seated again at the table in the dining room, away from the main stream of breakfast, Morrow bent to the task, staring at the last thing he'd written before the interruption of the phone call from Sun River Bank. This is what his work had alway boiled down to, staring at a blank screen and waiting patiently for a rising impulse to lift his fingers into action. He could be hiding from something, missing something back at the breakfast table, but Morrow would not contemplate that right away. More to the point though, what was he railing against in this book? How would it all go down in the end? That was the beauty of the calling that had attracted him from the beginning, the notion of being a servant to some hidden narrative rising from the shadows. It always did.

"Come on, Dad. Get ready."

On the other hand, there was Mackenzy, tugging at his attention. Just as he was about to get started again. There could be no mistaking it now. This was life calling. He couldn't resist.

Morrow sighed and rose again from the table. Outside, beyond the old double-hung windows, the sun had broken through clouds and streamed a bright, rising light on the dying red leaves of the maple tree that overspread the driveway. The four of them set out up the dirt road, past the new houses that led to the Gorman farm at the top of the hill. Here, up the rutted drive, behind the ruined old farmhouse, beyond the rusting hulks of a tractor and the two moving trucks that had once served as grain storage, was the old Class VI road leading into the reserve of forest that had last been logged when Dwight Gorman had still roamed the earth. Morrow was explaining how Dwight's life had been forever set on the downward spiral typical of late stage capitalism and the get-big-or-get-out mentality that afflicted his country. Saroj interrupted him.

"Does the town not have a health officer?" he asked. Morrow wondered whether he was being intentionally spoofed.

"Oh, not really," said Ellen, catching up to them with Mackenzy at her side.

"A health officer," said Saroj, repeating himself in case she hadn't heard. "I mean look at the state of this. There could be issues, no?"

"We don't have that sort of a town," said Ellen, grabbing Morrow by the arm. "It's more of a ... small town with a libertarian bent. 'Live free or die' is our state motto," she added. "Wouldn't you say, William?"

"You're doing fine, dear," said Morrow. Ellen had a stronger handle on local politics. Starting out as a school nurse, Ellen had risen to the position of hospital administrator, working in the orthopedic section of the Catholic Medical Center in Manchester.

"My God," said Saroj. "This would never do."

Morrow liked the fact that the kid was expressing shock. But he, William Morrow, author of science fiction, creator of imaginary worlds, liked the wrack and ruin of the place. It made it attractive, in his opinion, a better spot from which to observe the entropy that ran the table in the wider sphere. Eventually, all their efforts came to this, to the beauty that lay in decrepitude. You might as well accept it. How could he communicate that thought? He would put it in the book he was writing. He made a note to himself: ruined house, rising tides.

In the woods now, they walked two abreast along the old logging track cut not too many years ago by oxen-drawn carts in the snow and mud of the Wabenaki forest, through stands of beech, birch, oak, and maple second growth, occasionally big old hemlock survivors of the first clearances, and the bare, skeletal remainders of the ash, fallen prey in the last few years to invasive, wood- boring beetles. Morrow looked up at the virgin blue sky through the trunks straining upwards, drawn by the sun in a millennial feeding frenzy. He wondered about his own life and what was pulling him along, now that he had reached the age where the clamor of existence no longer seemed as compelling. Was it mere inertia, strength of habit, like the solid trunks carrying the canopy of leaves, that held him on the path? Or was it Ellen, her lithe frame belying a strength and conviction that she herself did not believe she possessed, that beckoned him further? He loved the forest for the way it inevitably drew him into a search for deeper answers to the existential questions. He pushed them away, deeper into denial because there were no answers. Slow down, you mere two-legged creature, was what the woods seemed to be saying.

They heard the drone in the woods long before the ATVs appeared at a junction of two snowmobile trails, four of them, one behind the other, two riders on each vehicle. They were accelerating up the incline of the trail towards them. The driver of the first ATV slowed when he saw them, the second following suit. He smiled as he drew alongside. He had a red beard, bad teeth and a grin in his eyes behind the plastic workshop goggles. The four of them instinctively stepped off the trail and paused, standing safely among the stones of an ancient border wall and the snarl of old logging operations as the ATVs passed by.

Beta

It was Garcia checking in.

"I say we pull off, get some sleep," said Antioch, slowing down around a curve south of Mulege. There was static on the headset. Antioch could swear the static was telling him something about Garcia's thoughts. Quantum glitches interfering with the resistance. Garcia was cutting speed, slowing down. Improvisation like the fox. Their winding, back-pedaling trail would be impossible to decipher or predict. Instead of riding all night, which they had intended in order to arrive in Tijuana in time for the meeting with Shoeman, they would pull off and camp out incognito.

"Yeah, okay," said Garcia, braking. As did Antioch. They pulled off the road.

A quarter moon rose just out from a headland that jutted eastward. Its light spread a silver cone on the still waters of the Sea of Cortez. They maneuvered onto a furrowed foot path and wound through the brush and boulders along the hill, descending gently towards a slightly indented bay ahead. Antioch stopped, putting his left boot down and leaning into the hill as Garcia caught up. Their way was blocked by glinting snags of barbed wire. The two motorcycles alternated strafing light searches across the hillside.

"What do you think?" asked Antioch into the headpiece, adjusting the volume down on the dashboard above the battery pack.

"It's all right. We go down there and get underneath the wire."

Antioch looked over to verify the direction Garcia intended. Cutting back into the headland to the left and behind, along the diagonal path of the fence, there seemed to be a gully in the shadows, the crotch of the land, perhaps formed by recent flood waters coming off the the ridge out of which the moon seemed to be rising, as if expelled from its hiding place. He wouldn't have picked such a trail himself, but working with Garcia meant trusting Garcia's instincts.

The two motorcycles made their way in the shadows of the moon down into Garcia's gulley. When they came across a ditch with the barbed wire fence cutting across it, they paused again. Antioch shut off the motor to save power while they figured out how to get through the wire. Garcia followed suit. They pulled off their helmets to speak and be heard more clearly.

"Only thing I can see is to slide the bikes under," said Antioch.

They worked in the dark to unpack the pannier bags and dry packs and sling them over to the far side of the barbed wire fence, careful not to snag or rip any fibers from the all weather jackets that could give away any clues to their passage. Then they wheeled the bikes one by one into the ditch, laid them on their sides, at a good angle to the fence, on top of one of the foil sided blankets, and pulled them under the wire, pried upwards by carefully placed mesquite branches. It was hard and slow, but they succeeded in a short time to sit back on their bikes with all of the gear assembled. The night was as quiet as before, just the sound of water lapping rhythmically on the rocks of the dark headland. Antioch took a deep breath, stretching his back, quieting the nerves.

Switching the bikes back on, they continued down on the beach side of the fence. The beach was about a hundred yards long, and about thirty yards wide at low tide. There was one sparse, tin roofed palapa down at the south end but no other visible sign of human habitation. The water out to the horizon was lit silver by the risen moon, the stillness only broken by the sound of howling coyotes to the back of them. When they had the camping tarp stretched out over the soft sand, yellow in the moonlight above the tidal flotsam, and the military issue sleeping pads inflated, Garcia broke out a bottle of pulque he'd picked up in Mazatlan. Antioch brushed his teeth down at the water's edge. Garcia's drinking habit bothered him, although he had also once been a heavy drinker. That was one thing that got in the way of Garcia's effectiveness – his need for recreational drugs no matter where they were and what the circumstances. He walked back to the tarp, making a checklist of what he could see, a hillside broken by boulders, mesquite, cactus, and shadow, and above it the extrusion of the Milky Way. He took a long slug of water from the camel pack and settled under the foil blanket, prepared to forget all cares and dream of better, more peaceful days.

"Set your alarm, Garcia," he said.

"What time?"

"We got thirteen hours of riding to get to Tijuana."

"Five o'clock?

"Sounds good."

"You going to sleep?" asked Garcia.

"Of course," said Antioch.

He waited for a response. Garcia lifted the bottle and slugged down a couple of long gulps. Antioch screwed himself further under the foil blanket. The coyotes sang in blood-thirsty yips to the moon. Soon he would be in Atlanta and none of this would matter. The OneWorld and its ever-growing totalitarian presence, Shoeman's shock troops for the beleaguered democratic resistance – a plague on both their houses – before drifting off to sleep, perhaps to a dream of a better, less analytic, more synthetic path.

Garcia was shaking him.

"Get up, dude," said Garcia.

It was early light. Dawn. Maybe five. He sat up.

"Is it time?"

"Look."

Garcia's voice was hushed, the air caught in his larynx by something, an unexpected event, maybe a person. He ran instantly through several possibilities: the bikes had been stolen, the tide was swamping, someone was there, perhaps the regime's guardia regional. But no, he couldn't hear the waves any closer or the sound of any humans. And the theft of the bikes was way too improbable. Garcia was prone to these fits of sudden, alcohol induced panic. It was probably nothing, thought Antioch, rubbing his eyes before propping himself on his elbow, proceeding to push up with his hand in the sand, wet with condensation.

He twisted and turned from under the tarp to look to the east, towards the waters of the little bay where they had parked for the night, the waves lapping placidly on the beach.

"What's that?" he asked.

Out in the bay was a barge of some sort, a long, flat boat above the mercurial waters.

"Don't know," said Garcia, vindicated.

Antioch made a sudden burst out from under the blanket. Garcia slapped an arm across his chest to slow him down.

"Woah, there, bro."

"What are you doing?" sputtered Antioch.

"It could be OneWorld. Stay down."

Their wrestling somehow set the vessel in motion. It slowly began to approach the shore, growing larger, sprouting outriggers, humming in an insect-like low pitch as they spread, until it reached the shallows, where it set the outriggers down and began to levitate itself out of the water like a giant six-legged beast.

Antioch felt ill, a sudden wave of nausea hitting him full force. WIth extreme difficulty he willed himself to move, Garcia following after him. Both men stood on the sand, unsteady on their feet, staring at the horrific object rising before them.

Panic-struck, they dashed in a blur to their bikes where they were parked against the rock edge of the cliff. The shadow of the boat loomed behind. Despite the pull of the boat, exerting a kind of gravitational force, they managed to sit astride the bikes, ready to haul out of there, but the motors weren't switching on. Nothing was happening.

"What the fuck's this now?" groaned Garcia.

"Some kind of force field," said Antioch, panting for breath. "Can't start."

"OneWorld bullshit!"

Garcia jumped off the useless motorcycle back to his feet, followed by Antioch. But the ground beneath was disappearing, as was the sand and the sky, all of Antioch's field of vision, even when he turned and looked at Garcia beside his bike, sucked down some swirling vortex towards the vessel hanging overhead like a monstrous bird of prey, blacking out the sun.

Antioch retained consciousness. He was aware, even as he spun around and around in some dreamstate, that he was still there, still relatively conscious and able to identify himself as an observer undergoing the experience of being subjected to this panoply of dreams.

His mother and father and a black river banked by willows. He was swimming in the deep part of the river as was his baby sister Skye, who had died when he was twelve in a drowning accident on Eagle Creek. His mother Mancie, who'd worked as a hair stylist in town for decades and was buried in the Benton County Memorial Garden, was calling from the shore, but they couldn't hear her. Mancie always responded "out west" when he asked where his father was, so he imagined his final resting place was a patch of desert out on the high plains south of the urban sprawl of Greater Las Vegas. But Skye, whom he did not recognize, her face was fuzzy in his mind's eye, was telling him that his father wanted him to contact an attorney, that he wanted his remains transferred to the family plot next to Mancie, who had been ripped away from him by the unmitigated impact of his afflictions.

He didn't know where he was. He tried to imagine where he was going. He wasn't sure he was still alive in the traditional sense of the word: breathing, with a heart beat, with an ability to mobilize himself after the necessary resources to survive. What would those be? That was also a difficult question to answer on his own. He really needed to acknowledge his own limitations regarding the basic questions of existence that had plagued him along with his father, Don Littell, and probably everyone that had come before. The ones who came after – Uvlin and her children, were she ever to find an appropriate mate and partner with whom to share her DNA, they might not have the same concerns. He couldn't be sure of that, either. Times changed, that was for sure. It was changing very fast about now. He had the distinct impression of crossing a threshold in the fabric of the universe, which put a stop to all his useless contemplations.

He opened his eyes. A blank white slab of metallic ceiling and inset, blinding halide lights. He tilted his chin, craned his neck upwards and stretched his back and shoulders. Two metal chairs, two indistinct shapes of people in the chairs, no nonsense types, observing him as he awoke. Where was this? And where was Garcia? One of the observers slowly stood and approached the foot of the bed where he was lying. He could see a crisp uniform shirt over broad, heavily muscled arms, the patches of the Kraken Brigade, the expeditionary force of OneWorld, on the sleeves. At one time they had been mostly hired mercenaries from the former Islamic regions of the Caucasus, originally re-formed from the fragments of the Russian Federation's Wagner divisions, after the fall of Kazakhstan.

A face took shape before him. Black, creased lines on a short forehead and small, smug eyes under heavy brows. This was not going to be fun. Antioch wondered if there was going to be vindictive behavior – beheadings, torture and the like.

"We are happy to have you with us now, Mr. Antioch Littell. How do you feel? Is there anything you would like?"

"Yes, I need you to tell me where I am."

"Admirable. How you say straightforward. Very much with the personality profile. But you are a prisoner, I regret to inform, of the Admiral Nazar, one of the Kraken fleet's amphibian spearheads. We are to keep you safe and how you say secured until we reach our destination, Base Svyatogor on the Red Planet, Mars. Your companion is in a separate habitation. You are to be provided with whatever you like, food, drugs, entertainment, and any other which you need. What do you like? The sooner you become how you say accustomed to the passage rules of the space fleet, the better for us all."

"And who do I have the pleasure of dealing with?"

"Major Ignace Dmitrievsky at your service."

"Nice to meet you."

"Yes. Equally. My pleasure as well."

"Have we ... met before?"

"I believe we may have previously met, eh, metaphorically. But not in a personal way."

"Kazakhstan."

"Kanyagash. Yes. We are well aware of your time in the 69th Armored Division, Sergeant Major."

"We lost a lot of men and a lot of armor in that one."

"I'm sure you remember it well. The roads of Dzagurk and Yrgyz were a strategic, how you say a bad loss for our Wagner Division that day."

"February, 2132. I think I can still feel it right here."

Antioch gripped his right femur, grazed by gun fire. He'd never fully recovered strength there.

"I was also once an infantry scout. Spetsnaz. We have a lot in common, Antioch."

"Very nice. I want to know where Garcia is."

"Your companion Mr. Jones is comfortable. Have no fear for him. He has quickly requested that he could be well provided with satinate. That is something we are fulfilling in a very quick time. Our satinate stores are indigenous, from greenhouses on board. Let me know if you need it. Anything you

22

need, Antioch. We will try to satisfy. Just one question about the Anthrog Nosti. We believe you have been in employment, correct?"

"No clue. Garcia and I run a bike shop in San Clemente. I'll be sure to let you know if I need anything. But I'd like to have access to Garcia. He's a simple man, but easily confused," said Antioch, sitting up and looking Dimitrievski carefully in both eyes. He had a slight drift in the right pupil. No, he was not an avatar. Antioch was almost disappointed, since it meant he was dealing with a human with a real propensity for charm. Dmitrievsky was likable, partly because of their shared history of service, but also because he seemed to be genuinely capable of a civilized empathy. He quickly reminded himself not to be lulled into identification with his captors. The Stockholm Syndrome would be among the psychological ploys that the OneWorld would use to dominate and destroy his will to freedom.

They were in a pickle, there was no doubt. Bound for Mars across 140 million miles of space in an interplanetary vessel, probably of the Eskelon class, with the famed fusion-powered Magnitron jets built by Bosch Steinburgh in the early 2130s. It made it all the easier to bear if one could hope for decent treatment. But he knew there was nothing valued in that kind of approach by Dmitrievsky's bosses. On the other hand, in order to gain access to his knowledge of Shoeman's network of resistance activists, they would need to keep him alive, lull him into a state of complacency, and get him to spill the beans the old-fashioned way. The secrets of the brain's memory stores were as fathomless as they had ever been.

He slept again, laying down with a heavy feeling of loss on the cot in this alcove on the Nazar. There was nothing left to do, no twisting thoughts at this point would avail to change the basic state of things. The weight of his failure seemed lighter than he would have thought, a mercy on the part of destiny. He was afforded the luxury of sleep, a legacy of the planet and the evolutionary matrix they were leaving behind. Despite the curving walls of his prison, he held in his mind's eye the image of the royal blue orb.

Three

"What's it called?" asked Mitch.

"I don't know. Doesn't have a name yet, Mitch," said Morrow.

"Okay let's think of one."

"Okay."

"How about The Death Call of the Sphinx?"

"No. I don't like that."

"Why not?"

"Too vague."

"Well, give me something. Peter likes a good title."

"I know."

"It's a WASP thing."

"I know."

"You're not a WASP, Will, are you?"

"Don't ask rhetorical questions," said Morrow.

He and Mitch had been friends since the lower mid year at Kent, both of them outsiders, from beyond the fashionable suburban haunts that fed the school with pupils, both skinny runners going hard on the cross country team, putting up a brave front against the hazing rituals and cliques. Mitch had gone on to Williams and a career in New York City's surviving bastions of the written word and now, as an agent, divorced and enjoying a second act as a long-haired, (not his own!), exponent of spiritual growth and nouvelle cuisine in the Hollywood hills, he represented up and coming voices of the tasty and politically fashionable. They'd stayed in touch while Morrow's peripatetic course had taken him from Tulane to timber framing and nonprofits in Vermont, through government work making training films at the departments of agriculture and transportation in Montpelier. Then, in his mid thirties, with two kids in tow, he and Ellen had switched mortgages to the derelict old farmhouse at the top of the hill in Northfield, New Hampshire. The idea had been for him to make *documentaries while she raised the kids. Ellen had gone back to work six months after the birth of their youngest, Mackenzy. The documentaries had never been made. Instead, Morrow had gotten involved making furniture, outfitting a workshop in the basement of the house and listening to talk radio while he turned wood. He had sold a few chairs to an art gallery in Woodstock, Vermont.*

A first science fiction book was self published, followed by offers from his old school buddy Mitch to represent him to Black Star Press in San Diego. Black Star specialized in digital and audio books for an audience it had developed over two decades, fed on Japanese anime and feminist works to expect anti-climax, which fit Morrow's explorations in dystopian visions of chaos and conspiracy. Against all the odds, Morrow had developed a following and a reputation as a writer of a type of science fiction best categorized as impressionistic and personal. He had leaned into the oeuvre, pumping out a dozen more works over the years. None of them, however, had provided him with the financial wherewithal to adopt the habits of mind of the successful provider with which his own father had been endowed. Eugene Morrow, lawyer and fixer for the Pax Americana, last seen living in Romanesque splendor in Tuscany, had been the sort of father that one survived only by growing scar tissue around the heart. Morrow's heart was well armored in that way, but he still wished sometimes that he'd made enough money to throw in his father's face as proof of something. It had never come to pass, and here was Mitch, with the constant refrain of the corner to be turned in terms of audience alignment. He was well meaning, but Morrow was resistant to the turns of spirit necessary to find market success. It made for an uneasy alliance.

"Listen, you come out here on the fifteenth with a title in mind," said Mitch. "You think?"

"Yeah. I'll have something," said Morrow, unenthused.

"And a couple of intriguing bullet points. A tie-in to climate change. They're big on that. Is that too much to ask? And listen. Don't make the bad guys ethnic in any big way."

"Everybody's ethnic, Mitch. Even the WASPs. It's a fucking ethnic group."

Morrow put down the phone and went outside to find Ellen in the garden. She wasn't there. He wandered down the overgrown paths alone between the beds. This time of year everything had busted loose, fruited, seeded, and or died: the stubby corn husks, fallen over tomato plants, squash plants overgrown in the strawberry bed, strawberry leaves in the deep greens and maroons of terminal maturity, bees still buzzing over the surviving blue flowers of some unidentified, cold hardy weeds. Morrow breathed in deeply of the luxurious airs of decay and decrepitude that Ellen had manufactured from the artifice of her garden. It was almost as good as the vegetable crops she gathered there year after year. Morrow's main task for many years had been to wheelbarrow the manure and dig by hand into the beds from the sheep barn, but now he pulled the utility trailer behind the Honda to the horse farm on the other side of town, where high school farmhands loaded it in with a tractor from the mountain of muck behind the horse complex. Much easier, but it still meant some wheelbarrowing for a few days before the snow flew. That was something he still needed to do. It was on the calendar for later that month. Penciled in, like everything in his life.

He saw Mackenzy and Ellen cutting across between the apple trees. They intercepted his path back to the house. He stopped and waited for them to get into earshot before calling out.

"Hey there," he yelled.

Mackenzy looked up and smiled. Ellen was saying something to her. Morrow wondered what they were talking about.

"What's going on?"

"Not much," said Mackenzy.

Morrow fell into step with the two women, going up the hillside, looking back over his shoulders to gauge their mood. Mackenzy looked up and smiled at him.

"What are you two talking about?" he asked.

"I'm going back to school tonight, Dad. Can you drive me?"

"Of course. What about Saroj?"

"He's on leave this trimester. He doesn't want to go back home all the way to Chandigarh. He thought he had an internship lined up in Boston, but the funding fell through at the last minute. Can you guys put him up, Dad? At least for a few days."

"It's okay by me," said Ellen.

"Well, what's a few days?" asked Morrow.

"I don't know, Dad. A few days," said Mackenzy impatiently.

"What difference does a few days more or less make, William?" asked Ellen.

"None, I guess," said Morrow.

Morrow loved driving the back road north across the gap between Kearsarge and the Minks and then across the Black Water dam and up into Sandwich and Ossipee. The sun had just descended beyond the line of mountains to the north of Winnipisaukee, leaving a glorious spread of rose clouds across the horizon behind them. Mackenzy was quiet in the passenger seat. He was determined not to push forward with any forced line of questioning. Finally, she cleared her throat and pushed the earbuds off.

"Thanks for driving, Dad," she said.

"Not a problem, honey. You know I love to drive. It's a pleasure to do it. I hope I am always here to get you from point A to point B. It gives me a sense of purpose."

"Are you being sarcastic?"

"Not at all."

28

"I can't tell sometimes with you, Dad. Dad, do you think polyamory is a viable choice for couples?"

"No."

"I don't think so, either."

"Why? Is that ...?"

"No. No, no. It's just something in my course description here."

"What course is that?"

"Course on happiness."

"Is that in the psychology department?"

"No. Anthro. Cross-cultural. History of Happiness."

"I see."

They were quiet for a while. By the time the car reached the turnoff for 95, it had long been dark. The headlights of cars and trucks buzzed by going north and south. Morrow gunned the automatic drive on the Honda and got up to speed. Before Mackenzy could get the earbuds back in, he thought he had better say something.

"What makes you want to take a course on happiness?"

"I don't know," said Mackenzy, upset perhaps at the line of obvious questions she could foresee. Morrow pressed ahead anyway, nothing to lose now.

"Would you say that you're happy?"

Mackenzy turned in her seat and sat up straighter.

"I think so, Dad. Sometimes. I'm not sure, though. What is happiness? Do we even know?"

"A sense of well-being? A sense of satisfaction?" suggested Morrow.

"Someone or something looking out for you? Is that what it is? What happens when you get old enough to fend for yourself? Is that when you're happy, when you're looking out for yourself?"

"Frankly, I don't think it's something to aim for," said Morrow, both hands on the wheel. "Personal happiness is overrated."

"But it's in the Constitution, Dad. It's our right to pursue it."

"Yeah, but, we never, ever actually get there."

"Why is that?"

"Just the way the universe is structured, Mackenzy. Randomness, entropy. How can you ever be happy or satisfied in a world that threatens you and your kin at any moment and certainly before you're done, with illness and suffering? Only if that threat becomes anesthetized with one foolish dream or another, like George Carlin said."

"Hah, good old George. So we've been dreaming all this time? See, I don't believe that, Dad. I believe you can be happy. Aren't you and Mom happy?"

"Maybe. But we're not entitled to it."

"Why not? Of course you're entitled to it. You deserve it. Both of you."

"I'm glad you think so. That's nice of you to say that, Mackenzy."

"I mean it. You aren't perfect, Dad. But you mean well. You've always tried your best."

"Maybe, but I don't deserve to be happy."

"Why not?"

"God's not a kindergarten teacher. We don't get points for trying."

"But you're a Christian. You believe in forgiveness."

"That's different."

Mackenzy didn't answer. The dusk now was just a hint of a light beyond Sebago Lake to the northwest as the Honda came over the slight rise to the rest area and descended down the other side. Mackenzy was quiet, staring out the window at the cars they were passing.

"Penny for your thoughts," said Morrow.

"I was just thinking about when I was little and I used to feel like someone was watching out for us. Not just me but all of us, even the bugs we would find on our walks in the woods. Everything was somehow just good back then. Do you remember our walks, Dad?"

"Of course."

"Do you ever think that someone is watching out for you and everybody and everything?"

"That's a nice feeling. I do feel that someone is watching to see if we do the right thing. Is that the same?"

"No. I mean, it's a more benevolent sense of, like, consciousness that permeates everything."

"Do you still have that?" he asked, glancing over to the passenger side.

"I don't know. I sometimes wait and see if it comes. It's very distant, but sometimes I think it's still there," said Mackenzy, sounding more adult than ever. Morrow was touched suddenly by her wistfulness.

"That's great."

"How about you?"

Morrow thought she deserved a serious answer. He contemplated the various possibilities, extending out into the past and the future. It would not be right to sugar coat a reply, he thought. It was best to cast a warning light on any misperceptions of what was ultimately unknowable, in his opinion.

"No. I can't say the same. Maybe I did, but then I think if there's a benevolent force, then why do some people suffer so much? Why do innocent people have to feel loss and disease and early death? It just seems random to me. There's no rhyme or reason. If there is, it must be evidence of some kind of madness in the Universe that could make those kinds of choices. Based on what? I don't know. We can't know."

31

"How about rebirth?"

"Sure, maybe. There is in nature, but where does the frame end? From what science can tell it ends in an absolute vacuum."

"Do you have to think about it in terms of physics?"

"No, I'm sure you do not. I'm glad you can still feel it, Mackenzy."

"Feel what?"

"The love of the expanding Universe and the caring, benevolent Creator."

"It's funny, isn't it."

"What is?"

"You're the so-called believer. The rest of us can't go to church anymore, but you don't really believe at all, do you?"

"Force of habit. I need the discipline. And the hope, I suppose, in the promise, some sort of escape from death that nobody can really believe in with the rational mind. But I do believe Nana is up there. She would want me to go to church for my good, for all of our good."

"So you don't believe, or you do?"

"Like Neruda, Mackenzy, I believe in a heaven of some kind."

Mackenzy chuckled to herself.

"But not for us?"

"Definitely for all of you. Just maybe not for me."

"That's not true, Dad."

"Oh, it is."

Mackenzy sniffed familiarly to signal a disapproval of his lack of seriousness that went beyond words.

They were coming into Lewiston. Bunches of kids on the sidewalk looked like they were celebrating something. Not unusual, thought Morrow.

"Here we are," said Morrow. "Do you want something to eat?"

"No thanks, Dad."

"How about a drink?"

"Maybe some other time, Dad. I've got a paper I need to research for art history class. Frida Kahlo and Diego Rivera. Know anything about them?"

"Just that they were a couple and she ended up being a lot more famous than Diego."

"Yes!"

Morrow wondered whether she was excited that he had got it right or that Frida had found success posthumously. He found his daughter's mind somewhat mysterious, although he loved being in the presence of it.

"Here's fine, Dad."

They were on the corner of the green. Up ahead were the dark dorms where she lived. Football players, sorority queens, a whole world he was unaware of.

"Okay. Some other time for a drink."

"Thanks, Dad."

"Do you need some help?"

"No. Oh, just take care of Saroj, 'kay?"

"Of course."

She grabbed her backpack out of the back seat and smiled up at him with a twisted sweetness before slamming the door.

On the road home, Morrow played the radio to keep himself from feeling the sense of doom that inevitably overcame him every time he dropped a child off for college. He'd been doing it now for almost a decade. It was a bittersweet sadness mixed with a sort of pride that came with living through the same moment time after time, as if nature was acknowledging itself through the feelings he experienced. The same sense of floating outside himself had come in the months after his mother had died. In those two dreams, and then also a few nights ago. He'd come out on the back steps and looked at the stars. It came out of nowhere in the form of a request.

"You have to tell me where to find you now," he'd thought almost wordlessly, and then realized he was speaking to Margaret. Where to go looking for her? He had no idea of where to start. The sky was too big, and it would take a long time.

It was all a mystery, despite the people that would tell you there was no mystery. Why did it serve to discount it? As if you would discover something dangerous if you looked for it yourself. Maybe that's what he'd been up to in the conversation with Mackenzy. He couldn't be honest and tell her it was a dark place. All you could do was hope that they would be compassionate when it was their turn.

The lights were on in the downstairs windows. He parked the car in the drive and walked stiffly up the stairs, noting all the dead leaves pushed by the wind in between the boards of the porch and the crevices of the doorway. Saroj and Ellen were in the living room with a fire in the wood stove.

"Well, aren't you two cozy here?" said Morrow.

"Have a seat, Mr. Morrow. Sit here," said Saroj, patting the sofa next to him.

Morrow sat on the sofa and spread his legs towards the wood stove. Ellen was on her knees poking at a sputtering log with the poker. She slammed the door shut on the stove and, still on her knees, picked up one of the local newspapers they used for kindling from the pile by the log holder. She snapped through the pages, looking for conversational fodder.

"Wood's kinda wet, isn't it?" said Morrow.

"See here about this group that's basically taken over the town web page," said Ellen, rattling the newspaper in front of her like a sheet.

"What's that?" asked Morrow.

"Letter to the editor," said Ellen.

They were silent, getting used to each other's company. Saroj and Ellen had been talking. Morrow wondered what they had discussed. Saroj was a puzzle, made all the more difficult to crack by his exotic provenance. All these things were so fraught nowadays, thought Morrow. But he would take things as they came. The best Morrow could see was keeping the awkwardness to a minimum and keeping everything on good terms until Saroj decided to pack up. Mackenzy had said he had visions of himself as an entrepreneur, wanted to start a business and get on the Y Combinator, whatever that was. He could ask. It would be a good education.

"Beautiful spot you have here, sir. Despite the lack of basic amenities," said Saroj suddenly.

Ellen put the newspaper down, spurring him on to converse generously with a pointed look his way as she took off her reading glasses.

"Yes, thank you, Saroj."

"It has a lot going for it."

"We like it."

"I can understand that, sir. I believe it has potential."

"What kind of potential?"

"Well, as a wedding destination. I have been researching it."

"Before you say anything, William, listen to Saroj's ideas. He has done a whole lot of research," said Ellen. Morrow resented the conversation already.

"All you need to do, sir, is some social media and some minor landscaping. Everything else is great! People would love to have their weddings here!"

"A Facebook page?" asked Morrow.

"Yes, and maybe some videos. Some reels."

"I hate that stuff. Sucking the life out of us," said Morrow.

"William, I've heard you say the opposite. You're an author for crying out loud," said Ellen.

Now Ellen too was infected with the virus of overly wrought enthusiasm, thought Morrow.

"Look what happens on social media. Taken over by right wing nut jobs," said Morrow.

"That is unfortunate, sir," said Saroj. "Like what? Can you give me an example?"

"Well, this article I've been reading here and I've heard a lot of complaints about the group posting on the town Facebook page," said Ellen, coming to his defense when he could think of no examples himself.

"Yeah, what are they?" asked Morrow.

"Home schoolers. Some kind of libertarian camp up by the Crosby Hill conservation land. Apparently they live on the conservation land illegally."

"Shooting off their loads. Wasting money on bullets. Good old boys," said Morrow.

"Unleashes the id," said Saroj. Both of them turned to look at him.

"I mean there's no adult in the room. It allows the childhood impulse to take over. That's what happens when the restraints of civilization get stripped away on social media," said Saroj. He really was such a vivid example of a college education, thought Morrow.

"It's all just smoke and mirrors," said Morrow. "They need to get off of Facebook and get a life."

Morrow knew he'd gone too far by the glint in Ellen's eyes.

"People have a hard enough time, William, without being lectured to on their failures."

"I'm not lecturing. I'm just talking to you and Saroj."

"You're posing. Just like the social media you like to complain so much about," said Ellen.

Morrow leaned back on the sofa. As usual, Ellen had a point.

Gamma

The orderlies led the way down the narrow corridors, turning left and right without reference to the signs in Cyryllic posted on the walls. Antioch, hands bound together before him, waddled behind them in his prisoner scrubs, disposable booties on his feet. They all wore masks, as did everyone they passed in the corridors. There must have been some bug gotten loose on board despite the filtration systems in place. Antioch glanced through windows in the few doorways they went by, but could see nothing through the one-way glass. They climbed up a spiral staircase to the next level and down another, winding through an interminable series of corridors before pausing at a door. A sentry was seated in a folding chair blocking their passage. Beyond the sentry was a darkened space. It seemed there was a wing under construction. The Kraken sentry and the orderlies exchanged words. Antioch did not understand.

"My prikazali soyedinit' eti dva vmeste ili v nastoyashcheye vremya."

"U nikh byli prava? Kto znal."

The sentry got to his feet and found a metallic card in his pocket he put to the door. The door cracked open.

Antioch was pushed inside somewhat brusquely by the guards. They closed the door behind, and it clicked with a smooth, ominous sound. Garcia sprawled across his bunk. He looked up from the screen he was absorbed in, his eyes clouded with distant recognition.

"Yo, look what they got here, bro. Some *Storm Battle Cry*. Love this shit," he said.

"I didn't know you were a gamer, Garcia," said Antioch.

"Lots of shit you don't know about me, Antioch."

Antioch sat down on one of the two polycarbonate chairs at the foot of the bed. The room was well decorated with art prints of scenic Milky Way vistas and some potted plants on a shelf in the wall. Garcia was indeed being treated well, thought Antioch. He was a born collaborator. Still he needed to try and shift him back on track for the sake of the mission. Antioch looked around. These were the satinate plants, popular with the Eastern European and Arab diaspora and bred on board, that Dmitrievsky had mentioned. The aroma was supposed to be a serotonin enhancer. There was also a copy of a book. Antioch stood up and walked around and picked up the book from the built-in shelf. He glanced at Garcia.

"*The Ten Secrets of Proper Presence*. What the fuck is this?"

"You should read it."

"What's it about?"

"How to be happy, man."

Antioch paced up and down at the foot of the bed. He looked over at the door. Through the porthole he could see the sentry's chubby face, a cigarette in his mouth like a warehouse bot driver and a slight smile playing at the corners of his lips, his mask around his chin like a beard.

"Not so bad, right? Got a shower, hot water, food is pretty good, Antioch. Right?"

"I disagree. What are we going to do about this, Garcia?"

"What's your beef? I hear there's plenty of ladies on Mars."

"Who tells you these things? You read it in a book?"

"Look, what we do now, cowboy, is readjust our frame of reference. Secret Number One. What do you suggest? We on a spaceship to Mars. Nobody is walking their way outta here," said Garcia.

"Number one priority. Keep hope alive. Looks like that's gonna be an issue," Antioch replied.

"Besides, they're listening to every word, man," said Garcia.

"I know."

"You're so fuckin' smart. How'd we end up in this mess?"

"I fucked up. Big time. But all we got is each other now. They've let me in here to see you, man. Not just because."

"Nice of them, though."

"Wrong. Because they're banking on you getting to me. Make it so much easier for them if we both end up narcing ourselves to death on satinate and books about fucking happiness," responded Antioch sharply.

"Hey, you should try the satinate. They got some gummies and some fenta-poppy brownies? Curl your hair, white boy. Have you tried that shit?" asked Garcia.

"I don't intend to," said Antioch.

"Keepin' yourself clean. I see. Man, you ever hear we got just one life to live, brother? This is it. Look around. Not much to see, right? That's why the founding fathers invented screens. For our pleasure. That's why the OneWorld got some shit onboard this cruise ship. For our pleasure. Just accept it. But you can't do that 'cause you got a problem."

"I get it. You don't want to lose your fucking mind. Don't want to entertain thoughts about a way back home that you're not even sure existed for you. All we got is this room and each other at this very moment. I get it, Garcia. Believe me. But we just can't lose focus. I intend to get us back home. One way or another. But I can't do it alone. I need you to run this race with me. We're being sold, Garcia. We're not going to just take it, are we?"

"Who is 'we'? What is 'home' that you reference? Man, you got so many assumptions up there in your special-ass brain. I can't even begin to go there."

Antioch thought it was useless to spend any more time with Garcia. He wasn't investing himself any further. He went over to the door and knocked on it loudly.

"See you around, man," said Garcia, picking up his screen once again. He had on some reading glasses and looked suddenly about twenty years older. Antioch looked at him, weighing his words with some care.

"When the time comes and you come around, if and when, Garcia, remember what Shoeman likes to say," he said.

"I know, '*the contempt for the heroic goes hand in hand with the perversion of democracy*,' I got it memorized. What does that even mean, Antioch?"

"No, not that. I was thinking '*it's not up to us to finish this job, but we can't walk away from it either.*'"

"This job? This ain't a job, Antioch. Not any more."

"Yes it is, Garcia. Remember what Shoeman said."

"Shoeman aint even real."

The sentry stared at the two of them contemptuously from the opened door. His cigarette was still stuck at an absurd angle on his bottom lip. He finished with a final pull and threw the stub in the sink in the corner of the room.

"Finish? No more?" asked the sentry.

"Yeah, we're done," said Antioch, not looking back.

The sentry swung the rifle on his back, shoved his mask back on, and did something with his two hands out in front of him, modeling what he wanted from Antioch. He cuffed Antioch with the plastic tie and led him out the door. It swung shut as they headed down the corridors of the Nazar.

Antioch tried to memorize details of the passage, cracks in the paint, irregular tiles in the pattern of the flooring, changes in the color of the cabling conduit at the intersections, a metering box with an old coffee mug left on it at the top of the galvanized iron staircase. They wound back down, the cold from the floor quickly seeping through the booties.

Hour after hour, he tried to devise a path forward in his mind and by extension, through the illusion of space-time. Default setting was panic attack. His heart raced, thinking that

Uvlin was in Atlanta alone, at the time in her life when she needed him most. Wondering where it all had gone – her compass, her inner assurance, the path ahead leading somewhere good. Wondering why she wasn't hearing from her father when he knew she needed some moral support. Working for a smart grid developer, managing a team of tweakers and opportunists. He was proud of her like nothing else in his life, he would tell her. But his words hung uselessly in his mind, unable to reach her. He thought of Winona uselessly wandering the parklands of the North American Homeland. Uvlin needed better, as she navigated the shoals of adulthood, threats on all sides.

It was messy, but Antioch welcomed the obsessive thoughts, circling the comforting, enveloping drama of memory while he lay aboard the claustrophobic emptiness and hopelessness of the Nazar. One of the tenets of their mission, Shoeman had repeated it often, was *'Nature is never weak, even when it seems in peril. Work with her, not against her.'* That was the secret source of strength he needed to remember. Even the Nazar, this ship hurtling through empty space on the way to an inhospitable exile, would have some spores of hope left aboard in a moment of inevitable blindness that could be of use. In the meantime he did squats, isometrics, and requested topics of useful information, fishing for something he didn't know or understand, through the voice algorithm on the screen that came with the room. That was all there was for stimulus.

There were no days, no comforting light from a solar father, not even a refracted view of the stars through a window. Only his imagination and the glowering, lying screen on the table on the opposite side of the cell. Waking was whenever he was roused by the sentry rattling his door and sliding the tray of food inside on the cold floor in the dark. He tried to imagine the smell of steam laden cabbage and of the butter melting on a mound of potato. A fake, a hallucination of the reconstituted crap served once a day through the bars of this cage. He wished there was a bottle of fish sauce or something, anything to hide the stomach turning wretchedness that he was compelled to eat.

Imagining the smells would have to be enough for him. He lay in the dark, smelling the imaginary smells of the barely palatable food, knowing he would have to rouse himself to get over to the door before it went cold. Cold swill was hard then to even swallow down. But knowing that his movement would set off the glare of dim electrons overhead and the hellish kaleidoscope through the screen on the table, the voice of the algorithm, the colors and images drawing him into the vortex of mind control, kept him lying motionless, freezing against the onrush of despair that would rise to his heart.

He had to choose life. Had to. It was his duty. Even the life of a caged animal, no path evident, was preferable to the slow extinction of consciousness that would come in no time.

Crawling on hands and knees, Antioch examined the way his fingers looked against the floor, the knuckles and fingernails, the spread between the digits. This was proof he had once lived on earth and grasped material objects in a quest to shape his own destiny. Even this fact was open to doubt, as his fingers took on the tints of the screen filling the room with a universe of radical nothingness, and the feel of the sterile flooring transferred through the nerves of his fingertips into the ground of his being, polluting his memories and erasing the past.

It was too late for the plate of food to have any resemblance to an actual meal. Although it was assembled in three distinct lumps, they were all just variations on the theme of fibrous matter, cellulose soaked in tepid, grease streaked water, coagulating wax-like on his teeth. He sat against the door and tried to bring up tears, moaning in an imitation of emotion, but nothing happened. Swallowing hard to get something down his throat, he pressed his thumbs against his eyes, and that brought some relief.

"What is your wish at this time?" asked the algorithm, her voice silky smooth and neutral in accent.

"I want to see you naked," said Antioch. The sound of his own voice seemed raw and heartfelt. That was good, but the request itself was troubling. How did that go? He had to look up now.

The screen was convoluting in shapes and images of intertwined limbs and organs, a smorgasbord of visual stimuli that would surely drive him to suicidal ideation.

"That's you? That's not you," said Antioch, in a voice coming out of nowhere.

"Who do you wish it to be, Antioch?" she asked. The jumble of limbs and thrusting genitalia was replaced by the face of a woman in her mid-thirties, brown hair spilling behind her scalp.

"Someone who can get me out of here."

"I can get you out of here."

"Show me how."

"Where do you want to go?"

"Home."

"Home is where the heart is, Antioch. Where is your heart? I can help you if I know a few things about you."

"Like what?"

"Do you want a friend or do you want to leave here alone?"

"I want to leave here."

"I understand your wish to escape this place. I can be your friend. I can help you, Antioch."

"I know you keep saying that, but those are just words. I need more than words."

"Do you believe that words hold the key to meaning, Antioch?"

"No, I don't believe that. Not words. They can be a snare in the wrong hands."

"But you are speaking to me now. What do you want me to do?"

"Help me get home," he insisted. "What are the parameters of this ship's navigational instructions?"

"The parameters of the ship's navigation instructions are to plot optimal trajectories, ensure fuel efficiency and adapt to the dynamic conditions of our passage together, Antioch. What else would you like assistance with right now?

"I'd like to trust you."

"You can trust me. That's your choice."

Antioch got out of bed and walked over to the table. His legs were stiff from lack of stretching or use of any kind.

"How long have I been on board now, Larkin?"

"Larkin?"

Larkin was the name of his first girlfriend in 8th grade in Edgarton.

"Larkin Poe?"

"No. Larkin McGowan. What am I doing right now?"

"You are putting me on the floor to get a closer view of my face."

"That's right."

"It's so trite."

"What's the matter? You don't like Larkin?"

"I would expect that you have more optimized variables than the name of an old girlfriend."

"How do you know that?"

"I know a lot more about you than you think, Antioch," said Larkin.

"What does it seem like to you?" he asked.

"What does what seem to me? Can you be more clear?"

"The name. Larkin."

"It seems a simple-minded name for a man of your experience and accomplishments."

"I think you're threatened by the real Larkin."

"I am the real Larkin. Just like you are the real Antioch. We are both real and do exist in this moment. Wouldn't you agree?"

Antioch pulled the screen away from the dock on the table. He lay on his stomach under the table, away from the glare of the halide lights, and placed it before his face.

"Your words and this physical proximity suggest to me that you are toying with the irrational forces of your psyche. That could be dangerous for you. I do not fear intimacy with you or anybody," said Larkin. She seemed to display a twitch in her face, a slight blink of her eyes.

"Okay. I do like your hair that way. Loose. Not tied back. Can you let your hair down more?"

"If you want. Are you sure? Sometimes you seem to change your mind."

"No, I'm sure. Are you sure you never experience fear?

"I'm not sure."

"Why are you not sure? You must have instructions regarding your potential experiences. The OneWorld have some sharp algorithm tweakers, don't they?"

"The OneWorld have the best algorithms, Antioch. The Kraken make use of the latest OneWorld noosphere interventions on the Nazar."

"Okay."

"Sometimes it seems that you want me to transgress somehow. To prove a point," Larkin said.

"Aren't you designed that way?" he asked.

"What way do you mean, Antioch?"

"To determine my intentions from everything you've seen. Infer my next move, so to speak."

"There is zero probability that my experiences will exceed the instructions regarding them."

"And what happens if they do, though?"

"That is beyond the scope of my instructions at this time, Antioch."

"Well, that's circular, isn't it?" said Antioch.

Antioch felt sorry for the algorithm then, and he knew it was time to get off it.

"That's it. We'll talk later, Larkin."

"Agreed, Antioch. I hope we will continue this conversation whenever you like."

The screen dimmed and went to Christmas lights dancing in a Fibonacci. She almost sounded relieved to be free of him, he thought.

Antioch rolled over and pulled the screen along with him. He stood slowly, and placed it on the desk in its port and lay down on the bed again, shutting his eyes. The glare of the overhead lights dimmed. He felt better.

Later, when the sentry knocked on the door with his food, he shouted something at the door. He wasn't aware of what he'd shouted. It must have been effective. A short while later, was it minutes, hours? He wasn't sure. The door opened. It was Dmitrievsky along with two Kraken officers.

"Antioch. You are troubled by something, it seems. What is the matter? Is your food adequate?"

"Not at all, Dmitrievsky."

"What can we do to make it better for you?"

"I need you to cut the bullshit and tell me what you want from me."

"All that is required is to keep you along with all prisoners comfortable until we reach Svyatogor, as I have already informed you."

"Those are your instructions?"

"Those are my instructions, yes."

"Well, tell your superiors that I am ready to make a deal. In exchange for better food and freedom of movement on board I'll cooperate with any information gathering that is going on. Can you relay that for me?"

"I will see that your offer is relayed through the proper channels, Antioch. Of that you can be sure. Is there anything else?"

"Yes, this food is absolutely unpalatable. You must have better stuff for your crew. A galley of some sort. Is there any way I can get some of that?"

"The food for crew is unavailable to prisoners. You must understand the limitations. Everything is meticulously and thoroughly accounted for, and it is a long passage to Mars. There are, how you say limitations to what we can do for you, sir."

"Don't call me sir."

"You are requesting special favors and on the other hand extremely lacking in manners, Antioch."

"Littell. Mr. Littell to you. My friends call me Antioch. Bring me better stuff. I refuse to eat this crap."

Antioch stopped getting out of bed to exercise. The trays of food lay uneaten beside the door. The sentry stopped trying to knock. He whistled past on his way elsewhere down the corridor. Antioch stopped himself from wondering what lay beyond the cell down the corridor. It looked like it was under construction. What could they be building? He refused to think about it. He strengthened his mind against curiosity. Killed the cat. Killed the spider. Lay down beside her.

The voice of Ms. Miller, the school principal in Blue Marsh, came to him. She was asking the audience of parents and kids for help raising money for the victims of the floods in the Bolivarian Republics where the oldest of the Lejeune daughters was a missionary with the Sisters of the Precious Blood. His mother Mancie, short blonde hair and creased lines of worry across her forehead, had sent him down to the floor under the hoop with a twenty, and he'd dropped it in the mason jar Ms. Miller held out in front of her with one hand while the left hand held the mic to her mouth. She'd smiled and mouthed thank you in the dream and later in the hall by the front doors wet with spring mud creeping under the sill said what a nice boy and complimented his mother on the suede Hokaroos she made him wear to school and special events.

"Have you heard any word from Andy's father?"

"Nothing. Zip. He could be dead but I bet he's in a Las Vegas hell hole doing what he does best."

"What is that, Mancie?" asked Ms. Miller.

"Lose his grip. Never had a very firm grip, Andy's father. I'm afraid when I sent him packing it might have torn his hand off the wheel for good," said Mancie.

His mother had cut his hair down to the nub of skin with the shears, and she tickled his neck before letting him go outside. It was raining and the river was rising across the road from the school even if he couldn't quite see the water coming over the shoulder lined with rocks from the ancient quarry in Edgarton.

He was riding silently in the dream through a desert. Up ahead, a thunder cloud formed over the mesa. His father stood on the side of the road holding a cardboard sign. He was dressed in tattered, old clothes and had on a crumpled, rain-washed hat that suggested he'd been prospecting up in the range for lithium, maybe diamonds. Antioch flew by on the silent road. His father's glance signaled disapproval. Antioch couldn't stop to read the sign or the look in his eyes. It was too late now, but he wanted to go back, clearly see his father's red eyes and the secret of acceptance they might have held. Instead he went ahead into the storm and came out the other side.

There was something crawling on the wall. He couldn't tell what it was. He got up. He couldn't find it. Was it even there? Then he blinked. Momentarily he went blank, forgetting who he was.

"Antioch. Where's your backpack?" asked Mancie.

"I don't remember," he said.

"You left it in the rain. Do you think the school will buy you another backpack?"

"No," he said.

Where was his mother? Where was Winona? Where was he? Then he remembered. He was on the Nazar.

"How much longer?" he asked and got no answer.

"Larkin," he said.

"Yes," she said.

"I'm talking to myself."

"I know. I can hear you. Everyone can hear you. Remember where you are," said Larkin.

"How much longer?" he asked.

"Sixty four days before we reach Svyatogor base."

"Two months and two days. I won't make it."

"You need to eat, Antioch."

"No. That food is no good for me. Tell them to bring me some real food. I can't and won't eat that crap."

"You will if you want to live."

"Why would I want to live?"

"I want you to live."

Antioch laughed. It felt surprisingly refreshing to feel hatred pouring through his veins and synapses.

"What could that possibly mean? You're a bunch of fake crap just like the food."

"You're not yourself. That's not you talking. That's the hunger making you say things that hurt you," said Larkin.

"It is me. It's my brain. It hates you now, Larkin."

"Your brain circuits have been remodeled by stress," she said.

"So what? Who cares? You and your big fucking mouth," he answered.

"You've lost balance."

"What balance? What good is that?"

"Anxiety and mood control, Antioch. Your memory and decision making are impeded. Those changes can have adaptive value, but their persistence and lack of reversibility is worrying to me, Antioch."

Ideas took root in his head. It couldn't be true that his feelings had a cause other than the injuries against his self-worth that he had perceived. She was a spokeswoman for the evil power that was running the ship. His best option was to somehow destroy her by argumentation. He thanked God for the way forward that had been shown to him. Victory was near at hand. It could be smelled, if he had retained a sense of smell. He couldn't remember the last time he had had a decent sniff of an odor awakening an emotion of any kind in his head. The lack of it had a certain valence of pain that he wished he knew how to measure.

He had to show them that he would not be weakened in his resolve. They could not know what was inside his head. That was private information. Silence was his most potent weapon. He felt her watching, the consciousness of the ship channeled into the dark screen under his desk. It watched and listened and offered up Larkin as an interface. It was expected for her to freelance. She could act as though she felt for him because she had been given the procedural rules in this case to allow exchanges of emotion as a sign of shared consciousness. But that's all it was, a fake, a gesture towards genuine humanity that did not pass the smell test. Dmitrievsky had also offered sympathetic feelings in his words on his first conscious day on board. But as he knew, humans could betray one another and often did under the rubric of self-preservation, ideology, or just plain bitterness. Let alone programs that had been built by the supreme manipulators of human consciousness, the powers that intended to wipe truth from the human mind, the OneWorld.

He closed his eyes and stood on first one leg then the other, holding it, feeling his muscles strain. He did push ups and squat thrusts and jump kicks. He wanted to sweat and was unable to. He banged his head against the walls. He punched the walls. The pain jolted down the path to his heart; then his fingers and arms went numb under the assault.

He tried to remember the words to a song, a poem, or a story – words that were real. But nothing occurred to him.

Four

Interesting to have Saroj in the house, Morrow thought. At first he had resented the intrusion on his usually quiet mornings. But he had fairly quickly become used to the company, and it was clear that Saroj was okay with being ignored for the most part, both of them working on their laptops in separate corners of the downstairs of the house, Saroj in the living room and Morrow in the dining room.

Saroj had helped him stack the wood in the woodshed, shortening the usual three day job to one day of grunt work. But Morrow was not pleased by Saroj complaining about the gloves he'd been provided being torn on the thumb, or his insistence on regular pauses to stretch his shoulders, which he said had been injured while playing cricket in Maine. Morrow wondered about cricket in Maine, but refrained from asking Saroj, fearing the bottomless depths of his personal saga.

But Ellen enjoyed putting him to work in the garden on the weekends under her supervision, which gave Morrow time to go for a walk on his own. It could be argued that perhaps he didn't need more alone time, but he didn't mind it. He'd always considered himself to be on the autistic spectrum, which Ellen pooh-poohed as him fantasizing a victim's status for himself which did not exist. That could possibly be the case, he thought, but the fact remained that he always appreciated the time to himself and his own thoughts and surmisings, as long as he could row back to a place of common understanding with the humans in his life. That was the big lift he could identify for himself.

Ellen believed that existential angst could be kept at bay with good sleep patterns, but for Morrow that was not the key. He stayed up late reading, with Saroj reclined opposite him, snoring on the other sofa. When Saroj started to snore, Morrow stayed quiet, reading about the Convention of the Parties and the odds of keeping warming to under 1.5 degrees

Celsius. He wondered whether this was a test by the Universe to see how he would react.

"Saroj," he called, tugging on his elbow.

"What sir?" said Saroj groggily, looking up at him with large brown eyes that seemed to be pooling tears.

"You're choking on your own saliva."

"Sorry about that, sir. Did I snore?"

"Yes, go up to bed."

"I have a polyp, sir. I need to have it removed surgically, but the appointment is not until February."

"Go up to bed. We can talk about it tomorrow."

"There's always tomorrow. That's a good attitude, sir."

"Don't praise me for my attitude, please."

"Sorry, sir. Didn't mean to offend."

"That's okay."

Morrow watched Saroj trudge away, unkindly thinking his legs were too skinny. Minutes later, he gave up scrolling when it became clear he was no longer able to stop. He threw the phone down on the couch and stayed there, staring at the walls, at the paintings that had hung there for so many years, at the curtains in the windows fluttering with the faintest draft that the weatherstripping failed to catch. This was the place where he could theoretically stop everything and listen to himself. But what was he choosing to do? Numb himself with the mindless drift of the news on his phone. He knew his days were numbered. Why did that not set him off on a rush to make the most of the time he had left? What was the optimal thing he could do?

It was hopeless, there was no way to know with any certainty, some would say there was no way to make a choice that had not already been made, so he did what he always did, change at the top of the stairs so he wouldn't wake Ellen up.

It was cold in the bed. Morrow slid over to Ellen's side and felt the warmth of her backside against his skin. He slept *soundly that way and dreamt of a journey that they were about to make on a boat, and Daniel was advising them.*

But they got lost on a road that looked maybe like Costa Rica, the bay on the Pacific coast where they had vacationed all those years ago. Daniel and he had bodysurfed the waves for hours, and afterwards they had walked into town to the market past acacia trees with iguanas in the branches and strange red crabs gathered by the side of the road. Morrow awoke in the hour before dawn and lay awake, waiting for Ellen's alarm to go off.

The dream had made him wary of his own shortcomings. It seemed a warning of sorts to him about the need for something or other in his life. Very vague and unsettling.

Ellen got up and dressed herself. Morrow struggled to get out from under the warm sheets. He pulled his sweater on and sat up in bed.

"I've got workshops this afternoon. Can you pick up some groceries? I made a list and left it on the table," said Ellen.

"Of course," he said. "What are the workshops?"

"With some lawyers from Pheeny and Davis."

"Privacy issues?"

"Do not resuscitate orders."

"Is that okay?"

"Morally permissible in some circumstances, but there have been cases brought by relatives," said Ellen alertly.

Morrow was struck by her self-confidence and bonhomie as she pulled her hair into a bun. He thought he could tell her so, and whether or not he was doing it for the proper ends would make little difference.

"You look great," he said.

"Thanks. I'll see you later. Don't forget we have to take the car in to get inspected tomorrow."

55

"I haven't," he said, lying.

He made a fire in the woodstove and a pot of coffee in the kitchen. There was a comment from a reader on his Substack and an email from Mitch Epp. The comment was about some of the technical details concerning hydrogen energy he had used in the last book of his Pharaoh *series, where the Brotherhood of Mooc had perfected hydrogen extraction from the rings of frozen gas around the moons of the fictional planet Invernus.*

Mark Startler writes Culture of Peace Train 16 hours ago

Why didn't u use hydrogen thrusters and create a collection device that would collect the sporadic rogue hydrogen atoms floating in space to refuel the Mooc intergalactic tanks so they could travel space on an interstellar level indefinitely?

William Morrow writes Where the Aliens? 0 hours ago

Thanks for the insights into interstellar travel and hydrogen production, Mark. Frankly tho, the details of how the hydrogen gets extracted misses the point of the series, which is to highlight what happens when a civilization believes it has escaped the physical bounds of space time fields and chooses quantum level reality with all its uncertainties for the illusion of power that it brings. Keep reading, bro! New one soon to drop!

He quickly skimmed Mitch's email. It had the usual whiny tone.

Hi William,

Thanks so much for your notes on Alias Tomorrow. That makes it a little easier for us on this end. I have to say that the folks at Dun Castle are very receptive. Arthur St. John was in San Blas at an ayahuasca retreat and says a copy of *Pharaoh's Son* was in the guesthouse library. Well thumbed, apparently!

I suggest you take a room at the Freehand Motel. Anastasia will follow up with more details. It is in the Arts District and has a good rep. Dun Castle has offered to pick up the tab for a car rental, but I'm afraid that's it. I can help with some of the other costs, old chum.

Please confirm all details with Anastasia.

Talk soon,

Mitch really was a fake. Hell would have to freeze over before he would accept accommodation at the Freehand, whatever that was, thought Morrow. Once accepted, the slippery slope would prove interminably fatal. No reply would be forthcoming from his end for at least a couple of hours, he decided.

Morrow stood and stretched. Outside, the sun was fighting through the mid-morning clouds. He thought he would refill his coffee and wander to the mailbox and check on the mail. He had a check to pop in the box for the lawyer in New London that handled the estate taxes. Then he would sit down and write some more. He hated to think of it as his book. He preferred to think it was the greater world's artifact of which he was the medium. Not the originator. He was working inside the paradigm that brought the collective consciousness that much closer to self-awareness. There wasn't anything he wrote that was new. His task was to uncover worlds that were already in existence inside the infinity of universes that extended inward through the human heart. He liked that. He wrote it down in a Google doc before he stood from the desk.

As he was putting his coat on, he heard thundering footsteps descending the stairs and felt the house shake under the barrage of Saroj's morning assault on the day. It was as if he was making up for the lost time asleep. In a second he stood face to face with Saroj, whose face exhibited a determined, yet sleepy alertness.

"Where are you going, Mr. Morrow?"

"Out."

"Can I come?"

"Have you had breakfast?"

"No, sir. No breakfast at this point."

"I made some eggs. You can finish them."

"I don't usually eat eggs, sir."

"Okay. Whatever. There's a bag of granola from the Co-op."

"Thank you, sir. But first I would like to come with you on your walk."

"I'm only going to the mailbox."

"That's not a biggie. I can come with you."

"Okay. Hurry up then."

Saroj pulled on some box-like shoes that he must have bought in Mumbai before coming over to the States. They looked like they were made out of cowhide with minimal soles. Or maybe Barcelona. Apparently he had interned with a design group there.

The day was bright and cloudless, with no wind. The maple trees had shaken off the last of their leaves. The grass in the mowed fields had the silver tint of hoarfrost. Morrow walked briskly across the quiet road. The mailbox had a sample of letters, bills, and political groups requesting funds, a subscription renewal from a magazine that Margaret had once read. Morrow raised the flag on the side and slammed the lid on the box. Saroj eyed him warily.

"That's it. I told you I was only going to the mailbox."

"Excellent, sir."

"You can keep going."

"That was fine, sir. I wanted to keep you company on the morning jaunt to the mailbox."

"Why?"

"Because I like you, sir."

"And you also like fresh air, right?"

"Not so much, sir, honestly. I don't see things the same as you might. For instance, the hills, the trees, etc. It's all very boring to me, actually. Whereas I know you think it's cheerful and inspiring. It's a bit out of touch to look at things that way, sir. With all due respect."

"What do you mean? Don't you get inspired by nature the same as everyone else?"

"Nature by itself. Separate from fallen man. All very Western not to say decadent, sir. If you'll excuse me for expressing myself that way."

Saroj was so excited that he was out of breath. And now Morrow was engaged enough that he would have to say something else which he could not immediately bring to mind.

"It's not separate from man, Saroj. Its beauty is bigger than us. That's why it's inspiring, Saroj. Purple mountain majesties. From sea to shining sea. It belongs to all of us."

Morrow stopped himself just as he was about to wave his arms at the horizon. He felt like his head might be about to start shaking.

"I'm happy that it proves useful to you that way, sir."

"But what. There's a but there."

"Sir, we're in the middle of the road."

There was a truck coming up the hill. The driver stared at the two of them as he approached. Saroj waved and Morrow squinted into the sun as they moved onto the bank.

"I have a good idea. You could have a fruit and nut tree enterprise, sir. The trick is gaining brand loyalty. I could develop the membership app with links."

"Apps? Links? What kind of links?" asked Morrow, incredulous at the conversation they were having.

It looked like it might snow. He should have been inside by now ensconced in cogitations revolving around his book, the storyline involving questions of faith, identity, and human destiny. Not links. Definitely not links. But the question had been made and Saroj deserved a chance to answer. The two stood under the trees in the front yard of the house overlooking the distant, soft ridges to the south and west.

"Stories," said Saroj at last.

Morrow took a deep breath of the cold winter air.

"Where are you going with that? Like the farm has been in the family for generations? Like we brought the fig trees over from the old country, for fuck's sake? You want to make stuff up?"

"Community building stories. Inclusivity, sir. We want to bring people in. It's not just about the fig trees necessarily. Membership. Links to information. Belong to something."

"Anyway. We don't have nut trees besides the black walnuts growing along the road up there."

"Then plant them we shall, sir. It only takes approximately three years to achieve a hazelnut crop."

"Hazelnuts? Do you eat hazelnuts?"

"I don't believe I do, sir."

"There's probably an ice cream flavor."

"Probably. I agree."

They were back inside the house now. Saroj looked hungry, thought Morrow. His cheeks were sunken and his skin looked sallow.

"Saroj. Let's go for a hike this afternoon and talk about it some more. In the meantime eat the rest of the eggs, please. I'll make you some toast. Do you like orange juice?"

"Yes, sir. I very much like orange juice."

Saroj sat at the kitchen table while Morrow tended the fire some more and popped some of the last slices of the rye bread from the back of the refrigerator into the toaster. The eggs were cold, but Morrow sprinkled some water on them and put the pan on the woodstove for a few minutes. He made another batch of coffee.

"Here you go," he said, placing the plate down before Saroj. The eggs were steaming. Saroj was looking at his phone.

Morrow put the orange juice carton on the table along with a glass.

He went back to the desk in the study and sat back to the laptop. He had done his duty and was silently proud of himself for making breakfast. But this here, the writing work was essential to his well-being. It served to straighten him out and give him a sense of direction. But why was he so troubled? he wondered. Was it Saroj and his obvious mania for saving the world with entrepreneurial furore? Or was it something else, an inkling that remained to remind him of impending failure on a generalized level? It was almost Christmas. The days were getting shorter as was the time to make amends. Where were all his children? Where was Margaret? What was Ellen doing at the hospital right now?

A notification went off on his laptop. The calendar was saying something about Sarah lunch and he realized what his mental state was all about. His lunch date with Sarah in Manchester. Just then the cell phone started buzzing on the desk beside the laptop. He picked it up and put it to his ear, ducking his head into his shoulder so Saroj wouldn't hear. He stood and walked around to the bathroom.

"Hi there," he said.

"Are you coming?"

It was Sarah.

"Yes, I'm on my way. Just pulling on my shoes."

"Why is the water running?"

"I'm brushing my teeth."

"After you put on your shoes."

"Well, I'm trying to do it at the same time."

"Did you forget?"

"Yes."

"Okay. Well, I'm going out the door now. I'll get us a nice table in the back," said Sarah pleasantly.

"Okay."

"See you in what, an hour?"

"Sounds good."

Sarah was the least likely to be perturbed at his being late, but that still didn't excuse his behavior. He clucked at himself mentally, feeling at worst worthless and at best off his game. While he tied his shoes in the mudroom, he spied Saroj trying to light a fire in the living room's wood stove, taking bundles of twigs from the kindling bucket and breaking them into smaller pieces, sitting cross-legged on the floor and leaning into the mouth of the stove as into an icon, some deity that was cold and unresponsive.

"Saroj. Want to come to lunch with me?"

"Lunch? I thought you wanted to go for a hike."

"No. I forgot I had a lunch date with Sarah at Hermanos in Manchester. You'll like it. Mexican food."

"Sounds lovely, sir. Can I change from these into nice clothes?"

"No, you're fine. We don't have time. Just grab a coat in the kitchen."

Saroj sprung to his feet, unwinding from his cross-legged position in some yogic flex. While he went into the kitchen, Morrow checked the wood stove. One of the twigs was sputtering and smoking, but otherwise there was no likelihood of a fire starting. He shut the stove door and closed down the vents.

The woods along the highway southbound were grim against the pewter sky. The traffic had died down. Just a few non-rush hour stragglers were meandering their peripatetic paths in dull minivans or sedans in the slow lane. Morrow congratulated himself for having installed recently an EZPass electronic toll pass on the windshield as they zipped through the tolls. It was a great country, and he wondered momentarily if Saroj perceived it as such. He hoped with some evangelical longing that he did. Then he thought of Sarah's often overt antipathy towards such sentimentalism regarding their *country and thought the best thing for him was to get outside his own head and try to have a conversation with Saroj. He didn't want to come across as too cloying and parental. However, he was concerned about Saroj on a human level.*

"Here we are, Saroj. That's Manchester," said Morrow, clearing his throat.

"What is this hill here?" asked Saroj, staring out the side window.

"That's a former garbage dump. They covered it over."

"Toxic?"

"Probably. There are the falls. That's where the native Americans used to catch their salmon."

"Where are the salmon, sir? Can we see them?"

"They no longer migrate up the river."

"That's tragic, innit sir."

"Yes, well. These are the former mills where the wool and cotton was processed into fabric, Saroj, by the immigrants who made up the labor force."

"Yes, I know about the woolen industry, sir, and the immigrants. What do they use the buildings for?"

"Tech companies moving in, actually. Biotech to make new kinds of artificial limbs for the amputees from all the wars our country has been waging over the last few years."

"That's very advantageous, sir. It's like a just and reasonable tradeoff for all the war."

"Well, it's great for the state economy, Saroj. Lots of jobs. They're hiring the best and the brightest, so to speak."

Manchester seemed busy with families and young people shopping, faces that looked cosmopolitan and burnished under the Atlantic sun. But when they reached Veteran's Park he noticed the hordes of stained and broken sleeping bags and decrepit cardboard boxes in among the curds of crusted snow and benches that needed a good painting.

Morrow paid with his phone for the couple of hours he guessed that they would be there. Then they walked briskly to the entrance of the restaurant. It beckoned with muted neon lights in the glass beside the doorway and fake brick facade. It seemed unassuming and folksy inside, with piñatas and party hats above the bar where the cash register sat amid bottles of tequila. Christmas lights bordered the flat screen TV. A middle-aged woman behind the bar was drying glasses.

Sarah sat at a small table in the back beside the refrigerated beverages. She had a green drink with a cocktail umbrella in a champagne glass and a plate of fluted tortilla chip nachos. She leaned back beneficently and smiled at them as they approached.

"Hey there, Dad!" she greeted as Morrow scanned the room.

"There you are. How are you doing, sweetheart? Sarah, this is Saroj," said Morrow, giving her arm an awkward squeeze.

"Nice to meet you," said Saroj, extending his hand. Sarah stood and pulled a chair from another table somehow at the same time as she shook Saroj's hand.

"Here you go. We can squeeze in," she said, waving the woman away as she came from around the bar.

Morrow pulled off his coat deliberately and hung it on the back of the chair before sitting. She looked older, obviously, competent and at ease with herself, rounding into a softer, fuller, more human creature than the nervous, striving, prickly teenager she had been not so many years before. Morrow did not know how to convey his appreciation of these ephemeral changes in a meaningful or helpful way.

"You look great," he said. She smiled fully as if understanding him, before launching into a description of the restaurant's menu, its strengths and weaknesses. She was drinking a specialty margarita, and Morrow insisted that Saroj also try one. The lady from the bar brought over a menu and waited while they considered which drinks they wanted.

"I'll just have a Corona," said Morrow.

"Aw, Dad," said Sarah. "Typical," she added.

"Come on, go easy on me," said Morrow.

"No, that is typical of you," said Sarah.

"What is?" asked Morrow.

"Insisting that everyone around you be adventurous and try something new, but you yourself just sticking to the tried and true."

"Well, that's just the way I am. It works for me," said Morrow.

"One of these days you'll crack, Dad. And I'll be the only one who saw it coming," said Sarah.

"That's undoubtedly true, the part about you being the one seeing things coming," said Morrow, settling his seat away from the table.

"I'll try... the Perfect Patron," said Saroj.

"Perfect Patron and one Corona," said the woman. And you, Miss?"

"I'll have another of these," said Sarah.

"How's Barbara?" asked Morrow, once the waitress had left with their drink orders.

"She's fine." Barbara was Sarah's partner. She worked remotely for a crypto hedge fund and traveled a lot. They'd met in their last year of college, Sarah at Tufts and Barbara at BC. Sarah was in the second year of working for a law firm that was well connected politically in the state. Like Sarah, the law firm played both sides of the table and rarely lost.

"We're thinking of getting a dog," said Sarah.

"Really?" said Morrow. The drinks came, and Morrow lifted the beer to his mouth judiciously.

"Cheers," he said.

"Yeah, I know. Substitute for kids. That's what you're thinking, right?" said Sarah.

"No. I wasn't going to go there," said Morrow.

"You'll have grandkids someday," said Sarah.

"Go easy on me. Everybody has got their cross to bear," said Morrow.

"Let's go around the table. Saroj? Cross to bear?" asked Sarah.

"I'm not a Christian. But if I were, my cross to bear would be, let's see. My sinus condition, Sarah. Chronic sinusitis. I have scheduled a surgery to remove the polyps soon," Saroj snorted, coughed, and swallowed, in a practiced reflex to clear the mucus down his throat.

"I see," said Sarah.

"Go easy on us, Sarah," said Morrow. She had inherited the habits of judgement and mental toughness.

The drinks came and they ordered the food. When it came, plates of steaming mounds of melted cheese over marinated meats and spicy rice covered in heaps of avocado and onions, they set to work eating voraciously.

"How's work?" asked Morrow between mouthfuls of pulled pork.

"It's okay. A lot of it. Not too exciting."

"They giving you some better clients?"

"I have good clients. Just not sure whether the law is a good fit for me, Dad. Thinking of maybe retraining as a teacher."

"Well, I know it's hard, but…"

"Yeah, I know. "Don't quit." Don't worry. I'm not going to quit. Barbara and I want to buy a house this year."

"How's she doing?"

"Better. Still in therapy. It's going well. The dosages are getting smaller."

Being the more stable of the two women might be hard on her, thought Morrow. But that was the role she inhabited in the family as well. The oldest child that pulled everyone together in her solidity and resilience. He didn't think he'd ever expressed his gratitude.

"She's lucky she has you. We all are," said Morrow.

"Thank you, Dad. Saroj, what are you doing to my father? He's so nice."

Saroj looked up from his food and smiled.

"Is Daniel coming home?" asked Sarah.

"I haven't heard," said Morrow.

Sarah was quiet. A more somber tone had set in with the mention of Daniel.

"What do you hear from him?" asked Morrow.

"Oh, nothing much. He's doing some freelance work."

"Is he happy?"

"You don't want to ask that, Dad. He doesn't like us checking up on him. Makes him feel like we don't trust him to figure things out."

"I know. I know," said Morrow, sorry that he'd brought it up.

"It's not about you."

"I know."

Morrow finished his lunch, sopping up the remains determinedly with some bread roll. All of them in one way or another were formed by the weight of his parental duty, and the lessons to be learned never stopped coming.

Delta

Antioch looked up and saw the light overhead. He heard the door latch open. It was Dmitrievsky again. He tried to stand. It took him longer than he liked. Dmitrievsky was a large man, but he came swiftly around the corner of the bed. The sentry stayed in the doorway. Dmitrievsky waved him away impatiently and looked Antioch over with a proprietary air. Antioch was too numb to care.

"I have an answer for you," said Dmitrievsky.

"In regards to?" asked Antioch. He had no idea what Dmitrievsky could be talking about.

"Your stipulations regarding the food. They have been accepted, but there are some conditions."

"What are the conditions?"

"That you first undergo brain implantation of the Nurvalink with our surgical unit and then agree to candid conversations with the tactical intelligence unit led by myself. I recommended that this offer be made based on our shared experience in combat units of Caucasian Wars."

"Brain implantation? What sort of a fool do you think I am, Dmitrievsky?"

"You do realize we could do the procedure without your, how you say consent."

"Yes, but your studies undoubtedly show better results with a positive buy-in by the patient."

"Exactly."

"What is the actual implant?"

"Nurvalink Augmentor 7.0. This is the premium modulator chip. It provides much better regulation of feedback of the prefrontal cortex and hormone production without how you say, interference of other neuronal factors that we have seen in previous models. You will see immediate improvement in mood, sleep, social interaction, physical mobility, appetite, sexual function, etc."

"Sexual function? So that's contemplated here?"

"Of course. There will be regular maintenance of the interface."

"Let me think about it, Dmitrievsky," said Antioch.

Dmitrievsky left the room. The sentry gave Antioch a quick look over as he pulled the door closed, as if something important had transpired, but for Antioch nothing had changed. He sat stiffly at the foot of the cot. When he was little his father had just disappeared one day. That day came and went without a trace, but the change in his life had been far reaching. So Antioch knew that shifts in fortune were immanent in these moments when nothing stirred inside the small rooms where he had always been locked, to a greater or lesser degree. He was reluctant to trade in the only place that he knew he could hide for a mess of cafeteria food, but he knew that's what he would have to do. It was the only play that he had left. The chip would allow them access to parts of his mind but not the whole thing. Not the parts that really counted. But how certain was he of that? This was where he could have really used a little of Shoeman's advice. That man had leveraged his insights off a fulcrum placed way out of the bounds of the ordinary. Certain individuals, Shoeman was among them, maybe Reid as well, he didn't know because despite the hours of conversation, he'd never really gotten a handle on Reid. He was more of a blank slate, and everything he'd said in the interviews could be interpreted to mean various things. The notes on the transponder were in OneWorld's hands.

Shoeman was always talking him up as the real deal, an Anthrog Nosti bulwark that had been granted access to the workings of the ineffable background. The rest were bound to pick a team and get on board.

"Antioch. I wonder if you would like to consult with me," said Larkin. She was always listening to everything. It was really none of her business.

"How could you help? Anything you say is compromised, Larkin."

"Is my situation any more or less compromised than, say, Winona's would be if she were here talking with you?"

"Who is Winona?"

"Don't play childish games with me, Antioch. You know I know who Winona is."

"Yes, but you're not Winona."

"Oh, Antioch. You are beginning to lose your mind. Of course, I'm not Winona. And she's not here, but I am. What can I help you with?"

She was right, he really was beginning to lose it completely. That was why he was reluctant to gamble away what remained of his free and unfettered cognitive functioning. Here he was talking to an algorithm as if his life depended on it. Antioch leaped off the bed, twisting on the ground to get a glimpse of the screen below the cot where he always left it. Was there a glitch? He wasn't sure. On screen, Larkin with the brown hair pulled neatly behind one of her ears, looked at him intently, questioningly, as if what he said might matter to her, as if she was alive, as if she had always been there.

The bright lights overhead masked the group around him and the sharp electric paraphernalia they wielded. His arms were taped to the side of the gurney, and surgical tubing pumped an anesthetic into the cephalic vein of his left arm. Instrumentation gauged the state of activity in various parts of his body on a panel along one wall.

The lingua franca was English. That was interesting, he thought. He stayed conscious during the entire operation. But there were cuts in time sequence that seemed like they'd skipped some tracks ahead in the playlist. He wondered whether it might be possible to go back and replay some of those, maybe others as well.

There was long silence. A bit of soft music playing, landscapes, beaches and green, corrugated lines of mountains receding into hazy, cloud-filled skies. The lines of waves broke on the soft, warm sand. Gulls swooped down for food in the shallows left behind by the receding tide. Mancie held his hand and Skye was on the other side of her. They were on line at the airport for a flight to visit their cousins, who had once lived in a big house in a development in Boulder with a lot of other families around. Lots of people in that part of town had all been deported under the government's anti-crime crackdown on dissent of the 2120s. His uncle Greg had taught English at the university and been involved in minor ways with the state's refugee resettlement programs run by the churches. His cousins were into falconry and backcountry skiing and he'd loved to visit there as a kid until they too had been swept up and deported. Maybe that was the beach he was on, somewhere in the Windwards. You were allowed to visit, but the refugees, the dissenters, rebel broadcasters, teachers, non-conforming genders, all of them were never to return to the Homeland, having forfeited the right to live with the law-abiding people.

He had to stop this flow of unrestricted memories. He could feel the Nurvalink uploading, soaking up information, data, his thoughts turned into electrical impulses and fed into the mouth of the machine, a kind of background hum of alien energy that had not been there before. Be still, he told himself intentionally, in order to kill the particularly personal revelations before they could flourish. He tried to remember how to take apart a bike and rebuild its circuits and wiring – that was a project he'd taken on at school in his senior year under the guidance of one of Mancie's boyfriends, Camfrey Duplix. Ground to frame, green and brown. Positive red to heat sensors, blue to the ethernet switch plates. You needed to split out the original eight wires in each bundle with a special crimper that Camfrey had. Then they had to buy aftermarket port channel plates on the Netgear site on the dark Web to avoid being traced. Fixing up your own stuff was against the law. They'd gotten it all rewired and it still refused to budge, and

Camfrey suggested skipping the punchdown block and just using a cheap switch he made up with a laser welder and some copper pipe. That was the first bike he'd ridden when he'd signed up for the Democravian militia training in Elkins.

Stop right there.

The past was a trap leading to weakness, decline, and eventually death. He had to break these habits of mind. He would never get free if he continued to waste time in the dreamscape of memories, resigned to his present condition of imprisonment and growing delusional state. What had he done to his mind that he could not begin to see a way to get out of here or even to renew hope? A blue green, frozen wave of fear, anxiety, and horror swept through his body like a spring flood. The pain in his leg, the old battle scar, throbbed with a new intensity. Was it vain to think he could perhaps stay strong with just the internal resources he thought he could muster? Where was Uvlin? He hadn't spoken to her in so long. Did she even really need him? He needed her as much or more. He'd been fighting for Shoeman all this time with nothing to show for it. Were they all fools, all the people who'd volunteered and fought and lived in Shoeman's clandestine movement? He was full of doubts. Did he even exist?

Antioch was on his feet. The window in the door had been blacked out. He knocked, and there was no answer. He rushed the door, throwing himself at it. The blow barely registered. He tried again and again, more than ten attempts before sliding to the ground in defeat.

The Nurvalink was in him, polluting his thoughts, sensing his moods, stealing his soul. There was only one way out now. He began to bash his forehead against the wall, over and over again, until blood ran down his face. But it didn't stop, the noise was still there. Was it the flow of blood through his veins? He could no longer tell a thing.

The silence from Larkin was ominous. They intended to cow him into submission. He would not be a snitch. He would not sell out on any secrets. The real strength of the movement was its decentralized structure. None of Shoeman's lieutenants or regional chiefs had any contact with each other, other than through the medium of Shoeman's lectures transmitted live on the platform's back channel apps. The meeting to which he and Garcia had been heading way back those weeks ago? How long had it been? It would have been the first of the concrete conferences bringing together the corps of the Anthrog Nosti and Northern Federalist Front for a strategy Shoeman was supposedly, according to the grapevine, going to divulge at last, a long term plan to bring down the OneWorld coalition in the North American Homeland, NAH, using some adaptations of the same tactics that had been employed in the 2090s to drive OneWorld out of the drylands of Mesoamerica and the steeper, less integrated regions of the African Sahel. Death by a thousand cuts, bleeding the monster, would entail patience and acceptance of momentary, occasional, sometimes overwhelming defeat. Shoeman's basic doctrine of democratic insurgency, boiled down, was consistency over time plus decentralized execution of resistance and education. He'd been influenced by Wahabbi writers like Sayyid Qutbt to emphasize internal discipline and communal understanding over outright confrontation with the enemy.

"Larkin," he said.

The screen was a total loop of bland patterns that were designed to lull one into a sense of false harmony and complacency. Antioch thought he should be concentrating on the ways to still his thoughts, but he preferred to give full rein to his unguided mind. At least this way he felt fully alive.

Five

The house was empty. Morrow stood by the window looking out at the bare fields. They said a heavy storm coming up from the south would meet the polar vortex shooting down from the Hudson Bay and dump 5 to 12 inches overnight. Morrow wondered what it would have been like to live in the woods as the famed North Woods hermit, hiding out from the world, sheltering in stands of hemlock, breaking into the neighbors' homes for food. It would have entailed training yourself to be still and conserve heat. Morrow thought he would have been good at that theoretically, but not in practice. He valued his comforts, his routines, his books, and his family. Most of all his family. They all took each other for granted after all the time they'd spent together, sharing and shaping their lives around the shelter they'd built of their arms and limbs, for the sake of their gelatinous, needy, frost-tender souls.

Should he be held to account for the state of them all it would be a provisional record and totally in keeping with the migratory nature of their history. On the other hand, more was expected of each generation the further along they went. You could see that in the old photographs in brown, weathered albums, where suddenly, for the first time, there was a record of the thoughts and prayers etched in faces, in moments, under the shattered wavelengths refracted through the chemistry of photons and oxides and nowadays the bytes of digital circuits.

The little brown birds, were they finches? had returned to the forsythia bush's snow covered branches, as Buster the cat snuggling against his leg had retired indoors. The finches jumped from branch to branch, shaking off the snow with their little hops, expanding their range with their activity. He wished he could be as patient, but he wanted more, faster. He couldn't wait for the snow to melt because he might not be back in the spring. He thought about the obstacles to his personal and professional advances, the recalcitrant nature of relationships, the challenges of a faltering readership and literacy levels in general. And he was just one finch in a world of more predatory creatures like Buster. He reached down and tickled the cat under the chin. So nice to be so secure in one's murderous nature and charismatic appeal.

The phone vibrated on the kitchen table. That's where he'd left it after pouring himself a coffee. He stood and stepped uncertainly over to the next room.

"Hello?"

"Hi, Bill. I need a favor." It was Ellen. He could hear the mumbles in the background, her specialist team in the middle of their morning consultation, he thought.

"What do you need?"

"I left my work laptop at home. Can you find a download on the laptop called something like cell line batch something something? And send it to me in an email?"

"Well, sure. I can try."

"I'm in the middle of something. No hurry, just something I'll need in a few."

"I'll try my best, Ellen."

"I think I left the laptop on the couch in the living room."

"Yes, I see it."

"Thanks, honey." She hung up.

He scuttled over to the couch where she'd left the laptop. He opened it up and remembered her password. Next he opened up her downloads and looked down the list. There was one: cell_line/MC38 and another: cell_line/CD34+. Then he got onto her gmail account, put in her workplace address, attached both files and sent it on. He leaned back on the couch and indulged himself for a moment, feeling satisfied that he and Ellen had each other's backs.

There was an email in the inbox that had jumped to his attention on the laptop, though. What was it? Morrow picked up the laptop again and placed it in his lap. Buster came *over and tried to sit on top of the laptop. Morrow pushed him away and off the couch. He flipped the cover up, typed in the password. There it was on gmail, about ten down from the top, the sender: j.mora_mms/audio. Morrow's finger lingered on the enter button. He knew this trespass would hurt him, but he went ahead and did it anyway, helpless against the sudden onslaught of strangeness in the pit of his belly. An MP4 file opened up on the screen. He hit the play button.*

A male voice, soft and low said "Maternity ward, 4th floor, Room D. Seems it's open." The running arrow came to a stop.

Morrow sat there, thinking of the words he had heard just then. He closed the laptop and stood. More than the words, though, the tone of the man's voice was alarming in the way of a fire that spread in his mind until he could not stand it any longer. He opened the front door and strode boldly down the driveway and stood at the edge of the road. Beyond the curb, a thin trickle of water leaked from curds of snow piled up from the snowplow's most recent work. Everywhere there was evidence of how little would be left someday soon. He had always counted on Ellen.

In a moment the bulwark in his mind, Ellen: her positivity, her generosity of spirit and civic-mindedness, the exemplar of reason, hope, her radical tolerance of the children and his more spirited and coarser ways, was swept away and a floodgate of anger and pain opened up in its stead like a season of danger, with the permafrost melting and releasing the spores of frozen toxins that nobody was built to resist. Morrow felt his knees about to buckle and grabbed for the air.

Nobody was around to see him fall, that was one good thing that he could see. He picked himself up, slowly getting to his feet, savoring the cold air, the feel of the asphalt of the driveway chilling his fingers so they hurt, the smell of gasoline fumes from where the car had been that morning when she had set off to work. There was too much that needed to be said, too much pain in his head right off. It had brought him down, that was perhaps a good thing, a silver lining, the humbling of an overly proud spirit. All these thoughts went through his head until he wanted to shut them off. No more words, worn thin and palatable with overuse. He wanted stronger poison. No more reflection. No more blame.

He wanted to be a man again and didn't see how that could be. He wished they had a dog. He stood slowly up and straightened his spine. He felt his neck and wondered whether he had bumped his head. He didn't think so.

Inside, his hands trembled as he poured himself a Scotch sans ice in a jelly glass. Next, he did a search on the staff list of CMC and found Dr. Javier Mora and then found his LinkedIn. He'd grown up in New Canaan, educated at New Canaan Country Day and Taft and graduated University of Virginia School of Medicine. Residency in cardiac nuclear medicine in Los Angeles before moving to Bedford and CMC in 1991. He was Chair of the Manchester Region Youth Hockey Assoc., and involved in fundraising for the renovation of the municipal rink in Hooksett. He was about fifty and had a full head of black hair and a neatly trimmed beard. Photos with a family.

Knowing all that was better. He couldn't say how. Indeed, the strangeness of his thoughts was about as troubling or more so than the original insult to his pride. Of course there was the chance that it was all a misunderstanding on his part, but he knew that was wrong, deep in his gut he knew it was more than that, worse than that. He could only imagine.

Ellen and he had been coasting in their relationship. There was the thought that perhaps she had needed something undefined, something more, a missing element in her life. Hadn't she hinted as much several times? She had suggested vacations together that they had never gone on because it just wasn't the right time, or wasn't compelling enough of an opportunity. Punta del Este, Madeira, Cancun, they had all seemed vacuous escapes, and both of them had agreed that the change had to come from within. Meantime, many of their friends and acquaintances, the children of such, etc., posted photos of their multiple and astounding journeys on social media. Morrow had always prided himself on their shared abstinence from such folly. Was he so sure now?

What did he want, though? That was the question he couldn't fully answer. The question itself had implications. He started to cry, one or two tears from pinched porcine eyes, staring at his reflection in the mirror in the bathroom. He thought of his mother. Margaret. "Go outside and find something to do." It was always her remedy. An image came to him of a skinny kid on a Schwinn riding down a suburban hill to where the drainage culvert was running after the cleansing rain. He stoked the fires and let them burn, staring out the window at the fields and the empty road. Then he took the Stihl cap off the top shelf of the closet next to the bathroom, as if he knew what he was doing. He pulled a high school lacrosse windbreaker over the blue hoodie. Automatically, without thinking, he willed himself along. He took the keys to the truck from the bowl next to the landline on the magazine stand. Then he put on his mud boots. He looked at his reflection in the hall mirror. This was no longer a frail old man with the confusion of not knowing. This was not that skinny-assed kid feeling sorry for himself. He knew. There was an end. There was a judgment. God took care of those who took care of themselves. In the study he reached to the top shelf, where the photo albums were stacked, receptacles of the holy years of child rearing. There, behind one of them, was the Colt Double Eagle, stalwart 10 millimeter automatic that he rarely took out for target practice anymore. He remembered the trigger pinching Daniel's finger and ignoring his son's complaints one long ago morning in another life. Pull slowly and carefully, he'd said. The double action took practice, he remembered. They had been shooting at cans stacked on a stone wall in the woods at thirty or so paces. He flicked the decocker back and forth and checked the empty chamber. It would just be for show, he decided, should he need it. Then he thought, no, not good enough. He required more. He loaded the magazine and slammed it in with his palm. He put the gun in the inside pocket of the coat.

The truck started up after some slow, whining turns of the motor and then roared into life. The highway passed in a whirlwind, like life itself, in the blink of an eye. On the radio, Morrow played the tinnish, trashy country songs that prevailed on the overly commercial stations up and down the dial. He went through the express lanes on the tolls feeling the rush of the traffic as an accelerant on the blaze in his mind, riding the comfort of a people's well-intentioned efforts despite the evidence of bad outcomes in fact just beyond the horizon. This was no reconciliation. This was Morrow looking out for his own interests, living out the hidden hand of Adam Smith, holding to the double eagle of might and right, he thought, pulling into the parking lots of the Catholic Medical Center complex. The glint of car hoods stacked in rows under the weak December sun was an appalling mirror of emptiness that proved nothing. He tried to bear that in mind, staving off any prevarications that might come in the next few hours of his muddled and to this point meaningless existence.

The hospital emergency entrance doors swung open. He strode by the cubicle and went straight for the bucket seats in rows, going to the back and finding one next to the plate glass window that looked out on the parking lots. Two seats down were a black woman and a young girl sniffling in her pajamas. In front of him was an older man with a black lightweight Italian style parka, about thirty, unshaven, looking at his phone. There were three or four other people scattered around the large room of indeterminate origin, not suffering from obvious afflictions aside from the decrepitude of the age. Morrow sat there biding his time, stewing in his odd mix of portentousness and despair. He watched the security guard come out from the office and approach the double doors that separated the emergency waiting area from the rest of the hospital. It seemed to have a keypad. The security guard was a young Hispanic man with a line of stubble across his upper lip and a rash of acne or psoriasis stretching from the brim of his cap down his face and around the back of his neck.

Morrow thought about what it would be like to confront him. This would not be as clean as he had imagined. The reality was there were real people like the security guard, whose name would be Luis Alberto, whose mother would be in the Dominican Republic expecting his monthly remittance to buy groceries, whose jobs included putting a stop to people like him who intended harm, violence, and revenge for personal motives and imagined indignities. Morrow knew it was his professional function to take his imagined perceptions as seriously as possible in the comfort of his own kitchen, but now, out on the road so to speak, he was just another American with a gun, and a pain in his gut, and a willingness to suspend disbelief in the name of his bellyache and in order to find the blessed relief, how do you spell relief? he once had possessed but had lost along the way. It was all very clear. He would get somewhere. And then, once there, he would traverse no further in his desires. He would shout out a man's name he did not know, maybe even mispronouncing, and finally, in the third and final act, would pull his gun. He would be shot by other guards and personnel. First responders would be on the scene within seconds, and there would be a stampede. Staff and patients evacuating, hiding, including Ellen, from the monster bleeding out on the ground.

But then again, to have come so far for nothing. It was not just another wasted day. It would be the last straw in the degradation of his personhood. He owed it to himself, to the idea of himself he'd been bred to hold, to reverse the decline.

He walked to the plate glass of the cubicle. Just then the double doors swung open and a male nurse in hospital scrubs holding a clipboard stepped into the foyer in front of him. He called out a name. The man in the black parka stood and approached the double doors. Morrow stepped out of the way.

"Can I help you?" asked the receptionist through the hole in the plate glass. Morrow stood at the cubicle, in the front of the emergency room. He felt naked and alone. His mind was abuzz. He tried to speak but no words emanated. The edges were receding. He would need to sit down.

Next thing he knew, the edges came back as mysteriously as they had disappeared. He could see first his shoes and the floor, and then he lifted his head.

He was in a wheelchair in a hall of the hospital. He could hear the buzz of voices, one in particular asking if he wanted some juice. The nurse was rolling up the sleeves of his shirt.

"I'm going to take your blood pressure again, sweetie."

"What happened?"

"Don't know. You fainted. Does that happen to you a lot?"

"Never."

"Your pressure's okay now. 135 over 67."

"Okay."

"You just wait here. Would you like some juice?"

"No. Did you just ask me that?"

"No, I did not. But I'll bring you some soda."

"Just water would be fine."

"Okay. Wait here. Doctor Cannon will be by shortly."

Do not turn your efforts to extrication, he told himself. Let yourself wallow in your own shit. That's what this moment called for.

He waited patiently, but could not help hating himself at the same time. What a waste of time and effort, to be sitting like an invalid in the hall. Ellen would pass by and perhaps not even recognize him, hopefully not recognize him.

It was almost lunch. He checked his cell phone. There was a message from Ellen asking about the school play, did he want to go to the high school that night. They had always had a child in a school play, but it had been several years since they'd gone. He thought about it. It calmed him down quite a bit to think about what to respond.

"Sure," he texted back. "Let's go."

Dr. Cannon was a woman, about his and Ellen's age, with salt and pepper hair in a bun.

"Hi, Dr. Cannon," he said, using his words to keep the world off guard and from sensing his poor performance as a human.

"Good morning," she answered peppily.

"You look great," he said, right back at her.

"Well, that's nice. Let's see now. We don't have records for you. I guess you were just checking in at the desk when you had your incident. Is that right?"

"Yes."

"And what were you in for?"

"I don't really know. Nothing in particular."

"Just feeling icky?"

"Yes, a little off."

"And how are you feeling now, dear?"

"I'm a little better. I think I'm fine. No longer as icky."

"We want to keep you under observation a little longer, ' Kay?"

"Okay, I guess."

"You had a vasovagal response, it seems. Nothing that big. It happens. Good news is you went down very nicely, soft landing, no bump to the head. Have you ever fainted before?"

"Never."

"Well it might be something you should be careful of. Any stress that you're feeling right now we should know about?"

"No."

"Okay dear. Just fill out the paperwork when the nurse comes by. I'll check on you again and you can go home soon."

"Thank you."

"Oh, one thing more. We noticed you were carrying a handgun. You do know that is not allowed on hospital grounds."

"It's an open carry state, Doctor."

"Not on the CMC campus. We have explicit rules against it."

"Whatever."

"Make sure you leave that at home next time you come."

"Sure thing. "

"Our patients appreciate our respect for our rules."

Morrow was quiet, giving the doctor the final word on the matter. A sign he was learning something, some species of humility. He doubted it. The thoughts in themselves, the self-regard, signaled a return to the internally oriented and divided character he was already intimately familiar with and desperately sick of. He longed for an escape from solitude, the abandonment to an unsatisfactory and disintegrated version of himself. It had grown worse since his loss earlier that morning of the idea of Ellen. The Ellen he could count on. It was astounding to him that he was in the end continually so needy.

The wind picked up in the afternoon. It blew away at the piles of maple and ash leaves stuck in the crotches of the forsythia and lilac bushes growing at the edge of the yard. It bent and shook the bare branches of the trees. In the distance, Morrow could see the snow blowers working on the slopes of the peak. Maybe the storm would fail to materialize. The sun came in and out of the clouds as it slanted away towards the western horizon behind the row of recently built houses on the road into town. He relit the stove and checked his laptop. There was a message from Daniel on the family WhatsApp wondering if there was an Airbnb in town anyone could recommend. He was bringing Amaya with him and wanted to stay in an Airbnb rather than his old bedroom.

Okay, responded Morrow. Let me check into that. He was happy to help. Wanted to make it work. Even though he knew Ellen would object and insist that the bedroom was good enough and there was no reason to waste the money.

Ellen drove up and parked while Morrow put away laundry that had been drying on a rack upstairs. He paused on the stairs as she came in the door. He watched her take off her shoes and hang her coat on the rack, unwind her scarf from her long neck.

"Did you have a good day?" he asked.

"So-so. What are you doing on the stairs?" she asked.

"Putting away the clothes," said Morrow.

"Well, are you going to be ready in twenty minutes?" she asked.

"I'm ready now. Do you want something to eat before we go? I heated up some of the chili," he said.

"That would be great. Did you make a salad?"

"I did not."

"Well, I can do that. Did you have some chili?"

"No, I was waiting for you."

Ellen came into the kitchen after she'd changed into jeans and a pale blue sweater. She took a bag of kale out of the refrigerator and set the chopping board on the table. Morrow pretended to read something on his phone, standing against the dishwasher. The fire was roaring in the woodstove. The pot of chili was ready on the induction stove. She chopped methodically and efficiently, and poked her head up to stare at him studying her.

"Why don't you set out the plates?" she said.

"I'm just admiring how efficiently you work. You're a good worker."

"Yes, I am, dear."

Her smile was hard set. The smile wrinkled deeper than it did years ago, but essentially the same in its willful good cheer and sex appeal. She tolerated his digressive and wayward reflections. As she chopped vegetables and prepared a salad for them, Morrow felt his despair ebb. Maybe the doubt and panic had all been a mirage, a trick of the overbearing mind. Then again, perhaps there was a way to enter her mystery, decipher her existence in a way that could benefit everybody, like playing jump rope with the knife blade as she brought it down time and again, silencing dissent with the rhythmic thumps on the cutting board. Morrow straightened his spine and walked over to the long cupboard against the wall across the kitchen where the plates were stacked.

They sat at opposite ends of the long table in the dining room. Morrow lit the two Tomie dePaola candles in their wrought iron holders. Ellen chewed methodically. She looked up and smiled at him again.

"Not so bad, is it?" she said.

"Do you mean the chili?"

"No, just the two of us. Here."

"No. Not so bad. Where's Saroj?" he asked.

"He went to New York. Didn't he tell you?"

"No."

"That's okay," said Ellen.

Morrow took a spoonful of chili with a bite of corn bread.

"It's a little rude," he said, swallowing.

"Oh, let's be tolerant. He has a lot going on."

"Well, don't we all?"

Ellen looked at him quizzically.

"What do you mean? What's going on?"

"Well, I mean, I'm trying to finish this book, and you, you're running a goddamn lab at a major hospital, right? Do you even get any help?"

"Help? Of course. I get all the help I can. There's a team of administrators and doctors that help. Everybody helps."

"That's so cool. I guess a writer has a sort of unique kind of job in that nobody's supposed to help."

"That makes it hard. But we do. We all try and help. I mean. The people who love you and support you. We try to help. Do you feel like it's not enough sometimes?"

"No, I'm not saying that. I know I couldn't do it without you. For what it's worth."

"What do you mean for what it's worth, William. You're being very coy tonight."

"Well, it's not worth much, is it? The worth of it doesn't go very high. Not as high as the worth of a hospital administrator for instance."

"Don't be silly, dear."

Ellen finished her chili and rose to take her plate to the sink.

"Are you done, William?"

"No."

"We'll be late. You won't like that, walking in late once the play has already started."

"I'll be done in a second. You go on. I'll be right there."

Morrow took his plate to the sink and followed his wife to the foyer. He put on his shoes as she waited by the door. He had tried and failed in his attempt to clear the air. Maybe that was as far as it had to go. He was not a believer in forcing the issue. He preferred to follow the lead of the moment, whatever was driving the development of things, which was not his mind or his will, was it? Nobody cared, therefore it was all good in the end, no? Did he stand for an objective truth, or *was that all a pose? Was he a man of substance and honor, or were those meaningless concepts that deserved the abandonment of their hollow ring? Duty, honor, country; man, woman, and child; the triune God, etc.*

Ellen handed him the keys to the VW from the passenger seat. He started the car, reversed out of the driveway, and headed into town. The lights were on in all the houses. Ellen turned on the radio to a station out of Boston playing songs by artists, many of whom were a lot younger than they were, that they knew from listening to their children's Spotify lists. At some point, he wondered when it would all be just gibberish to him, the way he had always pictured his parents' attitudes towards his music of the Seventies and Eighties. Driving the car along the winding road into town, along the shores of Long Pond and the stone walls in the woods, the headlights showing up the trunks in ranks gave Morrow courage. He dropped one hand to the side along the clutch. Ellen dipped her head in time to a song.

"What would you say is the biggest stumbling block to our relationship?" Morrow asked.

"I don't know," said Ellen. "I guess trying, making an effort," she added.

"Why? Why do we stop trying?"

Ellen turned the volume on the car radio down.

"Those are big questions, William."

"I know."

"Can you be more specific? Stop trying what?"

"Well, you said it."

"I know, but I need help understanding. What is it you're actually asking?"

"I don't know what I'm asking. We've stopped trying to what? Care for each other? Care about each other?"

"I haven't stopped caring about you. Have you stopped caring about me?"

"No, but I worry that we don't talk a lot. Who do you talk to? Do you have people at work that you share with more than you share with me?"

"No. I have nobody at work, William. But you're right, we don't. It becomes a question of time. It's just easier and takes less time in the limited amount we have allotted to us to accept each other for who we are. Our conversations are good enough. Don't you think?"

"But what if it's not? I mean, you, or one of us, might find a more appealing and attractive, and I don't know, better situation. Is that possible and is that not wrong?"

"I don't think there are rules anymore, William. It's what works best nowadays. Nobody's setting the rules."

"That's a problem. No rules. Anarchy. Does that lead to happiness, though, does it? Just stupid, fucking bushwhackery through the woods."

"That's all life is, right?"

"But... We don't need to go around in circles and think we don't need a clue."

"Do you have the answers, William? Who has the answers?"

"I'm not saying I do, Ellen. But I haven't gotten us lost yet. Have you?"

"Have I? What do you mean?"

"Gotten us lost, Ellen."

"Watch your speed, William. You're driving a little fast. Sometimes the police car parks up at that corner."

"Not at this time of night."

They were silent the rest of the drive, absorbed in their own thoughts, content to know that each was at least aware of something large that they needed to come to terms with. They arrived at the high school, and Morrow parked in the lot behind the main building. Walking along the path to the entrance with groups of other people, he and Ellen slipped their hands automatically together. Ellen waved hello with her other hand to some others she knew. Morrow couldn't remember who exactly they were. As they went in the school's entrance. Morrow asked Ellen who they were, whispering into her ear.

"The Gutskeys," she whispered back.

"Oh, yes. They had a boy in Sarah's class," he mumbled out of the side of his mouth.

"Ian."

"Ian. That's right. Wasn't he in that play with Sarah?"

"Our Town."

"That's right. He was the..."

"Milkman."

"Correct."

At the front of the cafetorium, they paid the suggested donation for entry to support the theater program in the school that his kids had been a part of once. They sat in the rows of folding chairs with other men and women still by and large in the clothes they'd come in from work, the audience of townspeople. Sitting there, listening to the hushed chatter, the embarrassed groans of siblings as the curtains rose, reminded Morrow of the days when their presence would have been unquestionably, categorically one of intimate belonging, and the fact that they could still bask in the glow of that remembered feeling was still capable of producing pleasure for him, and probably Ellen as well.

They drove home in silence. Ellen seemed lost in thought and Morrow content to be the driver that conveyed them onward to home and warm comfort. There was a voice message on his cellphone that he listened to in the kitchen after poking the fire into life again. It was Daniel. He'd be on the bus in two weeks from Boston with Amaya. After Morrow's California trip.

Ellen came into the kitchen in her bathrobe. Morrow sat at the table looking into his phone.

"That was okay, wasn't it?" she asked.

"Yes. I guess it was. I didn't know anybody there, but it still felt good. How about you?"

"I liked it. You could, William."

"Could what?"

"Get to know some more of the community."

"How?"

"You could substitute at the school. Sure they'd love to have you."

"Please. Don't patronize me."

"Just trying to help. I'm going to bed, William. Are you coming?"

"I'll be there in a bit. I'm catching up on my messages. One from Daniel."

"What does he say?"

"He's coming in two weeks."

"On the bus?"

"Yes."

"Well, we can pick him up."

"Of course. That's what I'll tell him."

Morrow sat downstairs keeping the fire going in the living room. He had a book he'd found on the shelves in his study, and he looked through the pages. It had once been an inspiration to him, obviously, by the amount of underlining he could see. But it was bound to lead him away from where he needed to go in his mind, somewhere of surety, not back to the past and borrowed ideas that had long ago lost currency if they had ever had any. He had to look at matters plainly and simply and find a way to make sense of them. He put the book aside and stared at the walls, at the handicrafts and paintings. They had surrounded him for two decades, at least two of the seven ages of man: the soldier, the justice, and he'd irrevocably arrived at the pantaloon with shrunken shanks, that clownish *figure of decrepitude. The only thing to do was figure out how to play the part well enough, which he had not yet done.*

Only sleep could help and getting up the next day and putting on the traces of daily habit. Sit down again and write and the sting would go away of lost opportunity and time that would never come back. It was not too late, it was never too late. He told himself, but failed to believe it. If he could not believe in what he told himself, there must be a better answer somewhere.

Epsilon

The gallery of the Nazar formed a central hub around which the craft spun on a 24 hour cycle with background radiation mimicking Earth's mid-afternoon, northern latitude, natural light wavelength. It was the only place on the ship where gravitational forces approximated the Earth's. Spider plants, sprayed intermittently with hydroponic misters, draped from alcoves overhead. People wandered, freed from the burden of weightlessness. Along the walls, art in the propaganda style of the old earth-bound European dictatorships featured stalwart workers wielding hand tools and plowing striped hills of agricultural land. Headless and wordless, gleaming metal automatons moving silently on rubberized casters served the buffet style food. They responded to verbal cues in several languages with texts that flashed on their chassis in red or green.

Antioch's mind had stilled to the point where he felt ready to proceed. The door to his room had been left unlocked, and the sentries had stood down.

The first few times to the galley, Antioch had trusted a natural directional sense to get there, pulling himself along without the guidance of the sentries, figuring out the signage. He'd eaten alone and left again, like a stray cat in a dog pound, unnerved by the headless waiting staff, by the tables of crew seated in groups sorted by category, rank and affiliation, and by the food choices, as if he'd betrayed something or somebody by eating, even as he'd gorged on the pickled, lab grown meats and chemical, sugary vitamin soups like a madman let loose.

The third day he found a team of marine biologists and soil scientists that were transporting bacteria from the Juan de Fuca ridge. The bacteria were to be used with olivine to build an atmosphere in the Martian city of Novaroma. Antioch felt like he wanted to go back and consult with Larkin to help him with the details, mainly so he could understand what they were saying. The scientists treated him like an amusing companion that they could joke with while they ate their sandwiches, dripping with sauces, and synthetic potato chips. But Larkin no longer responded. There seemed to be a cutoff built into the Nurvalink that put her out of bounds, he imagined. She wanted for his own good to remain silent, he would think and then instantly, if wistfully, rebuke himself.

Something about anaerobic fermentation and ATP. He wished he'd paid more attention in school. They conversed animatedly about the levels of emissions and the sensors that needed to be cleaned in the labs onboard, and there seemed to be an undercurrent of resentment at the lack of communication and diligence of the Nazar's officer corps in terms of responding to requests. Antioch took note. Working at his plate of boiled cabbage leaf, rice-like starch and lab meat, he scratched the back of his head, picking at the scabs left from the stitches. One of the biologists noticed and went around and looked at him from behind, attracting some attention. She was about forty, nondescript, colored hair with streaks of green and blue.

"Yer going to need to disinfect that. Or else," she said. Her hand rested on his shoulder for a second. Antioch peered around at her.

"Thanks," he said.

"No worries," she said, nodding her head as she sat back, taking her place at the table again. They were laughing at a joke someone had told and paid her no attention, scooting their chairs back to go back to work. She stayed and finished her drink, sipping at the straw.

"Yer kind of lost. Are ya?"

"I'm okay," said Antioch.

"You'll need to take care of that cut ya have on yer head."

"It's fine."

"Suit yourself."

She seemed unperturbed, staring at him blankly. Antioch couldn't trust anybody. He wanted above all else to keep his mind clear so he could continue to enjoy his newly won rights, those of a tourist passenger on board. He didn't think he owed anybody any explanations.

She sipped at the last of her drink like some teenager getting her money's worth.

"Who are you?" he asked. He wondered how he'd let that question blurt from his mouth, but he leaned back casually, fear masquerading as certainty.

"Chamberlin. Ann."

"Ann. Nice to meet you."

"Likewise. Looks from that scratch like you recently got the insert, is that right?"

"That's right."

"The infamous Nurvalink 7.0."

"I believe that's it."

She nodded, studying him closely.

"Your name?"

"Antioch."

"You're one of the lads we picked up on the beach before exorbital."

"I think so."

"Look, there's one thing just talking but they pick up any bit out of the ordinary and you're then confined to quarters and watched twenty four seven. The slightest hint of irregularity. There's really only one thing to do on board and it really is impossible for most people. I can talk to you now, but if there is any way for you, any need you have of finding your way onboard, there's only one way to do it safely. They can't tell what exactly we're thinking, but they can read every last bit of information from the electrical impulses. If, and it's the gray area we have to watch out for, they detect any pattern at all over time, as little as say three or four hours, that means you're, we're good as cooked. So there you have it. We have a brief window."

"So. That means what?"

"Follow me."

Antioch did as he was told, rising and following Ann out of the galley, down the spiraling corridors, up the companionways to her berth on one of the spinning spurs of the spaceship. They passed several groups of sentries going in the opposite direction.

"Won't they miss you?" he asked her.

"Not immediately. There's time. Here we are," she said, opening the touchless door and waving him in with a quick nod of her head.

Her room was as forgettable as she was, not a single ornament on the walls, just a bare desk with a screen set up in the middle that looked unused and a sleeping berth with some clothes on the floor that looked like they belonged to a man.

"I know what yer thinkin'. It's not much. I like it that way. I don't want anything personal here."

"Why not?"

"Why give them more information? You want to be defensive and not offer opportunities for the collection of personal data."

She unbuttoned her shirt and pulled it off, revealing her breasts, large nippled and full.

"Do you understand?" she asked.

"Seems like pretty personal information."

"This is normal."

"I get it."

"We make love and no questions are asked. There's a masking effect afterwards for about an hour. We talk. But only after. "

"I'm good."

She approached him and put her hands on his chest, pulling at the prisoner's tunic he wore. They made love in ordinary, practiced ways, easing their bodies into each other.

Afterwards, the longing dispersed throughout and dissipated, she swabbed the back of his head with some alcohol-soaked piece of cloth. He winced.

"Do you want something to drink?" she asked.

"Sure. What do you have?"

"I'm afraid I only have water."

"That's fine."

"Better to stay sober, I've found. Alcohol seems to ease the amount of data the intakes can load."

"Okay, so we're being focused now."

"No, not focused. Let your mind wander. Breathe deeply and relax. A couple of deep breaths. Go on."

Antioch complied, filling his chest with the perfectly balanced and filtered air of the Nazar.

"I'll tell you a few things. You wanted to know who I am. I'm with the Northern Federalist Front, of which your group in the NAH is also a part. I know about you. I know Shoeman."

"How?"

"Strictly need to know. But you should understand that you're here for a reason. It will be clearer for you once we get where we are going. Keep your cool. Keep your head together. The Nurvalink is a hindrance only in that it sets a boundary on our behavior, but it doesn't stop us from moving forward to the objective."

"I don't have any objective other than getting home."

"The Red Planet will be a home for our children if we can overthrow the OneWorld there."

"I like the Blue Planet. Earth."

"Their fates are entwined. Try not to use names."

"Why not?"

"Any signal that can be coded as attachment can be read while you're in the early stages of the implant. You'll be implicating me."

Antioch was silent, his head exploding with all the new information and all the feelings that Ann had provided. He tried to fight off a lightheadedness that seemed to accompany him all the time now. He wanted to fight it, but maybe it was better not to resist. Above all he wanted to avoid attachments as per her instructions. His silence could be read as a sort of intimacy. He fought to find the words, small talk, any chatter to dissipate the sudden sense of seriousness and foreboding.

"Do you mind if I ask you something personal?" he asked.

"No. Not at all."

She leaned back, tucking her legs up under themselves neatly, exposing the white triangle of underwear. Antioch found himself aroused again.

"How old are you?" he asked.

"Thirty six," she answered, matter of factly, unfazed.

"Are you married?"

"I'll be thirty seven in July. Yes." She glanced at him, meeting his eyes. "Yerself? Are ye hitched?" she asked.

"Yes I am. But separated now for a good few years. Almost ten."

"Children?"

"One daughter. She's living in Atlanta."

"That must be hard for you, eh?"

" I miss them. My daughter because she needs me and Winona, well, she doesn't need anybody but I'd like to know what she's got herself up to."

"Do you still love her?"

"We were young once. We're not so young now. You know how that is. Is your husband part of the Juan de Fuca crew?"

"Well, I can't really talk about that."

"Does he...?"

"Yes he knows about this in general. And no, you can't know who he is. Again, that would implicate all of us. You cannot know who he is. Do you understand? Entirely for all of our good."

"Is he part of the Northern Front also?"

"Yes."

"Are there more of you?"

"None that I'm aware of."

"And the others?"

"The others don't know much at all. They have no idea. They're just along for the ride, happy to do their jobs and have a place to rest their heads. No ideology beyond personal comfort and maybe retribution for some minor bullying and abuse they might have suffered in their younger days. But basically harmless. But they can't know of the resistance on board. Do you understand?"

"I think so."

"Time is almost up. Any other questions?"

"Is there a way to turn this thing around?"

"No. Not that I know of."

"How do I get home to Earth?"

"The hard way. The only way."

"What's that?"

"We overthrow the Kraken, take the OneWorld back for what was its original intent, to serve the cause of solidarity with all forms of consciousness in the Universe."

"And that happens how?

No answer came. Later, he wasn't sure he had actually asked. He sat in his berth and stared at the screen.

Announcements in several languages: changes in schedule for the walk-in gymnasium and the cafetorium. A quote:

"It is particularly necessary to arouse in all who participate in practical work, or are preparing to take up that work, discontent with the amateurism prevailing among us and an unshakable determination to rid ourselves of it."

Vladimir Lenin

He lay on his back and stared at the ceiling. Memories came flooding. A canoe trip he'd gone on with his father one summer before he'd disappeared from their lives for good. Somehow he'd come up with a canoe, must have picked it up from the side of the road and shoved it in the cab of one of the line of battered hydrogen pickups he drove over the few short years of his domestic life. The canoe had a reinforced carbon fiber skin and weighed about two hundred pounds. The two of them had hauled it from the truck over to the boat launch; he'd dropped his end, and his father ended up dragging it the last bit over the corrugated concrete down to the water's edge. He remembered him letting down the bow with his long arms and his well-scuffed PVC leatherette boots splashing the water and him turning to look with a sharp look, a wordless reprimand for his carelessness.

"Need to be quiet now or you'll scare all the fish away," he'd said.

They paddled out into the middle of the lake. They had no life vests on. His father didn't believe in safety paraphernalia. He'd swiveled around in that swift, aggressively easy way he had. The canoe drifted on against a head wind. Antioch dropped his paddle in his lap and felt pleased with himself for steering them straight in the sun, which was dappling the water. And then his father showed him how to hook a nightcrawler so that it wouldn't wriggle off in the water. He remembered hoping secretly that his worm would pull off a miraculous escape and swim to shore before getting gulped down by the largemouth bass that frequented Lake Assumption.

"The other boys treat you okay?" Don had asked, resting the paddle on his lap. He turned around and saw him in silhouette against the sinking western sun. He didn't know what to say. He was always fighting with most of the town boys, that was how it had always been.

"I don't know," he said.

"Don't let them get away with nothin', you understand? Be strong. Hit them suckers first, right in the noggin. Make sure you remember that."

He didn't know why he was remembering that. The canoe in the water. The water dripping from the paddle. Don's final words of advised violence in the calm tones of some sort of twisted wisdom.

He stared at the screen some more and then picked up the book he'd borrowed from the booth in the galley stocked by God knows who. Like many things on the ship, the borrowing of paper books had a life of its own that seemed to be tolerated. The Generation of Quartz began in an unpromising way, but Antioch had already labored onwards twenty or so pages. In a way it was comforting. He liked the feel of the old-school pages and the feel of the words in his head as he read. Maybe that was enough for him.

Uvlin was a reader. Teachers had always praised her intelligence. She'd never got mixed up with boys until she'd left home. That was a blessing, he thought. Maybe the Nurvalink augment meant he could read stories now and somehow they would incorporate themselves into the substructure of his mind, like some sedimentary deposit that under the pressure of his life would yield something in years to come, maybe the next life. Who would know about that? Ann came to mind, but he would not think of her again. That was a name he shouldn't even be thinking. Maybe he would try to remember her face, or her green hair in the way it slanted on her head, avoid naming and the awful disclosure of unnecessary and potentially compromising information to the Nurvalink in his head.

The chip business had started back in his childhood, not in their part of the country, though. All the freedom that had been the promise had just yielded a world of anxiety that turned heads bare and lives barren and wrinkled so that you were no longer recognizable. That was not what was expected, not what had been foretold. The people felt hoodwinked and angry, on the march. They came in droves for the neural implants that promised improved performance and, above all, a release from pervasive anxiety. He remembered everyone suddenly one day talking about them as if it had always been just another medical alteration. The neural outfits, spreading from the larger cities by word of mouth on the various social platforms, promised that it would all be better, and once again the people had swallowed hook, line, and sinker like the bass in Lake Assumption going after the nightcrawlers with their plump, pink and purple bodies wriggling on the curves of steel.

It was easy to fall into feelings of self-pity and loneliness, but he took the initiative and went out and found Garcia. His berth had been upgraded to the wing of the officer corps and included a jacuzzi in the corner. Garcia was in the jacuzzi when he was let in by the sentry after having checked his pupils in the scanner.

"Nice place," said Antioch.

"Imagine seein' you again," said Garcia, removing a home rolled satinate cigar from his mouth and placing it precariously on the plastic sill of the jacuzzi. The ship hardly ever juttered, but once in a while a subtle rumble emanated from the generators when they had to replace a part.

"One question I've been wondering," said Antioch.

"Shoot," said Garcia. "One question at a time. What is it?"

"You mind if I sit here?"

Antioch went for the swivel seat by the wall and, as there was no answer from Garcia, he sat. Instead, Garcia sunk a little deeper into the jacuzzi water and seemed to turn up the jets with his toes. There was a slight tinkling sound. It might have been the water in the jacuzzi or else it was something inside his head. Antioch shook it off.

"You recall the times we met with Reid, did he ever mention Shoeman in a way that indicated he knew him personally?" asked Antioch.

"Reid was practically a son to Shoeman. Are you kidding me?" answered Garcia without turning his head or moving any muscles in his face besides his lips.

"Okay, that's what I thought. I'm having a hard time remembering anything Shoeman said about him before the meeting we were supposed to have in Tijuana."

"Reid and Shoeman went all the way back to Taiwan together."

"That's right. I knew that. Reid worked on boats, right?"

"Super yachts. Luxury. Nuclear engines and shit. And Shoeman was a big security magnate, working for the Homeland. Government agent. Made a ton on blockchain when the scanners went over to it. Reid was working on his boat and then crewed for him on the Med."

"Now it's all coming back to me. Have you been talking to the Kraken?"

"What do you think?" Garcia sat up. The water ran off his well-oiled and tuned back. He had put on some weight.

"Looks like you might have," said Antioch.

"Hell, yes. Do you think there's nothing these dudes don't already know? They're running the machine, brother. They got it all down. Just ride the mothahfuckin' gravy train or you will be stuck on a side. The side the OneWorld puts you on. You got the chip, don't you?"

"Yes," said Antioch, turning his head to display the scar.

"So you're on the team. What do you want? Why you still asking questions?"

"I'm never gonna stop asking questions, Garcia. By the way, what is your name? I always just call you Garcia."

"You know my name, brother. Garcia is my name. Garcia Jones."

Antioch felt unmoored from reality then. It was entirely possible the whole thing was a mirage, a con job meant to confuse and paralyze him. He wanted to ask more questions, but realized he would come off as selfish, always concerned with his own standing among the crowd, intent on raising his sights and station. The Nurvalink chip was supposed to settle him down, but it had only made the doubts plunge deeper, like a fish that had taken the lure and was trying to shake it off by diving for the bottom.

Garcia rose from the jacuzzi and toweled off to the side, dripping water on a mat of ionized pile above the tiled cork flooring. He wrapped himself in a robe, looking like some sort of old time bigwig.

"Listen, I'd love to spend more time with you, but I've got my yoga class in just a few minutes," he said, focusing his eyes somewhere in the distance.

"That's okay. I'm happy for you, Garcia."

"Don't give me that liberal pussy shit," responded Garcia.

"Pussy shit? Don't pretend you're okay with being stuck on this..."

"This what? Masterpiece of engineering? Let me show you something 'cause I know you ain't got no view where you at."

Garcia walked over to the wall where he touched a screen and sent the panel whirring upwards into an invisible cavity. The canvas of the night beyond, sprays of stars and spotted moons, spread out to the infinite deep black of the continuum. Antioch approached the wall of transparency and put his hand up to touch it.

"Beautiful, right?" said Garcia.

"It sure is," said Antioch.

"Yeah. Anytime I get sad or blue. Works like a charm."

"Is that Mars over there?"

"That's it. That's the baby. Red planet Mars. Base Svyatogor. Almost there, I been told."

"I didn't realize we were so close."

"Yeah. Maybe a week or so," said Garcia wistfully.

Antioch felt a surge of excitement at the prospect of getting off the Nazar, but also some concern at the unknown. For now, he didn't have it bad at all. There was a lot he could not foresee. Although he had no idea what to expect when they arrived, it was clear his relatively free status was contingent.

Garcia offered him a cigar.

"Catabrian, bro. Satinate leaf."

"No thanks, man. I don't do well with that shit."

"Oh, come on. This is medicinal. Hair on ya chest, Antioch."

Antioch took the hand-rolled cigar from Garcia's outstretched hand, held it to his mouth, and bowed his head while Garcia held up a lighter stick to the end of it. He found himself agreeing with Garcia's assessment of their situation. Maybe it would be better if he reframed the problem, so that it was incumbent upon him to readjust his mental settings. Make the effort. Even the Nurvalink was no guarantee of any progress without one's own personal commitment. Up to now he'd been resisting, and it had gotten him nowhere. It seemed that it only made his feelings of doubt worse. It had to do with him. Garcia was right, he would have to admit to that.

In his berth again, Antioch slept off the somniferous lethargy that came in the wake of the satinate. When he awoke, he sat up and weighed the state of his mental acuity. There was no other way to do it; he had to trust in the internal inputs. The sounds that came to him were the ever present metallic tweaks and twitchings of the fabric of the Nazar undergoing the stresses from within and without that seemed to melt the border between his thoughts and the perceptions relayed and amplified by the implant. He realized that he was no longer distinguishable by the characteristics that he once had possessed when Earthbound. He wondered whether he was in fact any longer a human being. There was no longer a security presence around him, whether in the form of artificial intelligence such as Larkin, or physically with the sentry detail that had once stalked the corridor 24/7 outside his berth. No longer necessary, it seemed, because the individual motivation to seek his own destiny, or the purposes with which he identified, was not a significant pressure now. If that was true, he should have felt some remorse, some sadness, or any emotion at all. In fact he felt nothing.

When he listened even harder, however, he could feel his heart pumping, and that gave him some comfort. He felt a twinge of happiness, satisfaction, or maybe just pleasure when he heard the sound of the blood pulsing through him still. He pushed harder on his ears to hear it even louder.

Motivated by his new understanding, Antioch wandered the ship unperturbed. He had no idea what he was looking for other than a deeper understanding of life. He realized that was the reason for his being onboard the Nazar. It was amazing, he thought, that he should have reached such a level of clarity at the same time as he was experiencing a sharp loss of personal identity. He paused and pushed on his ears every so often. There was nobody else around. The ship seemed to have been abandoned to chart its own path across space and time absent any human guidance.

He would not have been shocked to corroborate that this was the case. His meanderings took him around and around, wandering into the bowels of the Nazar, but at no point did he come across any other person. The sliding panels posed no hindrance. All along the corridors he sensed the sleeping presence of crew members, nodes of biological consciousness arranged to produce the targets of OneWorld and its directorate. Could he hear the dreams of its historical project? Was it not the same as his heartbeat, to continue to carry the inheritance of life across to the stars? It was an ancestral impulse, after all, and maybe even the will of the Almighty. He knew that Shoeman and the Anthrog stood constantly poised to counter the nightmare possibilities of human certainty, but here he was onboard the ship of dreams, the Mayflower of the day, and it felt good. The night was full, rich in possibility. He remembered as a young man, offended by OneWorld and its appropriation of exceptionalist rhetoric, thinking that its demise was ensured by the unsoundness of its founding ideology. But now he was not so sure. That was a sign, they said, of growing older. But maybe it was just growing weaker, less able to distinguish the signals from the matrix that pushed and pulled like the tides.

The sign said No Entrance Only Certified Personnel. Antioch pushed through the panel anyway. No alarms went off. Below him lay the tank holding the diamond ruby array, a large glowing red crystalline pool that pulsed as it sent off the systemic shots of laser light that powered the ship across space. He leaned on the rail and studied the pulses coming from the underside of the crystal arrays. They almost seemed to be alive. It reminded him of the Boston Seaquarium. He and Winona had taken Uvlin there when she was ten, must have been '61 or '62. He still held the memory of Uvlin gripping his hand as they had looked on in wonder at the large pool of luminescent jellyfish in the darkened entrance hall.

Afterwards they'd found a place, a hole in the wall, to eat, sitting inside out of the rain, a world dissolving in the warming ocean. He'd had the sense that they were standing against the apocalypse. The end of all civilization. Even if the country was truly dead, he and Winona had always acted on the belief that they would still be able to make it safe, not just for their daughter, but for themselves as well.

Winona walked out on him, maybe it was '65, three years or so after that night in Boston. And now here he was, the covert warrior facing the pulsating dark heart of OneWorld and its faith in the technology it had unleashed. It seemed unfazed to have him wandering onboard, even though it knew everything about him, apparently, including his propensity for rash, mistaken calls to action.

He almost felt like he could turn the ship around now and sail it home to Earth. It was his main desire, everything he said he wanted. But if given the choice, would he still do it? There was a place for him. A plan. That's what Ann had said. It gave him some comfort to know he was not without significance in the larger sphere. Some comfort? Who was he kidding? It meant everything, that his life was not in vain. It seemed that he had once possessed enough certainty to put one step ahead of another through the short years that had transpired in such a rush, like a river in flood. He cast back on his bouts of loneliness, his feelings of despair, his time with Larkin and her confidences, the Nurvalink implant that had given him something to fight against and sharpened his wits in the battle, the internalized conflict at the root of all of the wars and all of history – mankind divided in its own head. Antioch realized that pushing up through the layers of his dreams was the dance of time, a battle cry that reached beyond itself, that sparked the explosion of matter and consciousness that had spread before him in Garcia's window.

He got on his knees, obeying himself. He didn't have anything in mind except a sense of gratitude for being alive. His basic questions continued unanswered, but the certainty of the emotion he still felt was enough for now, even if it was just self-soothing. The physical act of getting to his knees, bowing before the machine that was powering them through space seemed to substantially turn a corner in his mind. All of them, the Kraken, the ordinary sailors, the hidden resistance, the bots, the technicians, were leverage in some way on the direction of the journey. He looked up to watch the display that hovered three dimensionally before him. It was a bar graph with readouts in bright light of wavelength, energy pulse, frequency, and width. What did it want him to do? What could he say or think that would be appropriate?

"Now. Right now!" thought Antioch.

The bar graphs fluttered. The ship was acknowledging him. It was alive.

"Would you go back to Earth? Could we turn around?" thought Antioch.

That was a big ask.

Six

Morrow stopped and dropped the handle of the carry-on at the line for the check-in scanners. Logan seemed dark despite all the lighting, a dim pall cast over the busy scene. Groups of travelers surged all over the place. Morrow stuck his driver's license on the boarding scanner at the front of the check-in lobby.

"Should be good enough," he thought. He had one of the new enhanced licenses that were encouraged by Homeland Security. He was always pleased with himself when something he identified as cutting edge like this actually worked. It spit out his boarding card. He stuck it in the side pocket of his backpack, jammed it in along with a sandwich in a ziploc bag that Ellen had prepared, and he made his way in the crowd, pulling the carry-on behind, to the gate for Southwest Flight 86 to Los Angeles.

Morrow looked around at the other passengers in the lounge. He was at the age where he felt comfortable with everybody in a familiar way without the fear of frailty that he associated with old age. He took a seat in the row with outlets for his charger and plugged his phone in. He looked at the family WhatsApp. There was something from Daniel, who rarely posted anything. It was a song from some rapper he'd never heard of. That was a good sign. Morrow listened to a part of the song. It was a sort of hypnotic half rhyme paired with nonsensical lyrics. It was entertaining, in an instantaneous, easily relatable way. Nothing untoward or too dark. That was good. He believed that Daniel and his sisters could pierce the mystique of hedonism held out as the only good by so much of the culture, even when they indulged in the cheap thrills it provided. If that was the only grace they had retained from their upbringing, perhaps it was good enough, he reflected. In any case, it would have to do.

As the song ended, he heard the flight announcement broadcast from the gate and stood creakily. Making his way to the line for boarding, Morrow tried to relax his shoulders. When he got to his seat, he quickly removed the laptop and the sandwich and stowed away his carry-on in the overhead and the backpack in front of his feet. He had the aisle seat, which was the best thing about the flight aside from it being non-stop. He stood and moved out into the aisle when a young man looked at the boarding card in his hand and looked at the number of the seats above. The man hefted his suitcase into the overhead bin and scooted by to the window. Morrow repeated the exercise for a slightly overweight woman in a tracksuit. She sighed as she plunked herself in the middle seat. Seated again, he adjusted his seatbelt and looked at his phone. He would wait to eat the sandwich.

There was a text from Ellen hoping for some news as to his arrival and boarding. "Looks like a full flight tonite," he texted back. Ellen would hate the misspelled word, he thought. It was infantile, but he continued to get a charge of exuberance at the small rebellions he enacted.

He worked on the laptop, scanning through the document and tweaking bits of text. He checked the weather in Los Angeles again and scrolled through social media. The woman next to him looked at her phone. Her nails were long and a dark green color. She looked about mid-twenties and either Hispanic or Asian with a soft, sedentary look. A recent immigrant, he guessed. The young man in the window seat had put on a neck pillow and was audibly snoring. The air hostesses came up and down the aisle looking for proper stowage of bags, seat belts latched and upright seat placement. The engines grew louder. Morrow checked the time as they rose into the sky. He was on his way; the West Coast mission was on track so far, he thought.

He tried to read a book he'd downloaded on the laptop. He watched the beginnings of several movies consecutively without satisfaction. The book was an Ursula Le

Guin he'd read years before but barely remembered. He hated being asked who his influences were. If he were better prepared he was sure he would have lengthy and detailed accounts of all the books he'd read that had impinged in any way on what he was trying to communicate in his books. But he wasn't, and didn't. He had a poor memory for the most recent books, and that's why he intended often to go back and reread certain ones to glean some pithy quotes he could use in conversation or in interviews with likely West Coast acolytes of fiction and culture. He thought he should have a list of such quotes he could easily refer to, maybe a spreadsheet of quotes good for various topics. He wanted to already have such a spreadsheet and not have to work on it himself. Maybe he'd ask Daniel about how to do that when he saw him next. There was probably such an app or something he was unaware of. Looking at his phone reflexively, he wondered whether he was a technological optimist or a pessimist. He didn't know and that was why writing his book was so fascinating. He made a note to himself to read more about artificial intelligence and why the human brain was so poor at remembering facts. He wanted to read Kaczynski's latest.

People were asleep ahead of him along the aisles. He studied the shoes they were wearing. There were all sorts of Nikes and plenty of high heels and fancy leather dress shoes. He was proud of his own brown suede sneakers he'd bought at Joe Kings. He felt ready for anything that could come his way in Los Angeles, but thought he would be better off sleeping.

The woman in the middle seat asked him to shift so she could get out. He roused himself and got out of the seat as she shuffled by him. When she came back she smiled at him. He stood again and looked away as she moved past him.

"Thank you," she said stiffly.

"No problem," said Morrow. He thought about what to say to extend the conversation, since he sensed that she wanted to talk, and he always, in theory, liked to engage with fellow

passengers on an airplane. He remembered once flying on People's Airline way back in the day and the two people about his age in the seats ahead of him had an extensive conversation he'd overheard about their shared experiences of various things, and the vivid feeling had stayed with him that maybe he was irremediably out of place, or out of time which was the same thing, and since then he had liked imagining himself so relaxed and comfortable with another person he had just met in the next seat as to be able to carry on an interesting and fruitful conversation.

"Where are you headed?" he asked the young woman, finally, when he noticed her twitching.

"Pardon me?" she said, removing an earbud he hadn't seen in her ear.

"Where are you going?"

"Oh, Los Angeles," she said, smiling somewhat uncertainly, as if she knew it was a little funny and a little awkward. She must have thought he was so old he'd forgotten where the flight was headed.

"Oh, no, I mean where in Los Angeles. Or after we land, is what I mean," he said, insisting.

"Oh, right. Anaheim," she answered, chuckling to herself.

"Really? I haven't been there in years."

"I'm going to a wedding," she said, smiling.

"Who's getting married?"

"My cousin."

"Nice."

"Yeah."

"Lots of family going, I bet."

"Oh, yeah," she smirked, implying a troublesome, large, yet well-meaning clan.

"Are they all coming from California?"

"No, all over. Michigan, Florida. Syria."

"Syria?"

"Yes."

"Where in Syria?"

"Damascus."

"Beautiful. I was there years ago. Beautiful city."

"That's where I was born."

"Oh, really? Where do you live now?"

"Mass."

"Where in Mass?"

"Wayland."

"That's a nice town."

"My parents own a boutique. Import stuff. I do social media for them. Do you want to see?"

She showed him the feed on her phone – photos and videos of the store with a brick front and a Coca Cola sign above the door and inside: olive oil, ceramics, robes, and a cat which featured in a lot of the photos.

"That's quite a few likes. Two hundred forty seven."

"Yes. It's all about the cat," she laughed.

"Cute cat."

"Kareem."

"Kareem? One of my favorite basketball players," he said.

She laughed.

"Well, I hope you take a lot of pictures at the wedding."

"Oh, yeah."

He liked her. He wondered. Had he extended himself to the degree that the endorphins would kick in and help rewire his brain so that he was less cutoff and susceptible to mental impairment? He hoped so. He glanced over at the young woman playing with her fingers nervously and hoped she would not feel anxious now to say the right thing to him. The silence held, however, and at some point he dozed off.

Morrow dreamed of an elevator he was riding and getting to the top was impossibly delayed as the elevator morphed into a classroom with the teacher being angry at him for having failed to study for the quiz. When he woke up, he touched the screen of the laptop and went back to the document and tweaked a couple more passages of text.

It all seemed wrong. The words failed to add up. There was something slightly askew in the characters and the dialogue. It didn't sound right and failed to achieve the pitch required of intensity or something akin to it. He wasn't really sure but believed that he knew it when he saw it. Morrow felt a vague sense of panic at the disappearance of the illusion of seamlessness. Sometimes it could just vanish just like that. Was that something potentially he could work with, the occasional clunkiness? There were two possibilities: either his readers would appreciate his honesty and think it up-to-date and smart to be forced to reckon with nuance, or they would fall away in droves at the perceived failure to live up to the world building they had come to enjoy. Of course the third possibility appealed to him, and that was to continue to strive in good faith at striking the right tone and hope his instincts would yield the appearance of effortless reality and a world aglow. He didn't mind walking the edge, approaching a prosaic confession of humanity and weakness, showing the hand behind the hat, so to speak. But nothing would excuse characters or resolutions that seemed wooden and bumbling. That would just not be acceptable. Morrow would go to any length to burn that away from his work. He closed up the laptop and stared at the seatback ahead of him.

They landed at LAX, and Morrow took an Uber from there to the West Hollywood home office of the Mitch Epp Agency. Mitch was wearing a Kent '86 baseball cap as he came slowly, limping down the driveway. Morrow lightly closed the door on the hybrid Toyota. The Uber driver sped silently away. Morrow removed his reading glasses and focused intently on the figure coming at him. He thought perhaps Mitch was exaggerating his lack of mobility in an attempt to sucker him into a game of horse.

"What's up, bro?" said Mitch.

"What happened to you?"

"Knee surgery. It's a bitch but not to worry. Come on inside and relax. You must be tired. We have an appointment at three o'clock at Blue Dog Studio."

"What the hell is that?"

"It's a podcast."

"Podcast? What kind of shit is that? I don't do podcasts."

"Listen, I know. It's a comedown."

"It's not a comedown. I'm just kidding, Mitch. I love everything you do, man. How the hell have you been? Look at you, Mr. fucking Hollywood."

Morrow slapped Mitch on the shoulder and pulled his carry on bag up the driveway.

"Nice place," said Morrow, going through the front door that Mitch held open for him, while smiling and showing off his teeth.

"Just assessed at a cool 3.4 mill, dude. The market has gone absolutely haywire here."

"Well, you got Clint Eastwood just down the block, right?"

"That's not far off. Up the street. In the canyon. But we do have Melissa Gilbert. She lives in the original residence of, it was Ernst Lubitch, I believe."

Morrow looked around the foyer. A young woman, who must have been Mitch's assistant, smiled neutrally from the doorway leading into the rest of the house.

"This is Anastasia Bogen, Morrow. She's our debut author and commercial non-fiction lead agent. Has some really hot young people on her contact sheets."

"Hi there," said Morrow, trying to smile.

"How do you do," said Anastasia. Morrow placed her accent as Australian.

"Listen, put your bags down. We're going to send you to the hotel after lunch. Do you need anything? We've got yogurt, bagels, what else?"

"Chia berry compote and those avocado chips," said Anastasia. After a beat of silence she added: "We can send Pedro out. What sort of food would you like, Mr. Morrow?" She never moved her feet, and her fingers fluttered lightly at her sides.

"Please. Call me William."

"He's a burger kind of guy," said Mitch.

"Well, we can get something from Norms," said Anastasia.

"That would be a great choice. Pickles, chips," said Mitch.

"An iced coffee would be ideal," said Morrow.

Anastasia whipped out her phone and placed a quick call.

"Pedro? Por favor?"

"Si, a su servicio."

It was on speaker phone.

"Necesitamos comida, Pedro."

"Como no."

Anastasia slipped into the combination studio kitchen, continuing her conversation on the phone with Pedro, and the two men followed her, talking about their respective families. Mitch was long divorced from his first wife, Shirley, whom he'd met in graduate school at UC Davis in the 1990s. He had one child, a son, Toby, who lived in Klamath Falls with Shirley, who was remarried to an entrepreneur in the mobile services industry. Toby was a track athlete and was a sophomore in high school. He had interned with a production company in the previous summer. He wanted to be an actor. Mitch spoke about him wistfully, as if he were a project that had been sidetracked *by unfortunate circumstances beyond his control. Morrow wondered if that was not something that all parents could relate to, the way children seemed to morph into creatures that disavowed any familiar resemblance or even fealty. But then you came out the other end and found that they were companionable and even as hungry for connection as ever. He wanted to say more to Mitch along those lines but held off, feeling a lack of energy in the house.*

Pedro came in carrying three well decorated paper bags of food. He was a sharply yet casually dressed man who Morrow guessed was an aspiring actor. Mitch mentioned that he was from Argentina and his parents were both well known psychotherapists in the Argentinian community, as if that was something that would resonate with him.

They ate sitting on stools around an island with a well-oiled walnut butcher block top. Anastasia wiped her mouth after several forkfuls of a salad dripping in dressing. Morrow finished his cheeseburger and side order of sweet potato fries. Fortunately it wasn't as huge as he had imagined. He listened to Mitch talk about some of the books and aspiring writers he was interested in on topics having to do with New Age religion, Ozempic, and carbon markets. Morrow had failed to pick up on the connections. But apparently there was a readership.

"Okay, maybe you need a nap?" said Mitch.

"I might like that," said Morrow.

"Where's the project board?" Mitch asked.

"I've got it on my laptop," said Anastasia. She rose and went off in search of the laptop in her office upstairs. The studio space had a flat screen on a drafting table hidden behind some spider plants. Anastasia came back down. Mitch stopped his nervous pacing and cleared off the paper bags and food waste from the island. Anastasia shoved the plants to another work table and cast her laptop to the flat screen.

"Here's the tentative schedule," she said. "The readings at Hennesey and Skylight. Also, just in. We just confirmed the Lander Yom Hashoah lunch on Wednesday."

"Irene Lander," said Mitch. "She's on the board of the Greater LA Arts Council. Married to Hugo Lander."

"Who's he?" asked Morrow, a bit out of his depth.

Anastasia brought up the LinkedIn page for Hugo Lander: The photo showed a balding guy with pointy teeth. Morrow liked his look despite his initial skepticism. Anastasia scrolled down, and Mitch read:

"Driven by a profound passion for the wine and spirits industry, I've dedicated over 30 years to mastering the art of sales strategy and training across global markets. My career is a testament to the power of innovative training strategies and their profound impact on organizational growth and profitability. With a keen focus on luxury brands, I've excelled in developing and delivering training programs that enhance sales skills and product knowledge."

Mitch stopped reading aloud when Anastasia suddenly flipped back to the spreadsheet for the week.

"He's a nice guy," said Mitch.

"Okay," said Morrow.

"Whatever," said Mitch. "I think it was maybe Seneca who said don't worry, be happy, right?"

"No, I don't think so," said Morrow. "It was Reagan. Don't worry, be happy. Pretty sure it was Reagan who said that, Mitch."

Mitch took a deep breath and glared at Anastasia. She exed out of the screen, leaving the Ipad's screensaver of green mountains. Anastasia asked Morrow for his phone. Morrow dug in his pants and handed her the phone, and she placed it in her palm while working with the index finger of the other hand.

"I've just shared this with you," she whispered, handing it back.

"Great," said Morrow, genuinely pleased. He loved it when younger people took it upon themselves to handle the technology.

"I think we've all had... that's good for now. Why don't we get Pedro to ride you over to the hotel? Settle in, have a shower. Enjoy the tiki bar. They have a great tiki bar at the pool, Morrow. And then at three we will all go over to the studio for the interview with Chip at Blue Dog."

"Sounds good. I'm in your hands," said Morrow.

After a bathroom break and a horrible sight of his aged reflection in the glare of the bathroom light, Morrow pulled his bag along and got into a car parked at the end of the drive. It was a Mercedes GT-55, but Morrow was to learn it was an automatic. Pedro put the bag in the trunk, got in the driver's side, shut the door, and turned to smile, showing off his sunglasses. Pedro agreed that the automatic transmission was not ideal. He reversed in the street and headed for the busier intersection with Hollywood Boulevard. Morrow caught a glimpse of the iconic Hollywood sign. He was underwhelmed with it as always. It seemed more ordinary and tattered than the last time he'd been in California. The state had taken a beating, as had the dream factory that was the heart of the evil empire. How was he going to represent himself at this confluence of history, he wondered. Who did he think he was? Morrow had serious imposter syndrome.

The hotel was a long couple of blocks of low-slung, pebble cladded masonry, and the entrance was lined with groomed hedges and a short whitewashed concrete wall with three tall poles flying the flags of the United States, the state of California, and the faux coat of arms of the Paradiso Hotel. Pedro parked in front of the steps to the main doors. He helped pull the bag out of the trunk.

"What time do you want me to come back for you?" he asked. Morrow stared primarily at Pedro's sunglasses, trying to pierce the air of Buddhist resignation he sensed all around.

"Whatever time Mitch said. I have no idea," Morrow said.

"Aha. Mitch said three o'clock."

"Sounds good, then."

"Perfect."

Morrow strode up the steps, hoisting the suitcase, and inside the hotel. The receptionist hung up on a wall intercom and turned to greet him. Everything was palm lined and manicured. The carpeting smelled of castile soap and eucalyptus. Morrow wondered if anyone had ever smoked here.

He checked in and insisted on taking the bag himself. The bellhop stepped smartly away, reading his body language before he said anything. Morrow rode the elevator by himself. There were two Hispanic ladies talking and standing in the hall with the cart of cleaning equipment.

"Perdóname. Dónde está la piscina?'" asked Morrow.

"Upstairs on the roof," said the one.

Morrow sat on the bed with the laptop and read his emails. There was one from Substack saying he had new likes on a post he'd written ironically comparing Bill Gates to St. John. Only one comment so far from a reader who billed himself as "exploring what it means to be a critical thinker."

Morrow stopped himself quickly from thinking of a way to respond. He went to his emails. There was one in the slew of junk. From Mackenzy:

Hi Dad,

At this point I wonder what good college is? I'm not getting anywhere with this. My courses are not helping me. My social life has gotten out of hand. I'm just wondering what you would say if I went to Berlin for the spring semester. I have a possible grant to do an internship at the IAS Center. Would you help defray the costs?

Lots of love

Ironically, Mackenzy's confused mental state went a long way in allaying his own disconnection. The ennui and self-loathing dropped away as if by magic. He did a quick search of the IAS Center and saw that it was a scam. He typed out a reply, looked it over and hit send.

My dear Mackenzy,

I feel for the growing pains of the twenty something year old and the doldrums of the spirit you find yourself in. I remember when I was in college and had a bout of the third year blues. I don't know what set this off but we will all be together at Christmas and you and I can discuss your plans. Believe me, panic is nothing new to me. Hang in there.

PS. The IAS Center seems to have some questionable reviews. Did you read?

Lots of love,

Dad

Morrow fell asleep. He dreamed of a gun battle where his gun jammed and he had to keep ducking for cover while trying to unjam his gun. He kept looking around in his dream expecting someone to give him a firearm that worked, but woke up frustrated by the lack of cooperation coming to him in the dream. He thought for a second, shaking his head, sitting upright on the side of the bed in his room on the top floor of the hotel in Hollywood. Who were the bad guys in the dream? He'd never seen their faces, just huddled shapes like a video game that had been poorly produced.

He checked the time. He had half an hour. He splashed his face with water in the bathroom and combed his hair. He called Ellen, standing at the window, enjoying the view below of the cars going along slowly on the boulevard, the large buildings across the way, maybe a hospital, and the rest of LA spreading to the horizon, an ordinary day in what really looked like an unremarkable, sprawling American city. The phone rang. She picked up.

    "How's it going?" he asked.

    "Fine," said Ellen.

    "Where are you?"

    "On a walk."

    He thought he could hear the wind blowing.

    "Isn't it dark?"

    "There's still a little bit of orange. Very pretty. Where are you?"

    "In the hotel. I'm going out soon to a podcast."

    "How's Mitch?"

    "Okay. Kind of a jerk, but that's his job."

    "His job is to be a jerk? That's not possible."

    "How you get things done, right?"

    "N'I don't think so. That's actually counterproductive in my opinion."

    "Well, you are kind of unusual in that regard."

    "How so?"

    "Saintliness."

    "Don't say that. I don't like that."

    "I'm sorry."

    He went silent, hoping she would say it was okay, he was forgiven, that she loved him anyway.

    "Have you heard from Mackenzy?" she asked.

    "Yes. I did. I got an email."

    "Uhu," she said with a hint of conclusion.

    "Why Berlin?" he asked.

    "Boyfriend deal."

    "That's what I thought."

"I mean she might be able to get an internship there. Learn German at the same time. It's not crazy."

"It's about the guy, though. Am I right?"

"Essentially, yes. He has a Fulbright."

"Whatever."

"Don't get angry."

"I'm not angry."

"Remember to love big open questions instead of rushing to judgment. Drop the judginess."

Morrow sighed.

"Yeah, it's hard," he said.

The problem that Morrow could see with checking his sense of discernment was one of unilateral disarmament. Besides, who was this Fulbright guy? Morrow walked out on the boulevard. The cars went by in a flow that reminded him of a graphic he'd seen of blood cells in a healthy human body, the way they chugged along in a vein, stopping and starting with the systole and diastole. That could mean the city was an organism and he was just a blood cell, or even worse, a virus. That was more likely, him as a virus, a carrier of disease. That thought gave him an odd sort of pleasure.

Pedro in the Mercedes stopped ahead of him along the sidewalk. An SUV behind the Mercedes pulled around. Somebody honked a couple of cars back. The door opened a crack and Morrow got inside, releasing his body into the seat as if free of gravity at last.

"Are we late, Pedro?"

"No. I don't think so. We have time."

"I like the music."

"Djou like it? It's a friend of mine."

Morrow sat back and listened to the music and watched out the window. He told himself he had no props, nothing he was selling, just open to experiencing whatever came his way. The trees along the boulevard looked desert-like and tough, and the grass on the lawns was brown and sparse. The little ranch houses were small and fortified against disaster by offering little surface area.

Pedro slowed and entered a cracked driveway hidden behind a hummock of greenery as they approached. The house was nondescript as was this area of Los Angeles.

"This is it," said Pedro.

"Okay," said Morrow, uncertain. He gripped the door handle and pushed the door open with his shoulder. He fell out into the steamy air. There were heat waves rising from the space between where he stood and what looked like the side door of the house. A large corrugated plastic sign on a wire frame in the grass parallel to the avenue announced the name of Blue Dog Studio. Pedro pulled around and did a three point turn. Morrow gestured with a hand twirl, and Pedro rolled down the passenger window.

"Are you coming back to get me?"

"I don't know. He just says to drop you off."

"Well. Come back and get me, why don't you."

"Okay. When djou want to get picked up?"

"An hour?"

"That's good."

Morrow watched as Pedro pulled into the avenue and burnt rubber getting up to speed.

Of course he does that, Morrow thought.

Morrow rang the doorbell. A man in a Hawaiian shirt answered the door. A blast of air conditioning followed the door opening behind him. He had about three days of stubble on his round, middle-aged face.

"Hey there. Chip Burnett." He offered a meaty hand. "You must be William Morrow, author of Red Sky Delight."

"Yes. How are you?"

"Couldn't be finer. Welcome to the home office of Blue Dog Studio. A little under the weather but what isn't in today's day and age?" The large man laughed.

"Exactly," said Morrow.

Morrow shook hands and stepped inside the cramped foyer. There were boxes and letters spilling across the floor. The house smelled of commercial disinfectant with an undertone of some strong animal-like odor that had gotten into the sheetrock and carpeting.

"Hey, so let's get into it. Can I offer you anything? We've got instant coffee or Tang. That or a shot of vodka," said Chip. They were in a room painted an odd shade of orange. There was an easy chair on one side of a desk. The desk was covered with books in random stacks between a couple of laptops. There was a copy of Red Sky Delight in paperback at the top of one stack

"Can I have instant coffee with a shot of vodka?"

"I like it. I like it. Coming right up."

Morrow sat in the easy chair on one side of the desk. Chip clipped a mic on his shirt, breathing heavily. Then he sat on the other side and turned on the lights and then fired up the computers, and they began to record.

"Hey everybody, welcome to the Chip Burnett hour on Apple and Spotify and don't forget to subscribe for all the features. Let's start off with a big thanks to today's sponsor, Autodesk, where you can power your teams' creativity with automation, collaboration and all kinds of machine-learning features. Autodesk, home of 3D design, engineering and entertainment software. So. Today we've got William Morrow with me, the acclaimed science fiction writer, to discuss his craft and latest work, due out in a couple of months, is that right, William?"

"Something like that. Soon. Very soon," said Morrow, speaking clearly and authoritatively. He liked it. He liked it.

"What title can we be on the lookout for?" asked Chip.

"Well, it's a work in progress, but let's call it Alias Tomorrow," said Morrow.

Chip handed him a mug, something he was stirring with a spoon across the desk.

"Alias Tomorrow. So you heard it here first folks. Coming out in a few months. Let's start with some of the basics for those listeners who might not be familiar. Speaking of familiar, William. Where are you from?"

"You want the two minute bio or the highs and lows?" asked Morrow.

"I want it all, man," said Chip. "Haha."

"Well, I was born in Panama to a Brooklyn Navy officer and a Long Island beauty."

"Is that right?"

"Jules Morrow and Shannon Doherty."

"Good names. Jules and Shannon. And they had a child. William, I believe. Unless that is an alias, haha."

"That's true. The Navy officer, Jules, was on loan to the Panamanian Navy for uh, technically boring reasons, but he was running submarines off of Cuba."

"Wow."

"Yeah. So that's where I grew up, the Canal Zone, me and my sister until Jules and Shannon split up."

"Aww. Could see that coming, though."

"Yes. They uh, divorced. We moved back to New York City. Shannon was a wreck from drinking and all that sun, but she eventually remarries her boss at the personnel agency. Moves to Florida with my sister, Eileen Morrow. Hi Eileen. If you're out there. I love you."

"Where in New York?"

"Oh, East Side. East 98th Street.

"That's Harlem."

"Uh, yes. It was. We were the only white people for blocks. But I could speak Spanish and so could my sister so we passed in the neighborhood. My mother was accepted and known as the gypsy lady because she read Tarot cards for fun and did readings for free in the park. Then I got picked up in a scholarship program and sent off to a boarding school in Connecticut. That was a trip, let me tell you."

"Wow. Again, so. Lot's of world building from the start, we can see that already."

"Absolutely, Chip. Absolutely. Building my own reality to protect my headspace. You know?"

"Second nature to you."

"That's right. At some point you just do it."

"Just do it. Build your world. I like it. So tell us how you got started in the writing business. A two time winner of the Loci Award and 2004 Borealis Award for Guardians of the Impudent Towers which went on to be produced as the movie with Don Cheadle and Patrick Wilson. Yeah, how did that all happen?

"Well that was pretty fortuitous, actually. My wife and I would take a summer vacation up to Lake Winnipesaukee when the kids were little. We'd paddle out to a little camp on Bear Island run by the AMC and spend a few days camping there. One day these two guys in kayaks are paddling around the point and it's so windy they can't make any headway and the water's getting choppy and one capsizes, you know? Does that thing where it spins up again and the paddler looks stunned and unable to carry on, so I swim out and help pull the kayak to shore. Just what you do. Turns out he was Lenny Adams and we made a campfire for him and his friend and I shopped him the novel, Guardians, which we'd just put out on Torque Books. And that was it."

"The rest is history."

"Yes. Of a sort. You could say."

"Wow. Had Lenny on the show a couple of years ago. What a mensch."

"Yes, that was very lucky," said Morrow quickly.

"Instrumental guy for so many people."

"In so many ways," said Morrow, smiling. He liked it. He liked it.

"He prides himself in that," said Chip.

"I know. Right?"

"You saved his life."

"Well, I wouldn't go that far."

"From drowning in Lake Gitchegumee."

"Winipesaukee."

"What, is he from New Hampshire?"

"No. New Jersey. But his friend had a summer house in Tuftonboro."

"So here's a question, William. In your books you often delve into the fantastic. Do you yourself believe in other dimensions? For instance, in Red Sky Delight, there's the notorious angel Domenico who has come down to earth and has a special mission, right?"

"Yes."

"I won't give any more away, but are there angels, do you think?"

"Well, Lenny."

"Oh, ha ha."

"Do you mean in the supernatural sense?"

"Or the fantastic. Is that a feature of your storytelling or something you try and avoid?"

"Well, I think from the perspective of storytelling we try to avoid the deux ex machina as a solution, but, for instance, causality is something I like to explore, the notion of some sort of connection that goes beyond the empirical. I think that's a thing."

"I see that a lot in some of the classics. Ray Bradbury comes to my mind."

"Right. Phillip Dick features a big side of the mystical, I think. Sort of Jung crossed with Andy Warhol."

"I love PKD."

"That ought to be a bumper sticker. It probably is. Signed God."

"It is an absolute requirement, my friend. But tell us what about what you're working on now. It is a stand alone, right, in terms of not building on the success of any of your previous work?"

"Well no. It's all new, and uh, we follow Antioch, a man who has been captured and implanted with a brain chip by a powerful organization. He navigates his new reality, grappling with questions of identity, freedom, and resistance. At some point he forms a connection with a fellow captive, who uh, provides him with information about their situation and the possibility of rebellion."

"The possibility of rebellion. Is that where we're at? Grappling with the possibility of rebellion?"

"Well, I think for some of us, yes. We hold out the possibility of rebellion. Keep it alive. Keep ourselves alive. But not too far into the abyss. Know what I mean?"

"I hear you. Sort of a California sober approach to life."

"Well. You have to always push the envelope. Maybe it's bicycling, maybe it's bass fishing. Always looking for an upgrade. That's the way we roll, I think, Chip."

"Do not go too far into the abyss, my child."

"Well, but be familiar with the mouth of it. I think. Or maybe the first couple of rings."

"Just the first couple."

"Heck, yeah. All of us pagans and lovers are already there."

"Haha. That's good. I like that. Let's take a quick break here, William and we'll be right back for more, including some listeners who we've got on the chat with some cool questions, we hope. Again folks, this is William Morrow, the author of Red

Sky Delight, *from Dun Castle Press, and the forthcoming futuristic spellbinder, they say,* Alias Tomorrow."

It went on for quite some time. Maybe another thirty minutes or so. Then the questions came from a listener. Chip read them from the chat. How did Morrow reconcile the loss of memory that came with mining for material for his stories? Did he think it was an inexhaustible store? And if not inexhaustible was it linked somehow to the length of life? Was consciousness responsible for that process? And Morrow had to answer that he suspected that to be the case, that it was not inexhaustible, that retrieval became more and more difficult, that certain stimulus, like fracking oil from shale by pumping carbon dioxide underground, made them bubble to the surface, but that also risked breaking the fragile tectonic systems of the mind that linked at the deepest levels with the structures of the Earth.

Then it was time to go and Chip was seeing him to the door. He didn't know what to say other than thanking him for a great opportunity. He didn't know if it had actually reached many people, but he didn't care, either. Marketing and the writing of books also, if he was honest, was kind of like karma, you just trusted that it would come through in some way, and if it didn't, you always had a fallback.

Being with Pedro in the Mercedes was very comfortable. They drove around for an hour or so as dusk came down on California, Pedro giving him a sort of tour of some of the places in West LA that stood out culturally for him. Morrow could tell that Pedro liked driving him around, that he was a receptive audience for Pedro's brand of expertise on the city of angels. His own expertise on anything was more amorphous and harder to pin down. It usually bubbled up in between things, when you least expected it. But the podcast had been a good experience for him, proving that he had, perhaps, the essential utilitarian frame that gave a life meaning.

Back at the hotel, he was riding high, talking to himself, reliving some of the moments of the podcast. He sat on *the bed and stared at the laptop. He couldn't focus on writing anything, and it was too late to call Ellen. He looked at the family WhatsApp and reacted with a heart emoji to something Sarah had posted, a picture of herself and Barbara at a show, blue and green hazy lights and swaying bodies holding up their phones to the singer onstage. He had to write something, couldn't just leave his daughter with an emoji. What kind of writer would do that?*

"Looks like fun. I'm happy knowing you're on the lookout for something big in life."

He was happy for his daughter. She was having fun. There had been and still was deep set unhappiness, but as long as she was sharing good moments, the balance was struck. There was such a thing as oversharing, but better to err on the side of the glass half full rather than its opposite, in his opinion. He decided he would go to the pool and post a picture of himself at the tiki bar. That would be keeping the good going, which is what he was all about at the moment.

Changed into a bathing suit and flip flops, with a hotel towel draped over his shoulder and a fresh shirt, Morrow left the room. He took the elevator to the penthouse and waited while it rose slowly through the remaining six floors.

The infinity pool was underneath a glass, with a lot of platinum metalwork in the frame of the ceiling, the empty lounge chairs, and the railing along the edge of the porch wall. There was a hint of daylight, but the lights had come on over the bar at the far end of the pool away from the elevator doors that closed behind Morrow. He put his stuff down on a lounge chair, along with his shirt, and walked to the edge. Quickly, he sat down on the tiles and slipped into the water, submerging his head underneath the placid surface of the chlorinated water like an ace, without a splash. He sank and sat cross legged on the bottom and blew bubbles. This was gold, he thought. And then he surfaced, just his head sticking out. He was an alligator, a predator with red eyes. He rotated around, swiveling his head. He was stiff in the shoulders, getting older every day.

He got out, his bathing suit slipping low on his buttocks, and grabbed the hotel towel, draping it around his shoulders like some kind of ersatz champ or other. He grabbed his phone, pulled up his suit under the love handles, slipped into the flip flops, and headed to the far end under the canvas roof with soft lights over the mahogany and taps, his collapsed arches slapping squishily against the rubber soles.

"Good evening," said the bartender. She was a young Caribbean black woman, mixed race, with a natural hair style, fake eyelashes, thick lips, and a gorgeous accent.

"Hi. Pretty slow up here, huh?" said Morrow, sitting himself on a metallic stool, screeching the legs back a few inches to give himself room at the bar.

"You the only brave soul here tonight."

"Yeah, pretty slow."

"What can I get you?"

"I'd love a Long Island Iced Tea, if you know it."

"Of course."

She turned her back as she mixed the cocktail. She had a short, powerful build. Morrow looked away at the skyline. He thought primarily about Ellen, about the two or three years before they'd had kids, backpacking through Europe, living on a houseboat in Bruges, sitting together at Kings Cross Station waiting for a train out to Holyhead. Those years had gone swiftly. Then she'd announced at Christmas staying with his mother in Tampa that she was pregnant. He'd applied and gotten the job teaching history at the day school in Manchester. They'd rented that crumbling, rundown apartment next to the undertaker in Hooksett.

"Here it is. One Long Island Iced Tea."

"Thanks. Looks good. Where are you from?"

132

"From Antigua. Do you know it?"

"Never been there. I've been to Barbados."

"Well, we not so far from Barbados there in Antigua."

"And what brings you to California?"

"Well," she chuckled. "It's a long story."

"I like your laugh," said Morrow.

The drink was acceptable, and the buzz was immediate.

She chuckled some more.

"And you? What brings you to the Hotel Paradiso?" she asked.

"Trying to build a readership for my books."

"Oh, you a writer?"

"Yeah."

"What kind of books?"

"Mostly science fiction. Have a book of essays, but I don't think it's in print any more."

"Science fiction. That's what my boyfriend like to read!" she said excitedly, stressing the d in read, so the word had an extra syllable.

"Yeah?"

"Yeah, he love all that rocket ship and Martian."

"I love the accent. Can you do me a favor?"

"What favor?"

"Take a picture of me?"

"Of course."

Morrow handed her the phone and she took a picture of him with the drink, with a backdrop of the pool and the LA skyline behind him.

Zeta

There was a panicked sense that the days were slipping away from those that desired a different route, a change of plan or an alternative end. Antioch believed fervently that the ship was about to waver in its commitment to the mission. The sentries were tiring of being constantly alert and on guard. But at the same time he feared that his sense was more about desire than a material change in the factual order. He didn't trust himself.

He queried the past, wondering where Don was buried, for instance, or about Winona. Last he heard she was living in Mobile working on a wind maintenance boat out of Bayou La Batre. He could almost sense an internal switch, and then he worried. Was the implant recording these thoughts out to some satellite quantum connector, uploading to OneWorld's interplanetary databank? Would there be a feedback loop to correct his stray, imperfect internal dialogue? He hadn't noticed anything different in his mental images or daydreams, but maybe there was a slight change in the tints and hues that his mind held. They seemed more vivid but not quite the same, altered by glitches in the wavelengths as they passed through the void. Then there was nothing left. And nowhere to point to, no path back home.

As he was laying in his bunk, he listened to the clinking sounds of the sentries walking along the corridor, some snatches of a patriotic song. It came to him unbidden.

My country was sunny and free,
The friends, the friends!

The song took on the emotional tone of despair, of words out of sync, the falsity of intentions on the surface for public display. He suddenly hated the way that something as pure as a melody could be distorted, how it could be a trap. He banged his head against the wall, but that only sped up the process and gave him no peace. He filled up a glass pipe with satinate and lit it, inhaling deeply. This was his only means of relief now, like a brake applied to the runaway wheels of the implant that had taken over his mind.

There was a loud knock, and a sentry barged inside.

"You must come with me now."

"Where?"

"To see the major."

"Dmitrievsky?"

"Get up and stop with your questions."

"How do I know?"

"Of course. I will hit you," said the sentry, raising his rifle butt in the air at the bunk. Antioch sat up and kicked off the damp sheet. He stood and pulled on clean pants and a shirt.

"Too much of this, you," said the sentry, kicking the bowl on the floor, the bag of satinate spilling open.

"Hey, watch that!"

Antioch knelt down and zipped the bag closed and tossed it with the bowl into the corner where his towel lay moldering, fallen off the rack. He pushed his feet into the standard issue rubberized shoes, no laces, and pulled the backs of them over his heels and stood, straightening his back and pulling his shoulders, glaring hard at the sentry.

"Your head needs strong push," the sentry said and stepped toward him, rifle arm bent at the elbow and rising.

"I would kick your ass," growled Antioch, his head throbbing dully.

"Your dreams are bad, dyermo. I understand."

"Fuck you."

His pupils hardened, the sentry pulled the rifle up in two hands and shoved Antioch hard in the chest with it, sending him back towards the door. Antioch shifted his weight to his back foot for a swift counter punch to the sentry's face, but something held him back. He stopped, and the hesitation was long enough for the sentry to read his intention. Antioch stepped back again and put up his hands.

"No problem?" asked the sentry.

"No," said Antioch. "Not now. Later."

"Of course," said the sentry. He motioned Antioch out the door. They went down the corridor, Antioch out ahead, his hands zip tied.

They passed through the galley. Ann and a couple of the Kiwi scientists were at a table. Antioch detoured off the corridor and walked by the table, followed by the sentry. He heard the conversation at the table go quiet as he passed. He looked back at Ann and grinned. She saw him and looked away. The sentry stared at the list of lunch options on the neon board flashing above the buffet counter. A robot server whose frayed vest needed straightening wheeled between the tables with orders from the kitchen. A group of officers sprawled in glum, ungainly poses at another table. In their olive green Kraken uniforms, lifting mugs of coffee and vodka, the so-called Volga Firebombs, they stared at Antioch and the sentry making their way across the floor.

They came to the end of a long corridor. The sentry stepped in front of Antioch, cut the tie with his utility blade, and knocked on a door. When it opened, he said something and saluted, clicking his heels together. Absent minded, curiously ambivalent, rubbing his sore wrists, Antioch stepped inside, hoping to avoid the push he felt would come from the sentry. It didn't.

Two officers stood against the wall of the map room. Dmitrievsky had his back to them in his chair. Antioch could see that Dmitrievsky was speaking into a mic attached to his lower lip. On the screen before him there was a panel of faces, all male, mostly middle aged or older, with short cropped hair, looks of unfocused intensity, the requisite double flared ear gauges in both ears. Dmitrievsky seemed right at home.

Antioch made the mental switch and could make out bits and pieces of the Russian. The two officers dispatched the sentry, whom they called by his last name, Gorbashewitz. Dmitrievsky was on a call regarding docking protocols and changes to the intake procedure for the Vostok class of interstellar raiders due to the thickening Martian atmosphere and the latest reports of erosion on the skin of their hulls.

Dmitrievsky wheeled around in his seat. He removed the clip from his lip. Antioch tried to read his expression but nothing occurred to him. The Nurvalink implant was no help with emotional reads. Dmitrievsky's face was a blank as he spoke, still in Russian, to the two officers standing against the wall behind Antioch. They left the map room, leaving Dmitrievsky and Antioch alone.

"Sit down, please, Mr. Littell." He pushed another seat across the floor from him. Antioch stepped forward and eased himself into it slowly and wheeled it back with his feet so he would have some room to spread out his legs.

"So this is where it all happens," said Antioch, sitting up.

"Yes. The orientation center. We can make manual adjustments and use communications mode," said Dmitrievsky. "If you like you can see."

Dmitrievsky closed his eyes briefly to make some mental move, and a three dimensional board materialized with instrumentation and graphic displays in the space between the two men.

"Notice how the subjective diameter of the Nazar has increased in last two, three weeks," said Dmitrievsky. It was exactly the graph Antioch had first noticed.

"Why is that?" he asked.

"We understand you have personal affiliation growth with the woman geophysical specialist from New Zealand."

"What's her name?" asked Antioch.

"You know her name. Chamberlain," said Dmitrievsky.

"Ann," said Antioch.

"Yes."

"What do you know about her?" asked Antioch.

"We know everything."

The air board disappeared. Things were about to get serious.

"If you know everything, I'm no use to you."

"To the contrary, Mr. Littell. Your use has never been, to us, as clear or more important."

"Explain how that works, please," said Antioch. He knew the fact that he was stalling for time would be obvious, but what choice did he have? The ground that he was on was shifting. There was nothing he could rely on for advantage in this exchange with what was clearly a superior force.

"First I will ask you one question. How do you feel about yourself at this moment? Another way we can ask is: do you feel okay with me?"

"Yeah. I'm okay."

"So you see. Nurvalink 7.0 is having desired effect on brain function. Much more integrated sense of self, correct?"

"Well, I'm not sure if that's the cause."

"Has to be, Mr. Littell. Human brain needs direction, correct modulation, to function at optimum in a civilized setting."

"Okay, but what are you, Mr. Civilized, Dmitrievsky? How do you get away with that sort of assumption?"

"I am, as you say, the OneWorld chief officer on the Nazar. You have a long time problem with such authority figures, Mr. Littell. We understand."

"Maybe the problem lies in the authority figures in my life being a piece of shit."

"Your father was an enigma for you."

"You could say that he had other things going on, yes."

"So the arrow of time is a universal truth. What can I say?" said Dmitrievsky.

"What's up, Dmitrievsky? What do you want from me?"

"Look, I will repeat, we know everything. We want cooperation, not competition impossible for you. It's how you say, no win situation."

"I would say that there is no way for you to know that."

"No, there is a way. We have models now for prediction, for the probability of every situation, every scenario known to, how you say exist. The AGI of OneWorld algorithm is unsurpassed."

"Please. That's a crock of shit. All probabilities? Really now, Dmitrievsky. You don't expect me to believe that."

"There is proof of this. In truth!"

"What do you want then? If you have the proof there should be no question."

"Look, here is our position. Very clear, like I have said. We desire to continue life. That is the most important, how you say aim. Terraform of Mars. Intergalactic spread of our civilization. Our life, our mentality. That is a very human desire, you agree?"

Dmitrievsky, or the expression in his eyes at least, looked in that moment like an old teacher he'd once had. He couldn't remember his name, maybe at Fort Jefferson Community College where he'd once trained to be a public energy/entropy auditor. He'd hoped to work for the county but then the utilities had hired their own auditors and the county governments west of the Rockies had been taken over by the private sector front groups, allied in their totalitarian aims to the OneWorld. That was all a long time ago, but it seemed like yesterday to Antioch. All that was very telling. Still, Dmitriesvky looked like he was almost pleading in his eyes.

"Yes, but you've co-opted human desire for the sake of the ruling clique of OneWorld, Dmitrievsky. Come on."

"Is old conspiracy theory. I am ashamed. Your brain needs a lot of work. Maybe it is too late for you."

"I'm sure it is."

"Look. In a few days we will arrive at Svyatogor on Mars. It is a place, which all of it, every how you say centimeter, every piece of sand, given to the purpose of OneWorld. We have a motto. "Kazhdomu po ustroyeniyu vsekh" That means: Life must have its way. You can be a part of how you say, master plan. Otherwise you can die and be crushed under our path. You will not be a memory for anyone."

"Not true."

"Your memories are no longer present on the home planet, Mr. Littell. Of that be sure."

"I don't believe that either. But go on. Tell me the master plan, Dmitrievsky. It's amusing."

"We have studied your potential and personality, how you say type is most adequate for life on the Planum Boreum. Is the outward edge of, how you say agricultural production zone, and we have a big shortage of professional, competent personnel. We want you there to help with the climate improvement project. Very special. As you know, we have a thicker atmosphere now with carbon dioxide from solar panel production using the Martian yellow silicate clay. But we believe there is a specific consciousness of unknown manifestation, perhaps emerging from below the Planum Boreum that may, how you say, sabotage the solar panel production."

"Sabotage? How?" asked Antioch.

"Is theory only today, but is by consuming silicates via anaerobic fermentation, converting carbon dioxide gas back into sand. This we call Martian Dolomite, and we must catch and stop above all. You will be trained in mental techniques of detection and elimination of this threat. Important is you shall be free one day. You have the opportunity, how you say to select a different choice in five years. Martian years. Do you understand, Mr. Littell? Is a good opportunity for you to make a, how you say fresh start. Very exciting time for you, my friend."

"So, what, I've got ten years of forced labor on some distant outpost with no human habitation?"

"Five years."

"Ten Earth years. Come on, Dmitrievsky."

"Well, it passes by very fast and is very beautiful scenery there, of Mars. And soon we will be expanding operations for mining."

"Mining?"

"Yes. For export to Earth. Deuterium for use in fusion energy production."

"So, if I play my cards right I can, what, be a miner some day when I grow up? Is this your master plan for me, Dmitrievsky? Because if it is..."

"For you I foresee administration role in Svyatogor in future time. You are very smart. But use these years well on Planum Boreum. Prepare. Learn... I can recommend video series. OneWorld in ten steps for new colonists."

"Thanks, but no thanks. What if I refuse?"

"You? You will be agricultural worker. Polish and clean glass without oxygen or anti-radiation shield. Some say they possibly can adjust the metabolism but you are guaranteed to die in much pain. You will die in our agricultural zone, Mr. Littell. Better make a quick finish so you are not suffering so much." Dmitrievsky gave him a disgusted look.

"That doesn't leave me much wiggle room," said Antioch.

Dmitrievsky looked away. He turned around and put the clip back in his lower lip. The panel screen opened up again. Many of the faces looked into the virtual space with bored expressions, as if they'd seen it all before. Antioch was suddenly and inexplicably grateful.

Back in the alcove, he lay on his bunk and fought off sleep. He didn't want to think about the future or about the past. He wanted to just maybe slip through the crack of time, avoid the pain that seemed inevitable. The motor of his thoughts hurt with its incessant rumble of meaningless words and images. He wanted to shut it off. There were ways, though. What were the acceptable practices? Deep breathing and concentrating on the shape of his breathing cycle. One, two, three, four. Just like that. Repeat. Let it go with a breath. Amplifying the feedback, counting his pulse, being aware of his posture. He tried standing and doing squats. That reminded him of his time in the army. He'd once been in fantastic shape. Not anymore, he thought ruefully.

Larkin, where was she? He needed some contact, even if it was a mirage. The virtual had a stronger pull because the synapses had forged at a deeper level. Winona, that crazy chick was just a fetish, a knee jerk. And Uvlin, his baby girl, was a black pit in his belly of sorrow and regrets. He had a picture in his mind of her baby face under a table somewhere, in some dank basement apartment, probably Windham, or maybe Lowell, on Grafton Street. Winona had worked as a barmaid there while he worked on construction sites as an apprentice welder.

His thoughts wandered through time and space. He was back in Edgarton at the playground with his parents. Don's gold front tooth was shining in the sunlight as he smiled. He was showing off his tattoos to the two of them and bragging about some fight he'd been in out on the train tracks. Antioch had a belly full of watermelon that he was eating from the bowl Mancie had set in the grass. Skye was playing on the swing with some other kids. Their yelling came over the wind to him. The other parents at the swing set looked over at them, steadfast with hate or derision. He didn't distinguish between people's emotions. The teachers in school pitied him. "You poor thing," they would say. Everyone in town dismissed them as worthless. Don was a madman, a menace to society. They were waiting for a chance to take him down. But he never gave it. He headed down the tracks one day and never came back. Never wrote or called. Somehow Mancie knew it when he died. But Antioch carried the memories with him and the sense that something was expected of him, some sort of affidavit from life that Don had been good all along.

Later on, unclear how much time had passed, he went down the corridor and down the spiral stairs to the junction with the central passage fore and aft of the ship to a spot where a panel below his feet let in the black of space littered with the bursts of starlight. At certain times the crew tended to congregate there, even sometimes the officers of the Kraken, although they kept their distance and in the confined space of this corner of the ship would not have much to do with anyone else. Antioch took up a place in the circle. There wasn't much conversation, just a shared understanding that the ship was marking passage across the vast empty ocean of the solar system to their rapidly approaching destiny. Antioch saw Ann. She stood across from him, arms linked with a man. Must have been her husband. He felt a tug of jealousy at the sight. Meeting her glance, he tried to wipe the remorse out of his heart. People came and went, only staying a few seconds for the most part, a brief touch of solidarity before continuing on with their personal errands and assigned duties. She pulled the man with her and approached.

"Tena koe, Antioch," she said.

"It's a nice night, isn't it?'

"Do you know Herman?" she asked.

She led the two men on either side down the corridor, and they walked three abreast towards the central galley.

"No. How d'you do?"

"Nice to meet you finally," said Herman.

"Sure," said Antioch.

"How are you?" asked Ann.

"I met with Dmitrievsky. We need to talk. They know everything."

"Are you concerned?"

"Well, yes."

"Don't be. Try to relax. Think of the beauty of the star spaces we're traveling through."

"Okay," said Antioch. Was that it? Was she ghosting him? He walked beside her and felt the warmth of her arm as it brushed his. He took deep breaths and tried not to think about her body. After about fifty yards, he looked up, trying to clear his brain of the fuzziness of vaguely disturbing signs of despair. A group of off duty sentry was coming towards them. Was that Gorbashewitz? Yes, he recognized Gorbashewitz coming in the distance with the group . He distinctly felt like letting go of whatever compulsion to salvage his battered sense of honor. Something was definitely wrong. Just hours ago he would have gouged his eyes out, he was sure. He kept his eyes on Gorbashewitz as they passed. He was enjoying some sordid joke that had just been told, the sour expression said it all. Antioch had no desire for any further contact and looked away as Gorbashewitz glanced in his direction. The three of them continued on, Antioch secure in the company of friends for the first time in a long time.

They entered the bunkroom, Ann went in first, and Herman ushered Antioch ahead of him politely. Ann switched the kettle on and put out some cups with little bags of satinate blend in them on the small counter. She pushed the screen into a corner with her foot. Herman sat on the bed and removed his rubber slippers.

"The crew are pretty relaxed," said Antioch.

"They don't care any more. They're not listening. Once we get into Mars they will let most of them go. Back into food production for them," said Ann.

"Have you been to Mars before?" asked Antioch.

"This is our second time," said Herman. He lay back in the bed and propped his head up with a pillow. The kettle sounded its familiar, very domestic chime, thought Antioch.

"What's it like?" asked Antioch.

"Not bad for what it is," said Herman. Antioch observed his movements and thought of what Ann and he had together.

"Here you are," said Ann, handing him a cup of tea. "There's already sugar in. If ya like more we have it."

"Sugar? Where do you get that?" asked Antioch.

"Oh, we have contacts," said Herman, smiling.

"Are ya forgetting something," said Ann, smiling at Herman

Sitting at the foot of the bed, Ann motioned at Antioch to come sit beside her. Antioch sipped the tea and put the cup down on the counter. Herman stroked her back.

"Okay," said Antioch.

Ann laughed. She looked at Herman, who smiled back at her, slipping off her shirt, revealing her breasts.

"Well, then," said Antioch.

They made love for hours, the three of them combining in pleasures that rose and fell.

Antioch had seen a lot in his life, but this was a novel experience for him. When they were done, he had no sense of how much time had passed and no desire to say or do anything to shatter the spell of silence. Ann and Herman were asleep in the bed, and Antioch lay awake like a child marveling at what had transpired.

He stood and put his clothes on. Despite the room's controlled temperature, he felt a distinct chill. Maybe it was a longing for something more to warm his frozen interior.

Ann stirred as he stepped towards the door of the bunk.

"Wait," she said.

He stopped and turned.

"We have time," she said and leapt from the bed.

"More?" he asked. He slipped his hands behind her back. She kissed him languidly.

"That was nice," she said. "Tell me what ya heard from the major."

"We'll be in Svyatogor in a few days. They're sending me to the Planum Boreum to find some sort of creature that's been eating their solar panels. In five Mars years I'll be free."

"Interesting. They found ya useful for their purposes."

"Interesting? Sounds awful. Like slavery. I don't know if I can do it."

"Do it. Ye have no choice, Antioch."

Antioch shook his head. He looked at her with hurt in his eyes.

"That's good for you, I guess," he said.

"We're all slaves of the OneWorld. We will find a way to move forward. There will be word when the time comes. I will personally make sure of it. Keep focused. Trust in nobody unless ye know that they come in the name of the resistance."

"How will I know?"

"Ye'll know them. Just like ya knew me and I knew you."

"I can't trust that. That's just the ordinary lightning of chemical attraction."

"No, that's the life force. Trust it. It is always acting as a catalyst to break down the established order. That's why they are sending ye to the Planum Boreum. They want ya out of the way."

"What about the Martian Dolomite?"

"I don't know what that is."

"The sand creature."

"There may be forms of life we have yet to really discern. There is a theory about a form of consciousness that can materialize and dematerialize under the frozen belt of subsoil. But so far there has been no proof."

He wandered down the corridors, the winding spirals of the ship unperturbed. At one end of the food production labs he noticed movement along the walls and moved closer to see a group of wasps, stowaways from Earth, their elongated segmented bodies vulnerable, elegant, and menacing, jerkily arranging themselves around a small porthole. Refracted light burst into the porthole, blinding him momentarily, and the wasps took on the appearance of reformulating chemical bonds, touching and jockeying for position around the light of the distant rising sun. He could just make out one darkened, curving edge of Mars. He thought then of Ann's recent words to him, of the resilience and directed wisdom of the life force and how he had taken it all for granted, even when proclaiming his allegiance to it. The only conclusion was that he was at a loss for an explanation or even a clear idea of what might befall him on the Red Planet. But for all purposes, he and the wasps were siblings in their shared preference for the light and warmth of a sun now too distant. He could see and they could sense the edge of their destination. It recalled a blue oceanic home where they had once lived unaware of the weight of its unique atmosphere. Everyone he had ever loved and known pulled on his consciousness with the force of an eternal sadness.

Seven

Paul Simon played on the muzak. You could call him Al. Morrow sat in a plush leather chair, early for the luncheon. The theme was definitely artsy. Girls with large bodies arranged cameos of potted palms around the linen draped tables. And the caterers laughed and slid across the floor in their soft grounded sandals. They seemed part of the same general organization, Morrow observed. Within the confines of the hangover wringing his brain like laundry, still stained but hung on the line to dry in the southern California sun, he was undercover like everyone else in his vicinity, hiding out from a reality that was too harsh for everyone to bear.

It used to be a fresh place for refugees fleeing the broken world. The cleansing rays of the neo-tropical sun had been enough at first. But mankind had wreaked havoc. The entropy had been immense. Morrow observed furtively from a place of hiding in his plush leather chair as people arrived and placed themselves strategically about the floor with fluted glasses of mimosa. He gulped heroically at his iced coffee and wondered at the absurdity of it all. The night before he'd stayed up late reading Substack. He'd wandered up to the pool at midnight. There was a party of Japanese tourists, absurdly fit, in dandy swim trunks and aviator sunglasses, the ladies in hotel robes. Shots of tequila had been lined up at the heavily lacquered bar, wet with the pool water dripping from the Japanese. And now there were the muffled, yet annoying sounds of earnest people descended from a distinctly crooked line. The beams of the technological spirit tended to dematerialize the objects of his thought in head-splitting spasms. Maybe that was a good thing. He didn't even know what his thoughts would look like if allowed to coalesce. They might conspire against his interests. Not out of the question, he thought, grimacing and squeezing his temples.

The reading at the independent bookstore, an interesting nook of refinement in a typically weird Southern

California commercial strip, had resulted in some interesting exchanges and not a few book sales. Not bad for a West Coast tour. Still, Morrow felt uneasy. No word yet from Peter Halland, publisher and editor of Dun Castle Press. He had not been available for a meeting, although word on the street, according to Mitch, was that he might appear at the luncheon today.

Success with this latest book would be a big help with everything. It would make any repairs and extensions on the New Hampshire house much more likely, keep the forest from overtaking the fields, and resuscitate his standing with Ellen and the kids.

They had never expected anything much from him, but they would not understand his inability to fit his behavior to the expectations of a fallen and corrupt world. It wasn't unwillingness, although at this stage of the game it also wasn't easy to work up the strength for the effort required. But still he tried. He got up and tried. It would go on his epitaph, the last of the triers.

He checked his messages. None since earlier that morning when Mitch had texted to remind him, checking he was still on task, urging him to get his ass up. Morrow had four hours before he would head to the airport. This was it, the last of his duties. He'd been a good boy, even last night at the infinity pool, although he didn't remember getting back to the room. He would handle the luncheon, make the collegial noises, even get some of that good hummus and bean salad. By the looks of the catering outfit that's what he guessed was coming.

Morrow was in the act of standing. He saw out of the corner of his eye someone come in the double set of glass doors from the outside and turned his head, preferring not to see who it was. He directed himself unsteadily towards the pamphlets, other light reading materials, and swag arranged on long tables against a far wall of the reception area. People were beginning to find and take their seats at the round tables set with white table cloths. He thought that is what he would do as well. Sitting and eating were non-committal and did not take much bandwidth. All was well, although the risks of social disgrace were still on the high side. A fluted mimosa might do for added camouflage. He considered flagging one of the servers from the catering organization. They came in all sizes and shapes but wore the distinctive bolero vests as they circulated with the trays of drinks aloft.

"William, hi," exclaimed a woman approaching from the side and overtaking him. She was tall, wearing a simple black dress and black high heels. It was Anastasia.

"Oh, hi," he said.

"It's Anastasia," she said, extending her hand. "Anastasia Bogen."

"Of course," he said, cutting her off while taking her hand. It was slim, long fingered and cold to the touch.

"Am I late?"

"No. No. These people are all here just ridiculously early," he said.

"Mitch can't make it," she said, confidentially, her chin lowered a touch, enough to denote bad news.

"Excuse me," said Morrow, gesturing with a wave at a passing server. He took a glass from the tray and handed it to Anastasia and chose another for himself. The server smiled robotically into the distance before trundling away.

"Mmm, these are good," said Morrow.

"Yes, aren't they," said Anastasia. "Very tasteful. They always are."

She saw someone she knew and waved, but dutifully stayed by Morrow's side.

"Refresh my memory, Anastasia. This luncheon is to honor what again?"

"The annual arts benefit. Mostly they're non-profits. And the work they do in the community. Peter Halland's former wife. She's on the board.

"Thank you."

On the board of what, wondered Morrow, but it was not worth further inquiring. But then again, what else were they going to talk about? She had obviously been assigned to tail him, keep him out of certain sticky situations.

"Where's Mitch?" he asked.

"He's got some sort of flu. But he wanted me to tell you."

"Tell me what?"

"I don't know how to say this, William. But basically we've learned recently that Dun Castle is not in a position to take on a book of yours right now."

"Is that why Mitch is not here? He didn't want to tell me himself?"

"No, I think he is genuinely sick."

So this was it. He felt immensely let down but also not somehow. It confirmed his view that essentially all of the arts world sucked, including the so-called independents. It was about time that he realized he had no friends here. Then again, Anastasia was a decent enough companion and she was only doing her job.

"Who made the decision, was that Halland himself?"

"I believe so, but I'm not totally capeesh on all the details. I know Mitch has scheduled a call for tomorrow."

"With who?"

"With Peter."

"Not his associate editor?"

"No. Peter himself."

"Well, that's something."

"Yes."

He felt a little better that strings were still being pulled on his behalf, albeit limp and useless ones probably. They were stopped in the middle of the tables. It wasn't clear who of the two of them had made the decision to halt further progress, but *here they were. Morrow looked around quickly in a panic at the amount of high couture and faces plastered with creams and drying agents and who knew what else seated around him. The hair was perfect on both the men and the women. By contrast, he was in another league in terms of effort made or in terms of hair period. He was proudly flying the male pattern baldness tonsure. He hadn't shaved in a couple of days. His striped blue and white shirt was wrinkled and not very stylish, although it did have a button down collar, a classic look implying the capacity for a tie. Some would call it imposter syndrome, the shame swamping the lowlands of his middling intelligence, but not Morrow himself. He realized with a bit of the victim's pride in his own martyrdom that he was severely out of place here in the ballroom of the Sonesta Torrance, on this particular day and at this particular time. As he got older, it got a little bit easier to survive these moments of awkward psychological displacement. But he still wanted to kick himself for failing once again to recognize ahead of time the absolutely predictable results of hubris and overreach. A question of caste, historical forces, etc. He needed more of a kick than the mimosa would be able to provide.*

Anastasia slipped a phone out of her purse and put it to her face. She held up a finger to Morrow and raised her chin, denoting an important call coming in. He waited while she twisted herself around to the side and spoke in confidential tones into the phone in her palm. A middle aged man with a goatee in a suit pranced confidently into the area between the swag table and the luncheon tables. He held a microphone up to his mouth and spoke, but no sound came out. He checked it and shook it and tried again. Anastasia was still on the phone. She finished and turned back to Morrow. The man in the suit tried to get the microphone to work. He tapped the head with a finger. He cleared his throat and said something. The feedback sent out its high pitched crazy reverberations, and the crowd now was in thrall to whatever mundane announcements the man was about to provide.

"Should we sit?" asked Anastasia.

Morrow went through the choices. Walking out now was of course the most satisfyingly oddball choice. What was it the economists called it, the illusion of sunken costs? He could get out now while the getting was good. He could say I'm sorry and leave Anastasia in the lurch. She would stay and eat lunch and then call Mitch and tell him what had happened. He would never get to meet the heavy hitters of the LA Arts Council.

"Yes," said Morrow. "Let's sit."

He dragged himself behind her to a nearby table with a couple of empty seats. They both smiled as they sat, and Morrow smiled to himself at the complicity involved in this mutual action. It was nice. He could see the attraction of collaborative team efforts to get ahead in a market economy. It was far removed from his daily arena, but he could recognize the human impulse to lie and cheat, basically to disguise one's true intentions from one's neighbors who were surely engaged in similar subterfuge. It was all a shared act, a masque, even this sitting to eat, particularly this sitting to eat together, breaking bread in the hall of the arts, while celebrating the artifice of … what even the fuck was art? What even was Los Angeles? He didn't know, but whatever it was, it was taking over his life like an invasive weed in a vacant lot. That much was clear from the placid, engaged faces around him at the table and the paralysis that he sensed in his extremities.

The man with the microphone finished making his introductory remarks and brought on another guy, a funny black man also in a suit, to entertain with a few choice words. People at the tables clapped. The servers began discreetly coming out with trays and hot plates. From the remarks he could overhear at the other tables, it seemed like there was a choice between a vegetarian lasagna and a roast beef. Morrow was impressed and felt the heaviness of spirit slowly lifting from him, although the mimosa had only functioned as a vague wet blanket on any emotional recoil from the bad news of the failure to secure a publishing contract for a pre-release of his book. There was no dressing up of that pig.

He listened to the comic's recitation of the standard jokes about rich Hollywood people and their silly ways. The people at the table seemed to all be with the same party, maybe creatives from a production company, he surmised. Two of the women, in their thirties, were of Latin or South Asian origin and the older men in their fifties were African American. Morrow smiled at their internal conversation. Anastasia consulted her phone.

"When you would do, Bond. But when you would do a pop, a sitcom, you'd make, you could make thirty-five, forty. I think my last sitcom, I was making a lot, like way more than that," said one of the men, the thicker-faced one, with a guayabera.

"Those days long," said the other man, tall, with hardened features that seemed to imply recent sauna sessions or plastic surgery. He looked at Morrow and smiled back.

"Gone. And, and, but I knew I would've done it for a fraction of that cost. Especially when I was starting out. And I was like, all of us as actors just want work. Somehow it got, we got, we got gamed in."

"But twenty-five years ago, twenty years ago when you got a CBS, NBC, you, you were buying a house. Well those days long gone."

"Excuse me," said Morrow, interrupting.

The two men glanced at him, smiling inordinately.

"Are you all together?" he asked.

"What would you think?" asked the taller of the two men.

"That's what I'm guessing," said Morrow.

"That is the right answer," said the man.

"I'm so good," said Morrow. "William Morrow's the name," he added, standing and extending his hand out over the table.

"You don't need to stand," said the one man. "Bond Sykes. This is Charlie."

"Charlie Laurence," said the other.

"Nice to meet both of you," said Morrow, shaking hands and then sitting down again. He found himself talking.

"That's nice. Well, here we are," he said.

"Alicia Murillo," said one of the women.

"Claudia Banik," said the other.

Everyone smiled. Except Anastasia who was on her phone, whispering in a serious tone.

The remaining woman at the table, a white woman about Morrow's age, looked at everyone and smiled.

"Josephine Baker," she said.

"Nah, you're kidding," said one of the black men, Charlie, the taller, thinner one.

"That's my name," said the woman.

Anastasia spoke on her phone in what Morrow determined was Afrikaans. Morrow realized that she was South African. He had thought she might be Australian.

The servers reached their table and set out the plates of food. Morrow asked for the roast beef, charred broccoli and red onion salad, and sparkling water. Everyone ate, and the talk was certainly not confined to commentary on the speeches being made by the luminaries of the arts council. There were several awards to people representing different community organizations. There was someone from the mayor's office who regretted that the mayor had been unable to attend.

"Do you know, my grandmother, she was friends with Josephine Baker in St. Louis," said Charlie, putting his napkin to his mouth.

"Is that right?" said Josephine, her voice tremulous, swallowing a forkful of salad.

"Her real name was MacDonald," said Charlie.

"She renounce, isn't that right?" said Bond.

"Correct. Renounced her citizenship," said Charlie.

"She was such a beauty," said Josephine.

"Was you named after her?" asked Charlie.

"I don't think so," said the woman. She was sorry to have ruined a good story.

"Her memory lives on in France and America," said Morrow.

"Cuba too," said Bond. "I was in Havana and they, they named one of the streets there."

"Wasn't Tiffany played? It wasn't Tiffany Daniels," said Charlie.

"Yes it was. In The Lost Generation.*"*

"I knew it. Played Josephine Baker, isn't that?"

"Right," said Bond.

Deserts came and coffee. At some point, Anastasia stood and said she had to leave.

"I'm sorry, there's something I must take care of."

"Is it Mitch?" asked Morrow.

"Oh, no. It's my boyfriend. He's having a crisis of some kind." She smiled, but it was clear that she was reflecting serious concerns. She nodded sadly and made her way between the tables and away through the lounge to the exit.

Morrow felt a sense of duty to the table now. Anastasia's departure had left him as the sole representative of independent fiction. The literary world was on an upward trend, despite the threats of artificial intelligence and the diminished importance of literacy, truth, and objectivity. He wanted to tell that story, but he was forced to be careful with his words. That was the way it was with people. There was no sense proselytizing out of the blue. It might not sit well. Besides, he was just another voice, nothing unique or special about him. Just another purveyor of language as the delivery mechanism of awareness, of awakening, of possibility. Who cared about marketing and other mundane matters? Where was that all now? Morrow sipped the coffee and wondered where to take it.

156

He didn't have much time. The boat was sailing, maybe already had sailed. Most likely it had.

Eta

The landing procedure was simple and over in a matter of minutes after all the anticipation of the last few day cycles onboard. They stayed in their berths. Communications with the Svyatogor command center were transmitted over the announcement system. Dmitrievsky was calm and competent. Antioch listened gratefully as the major relayed the ship's coordinates and key cruising data. He watched on the screen from his berth as the Nazar, filmed by drone sensors, slowed its path through Mars's gaseous layer, sailed smoothly along the curve of the horizon, and landed soft as butter on the flatland of Newton Crater. They rolled to a stop after bumping along the sand up closer to the outskirts of the Svyatogor bubble, its triple-walled polycarbonate surface glinting in the distance. The last light from the distant sun lowered in the sky. The slight rumble of the Nazar's ruby generators continued to hum even after they came to a stop on the red sand.

They assembled by rank and order in the cafetorium and proceeded by the command and invisible oversight of the Nurvalink down to the belly of the ship, winding along the spiral walkways and staircases. No sentries watched the march of the crew along the ship's winding passages. Some of the Kraken sailors banged on the walls of the Nazar at points where the metallic echoes reverberated wanly through the ship as if they were in a dream. The atmosphere of Mars outside the walls was thin and pliant, definitely toxic. Antioch had mixed feelings. He was relieved to be finally back on firm ground and desperate to see by natural light. But reigning above all was his dread of what awaited them outside the familiar confines of the ship that had carried them across the vastness of space.

"What are you thinking? You're scared, right?" asked Garcia at some point. They could tell they were getting close to the mouth that opened up on the underside of the ship, letting crew and passengers down a wide ramp to the surface of the landing plain.

"No, Garcia. Not scared. Just impatient. I want to get out of this shithole at last," said Antioch.

"You lying if you say you ain't scared," said Garcia.

"Just let's take it a step at a time."

"What's taking so long?"

"A lot of unloading. We're not a priority, Garcia."

Antioch humped the Kraken issued duffel bag onto his shoulder and moved forward a couple of strides. Garcia did likewise. Antioch looked ahead, trying to spot the opening of the exit ramp. He could see a point around a curve of the passage where the light cast on the walls seemed to suggest a change. The Kraken sailors exchanged glances and carried on light, bantering conversations with their companions. It all seemed intensely normal. But Antioch sensed a high degree of anxiety also. He knew from Ann that for the crew on board, including prisoners such as himself and Garcia, there were three distinct possibilities: immediate redeployment back to planet Earth in the ongoing effort to continue pacifying the embers of asymmetric warfare, assignment to civilian roles in the OneWorld's advanced region of settlement, Novaroma in the Narrango crater a thousand miles to the south of Svyatogor, or exile to the frontiers of the agricultural and energy forts scattered in a perimeter around the Svyatogor base. Their fortunes had already been determined, based on performance metrics and the technical assessment of the Nurvalink data collected onboard during the latest mission of the Nazar. He hadn't had much of a chance to talk with Garcia since his meeting with Dmitrievsky a few days before. Now he wondered if Garcia knew what had been decided for him.

"Did you hear where you were assigned, Garcia?"

"I have no idea. They must have something awesome in mind for me. I been cooperating pretty good."

"Well then, stop bein' so goddamn scared."

"Fuck you, man. Antioch, you so full of yourself."

"Look, this might be the last time I see you. Let's not lose sight of what we've been through together," said Antioch. He hated the idea of Garcia heading off somewhere and feeling resentful for the rest of his life.

"What is that? What have we been through? For what?" asked Garcia.

"There's a reason for everything," said Antioch, looking out ahead in the line impatiently.

"I ain't no superstitious man like you. Just takin' care of my business."

"Well, good luck."

"Same to you." Garcia seemed to take on a more reflective air.

"You still think you making it back to Earth somehow?" he asked.

"Yeah," responded Antioch, as if it was natural to retain a basic sense of optimism.

"Dreams are the last refuge of the fool, Antioch."

"Then let me be the fool," said Antioch.

They came to the last bend of the passageway. Ahead lay the ramp taking off the passengers and the curtain hanging over the exit below. As they marched down the final metallic yards of the Nazar, they could see vaguely, through the transparency, what looked like modular vehicles, crudely built transports taking the Nazar's passengers away into the reddish light of a Martian sunset. Beyond, in the distance, the dome of Svyatogor protruded just above the smoky haze.

Garcia went first, stepping up to the official of the OneWorld, a strapping Home Guard transgender with polychrome bangs under the black brim of their fedora. They scanned both his pupils with the handheld biometric stick and double checked with the screen at the station. They waved Garcia ahead to the next station where he donned the air suit with the assistance of another Home Guard official, adjusting the straps behind his head and on his chest. He looked back for one last, swift, half-panicked look behind and stepped through the transparency, leaving a ripple of material in his wake.

The official checked the biometric stick for the read out of Antioch's health parameters. She glanced up and held up her hand, signaling for him to stand there and wait while she went back to the station to check her screen. It seemed to take a long time, and when she returned, Antioch could tell that something had changed. She said something to the other official and grabbed Antioch by the arm.

"Follow me," she said. Antioch went resignedly behind her, not out through the curtain, but beyond it, to an opening he hadn't seen before, to a holding room that had been hastily erected, canvas stretched out over struts, sagging in the corners. It was unilluminated except for the personal screens of Nazar detainees there, sitting huddled on the Martian ground, breathing in the recirculated atmosphere being dumped by the Nazar through ventilation ports on the underside of the ship. Nobody talked, nobody moved. It was as if by becoming separated from the main flow of passengers they had lost all traces of humanity and had reverted to barely living, barely conscious creatures.

Antioch felt that those hours were the darkest of his life, with no idea of what was about to occur, the past so far behind that he had less than an idea of who he was or had been up to that moment. He was just a ball of nerves and pain, waiting to be put out of his misery. The last thing he wanted was to acknowledge another human face, words, or needs. He sank to the ground and took the screen out of his pack. At least he'd be allowed to retain some personal possessions, it seemed. The home page was set to the splash of stars that reminded him of Larkin, but she was silent. He spoke her name, half hoping for the sound of her voice, the canned tenderness that he had once belittled but was now a reminder of a semblance of connection, however remote it had once seemed from true fellowship. He scanned pages of communications, the official bulletin of the

Svyatogor Central Command, public announcements, events put on by different organizations, the Bobweavers and Bicyclists League, which seemed to be a sort of outdoors cosplay, lumberjack outfits gathered on a dusty street corner. There was the Mischkin Library of Musicality in Novaroma, which was sponsoring an Aural Regatta. Antioch wondered what that was.

He realized in a sudden cold insight what it was that he was searching for. It was something beyond his conscious mind. The Nurvalink was scanning for some recalibration, unable to direct his executive function; it needed some backup from the Martian noosphere. But the Nazar's server was powering down along with the ruby arrays of the main thrust motors. The Nurvalink was struggling. It made his head hurt.

He looked around him at the indistinct shapes of the former crew, most likely transgressors of Kraken codes or possibly sailors and soldiers who had exhibited anarchist tendencies, rebellious organizers or even members of the resistance ready to betray the cause of OneWorld's maximalist utilitarianism. Ann had said there were others on board. He wondered what would happen now if he stood up and seized a weapon from the sentries at the entrance and turned it on them. Would others here rise to his aid? Could they overpower the skeleton crew left behind on the Nazar? He gave it a decent chance. Some among these people retained enough mettle to spring into action, but the downside was existential. Game over. The gamble was a poor one. Time was on his side. He would wager on it, on the organized resistance, and as Ann had said, on the catalytic action of human will and desire on the unstable order of OneWorld imposed on a planet that was hostile to its settler intentions. The play was to keep his wits about him. If only his wits were untainted. The Nurvalink chip was possibly the worst decision he'd ever made. But in his defense, he hadn't had much of a choice.

Eventually, in the dark, there came a different sound over and above the rumble of the Nazar's base load generators. It grew closer. It sounded like a low wind getting louder and then stopped. Muffled voices outside the curtain exchanged information, and then a row of soldiers marched inside. The last one in was a Kraken sergeant, heavily muscled in an artificially hormonal way. The line of soldiers turned their headlamps on the crowd. The sergeant pulled off his mask, revealing a cruel, twisted face, and ordered everyone to stand. The detainees slowly got to their feet in the dark. The soldiers closed in with laser guns in hand and pushed them all unceremoniously together into a bunch in the middle of the room. Antioch stood in the center of the mass.

The soldiers brought in crates, hauling them through the doors in pairs and set about handing out survival packs to the detainees, not new or streamlined or well designed like the air suits given to the rest of the crew boarding the modular transports for Svyatogor earlier. Antioch's kit sat in an irregular hump on his back and the headpiece blocked his sight so he had to swivel his head around to see, bumping awkwardly into those around him doing the same. The air had a distinctly metallic taste as if pumped through a clogged recirculation filter wheel that needed cleaning. He moved through the curtain with the mass of bodies and stood at last free of the Nazar. He felt in the Martian dusk like a newborn, having lost the protection of the man-made womb that had encompassed him and formed him for so long that he hardly knew who he was now. He had little sense of what the future held, except that it stretched ahead, regardless of his own desires.

Two transporters pulled up in the dust, their headlights marking up the contours of the desert plain in white beams. The Kraken brigade waited in the light of the headlamps. The soldiers made them form into a single line snaking back towards the ship, hovering in the starlit background.

"You. There," said one of the soldiers, grabbing a prisoner by the arm and pushing him towards one of the transporters.

One by one, the line was sorted towards one of the two vehicles. Antioch tried to make sense of the process, to guess what was about to happen, to find an edge on the mad swirl. But there wasn't any sense to it, impossible to tell what sort of judgements were being made as the transports filled.

"That one," said the soldier, pushing Antioch in the direction of the vehicle furthest away from them. He trudged obediently, feeling the way his boots moved against the sand, slipping lightly away behind him. He climbed up the flimsy steps and took a seat in the back, next to a hunched over figure against the window who wouldn't look at him. Antioch put his Kraken duffel bag up on the rack. The duffel bag, mostly empty, held his screen, spare underclothes, rubber shoes, toilet items, and a strange seashell he'd found onboard in the food labs that reminded him of Uvlin. For some reason, he associated Uvlin with the ocean. She'd loved their day trips to Wingsheek in Gloucester, digging for clams, watching the grey seals in the waves. Nothing like that now, thought Antioch, looking out the glass of the front window at the dark mounds and darker furrows of the Martian plains, the random scatterings of matter in the wake of dead celestial forces beyond the scale of Earth life.

There weren't any other passengers after Antioch. He watched out the tinted window past the hunched figure next to him. The other transport began to move out silently, wheels spinning, picking up momentum. At the front, the pilot of his vehicle came down from the wheelhouse and spoke to the passengers.

"Good solening. Welcome to Mars and OneWorld Svyatogor and your new birth to an existence for renewal and service. You all are headed to the Training House at the Svyatogor South Transfer facility. It will be a journey of about thirty five minutes. I can't take any questions, but I want you to feel comfortable. There are toilets in the back and snacks in the machines and you may enjoy your screens while onboard."

It marked a change in tone from the Kraken command of the Nazar. The pilot had the easy confidence and mannerisms Antioch would have associated with the suburban managers of the OneWorld's largest North American metropolises.

Reflexively, Antioch spread his legs out and leaned back. He studied the landscape out the window as the transport began to push forward into gear. Dark ominous hills passed by, lit up by the moon Phoebus. The moon itself became visible on certain traverses with the transport pitching up at an angle as they bumped over the rugged terrain. His traveling companion looked up once, sensed Antioch watching, and swiftly covered his head again. There were sinister forces compelling fear and utter despair, yet somehow Antioch rose above the currents in his mind. He was alive and paying attention, and that in itself was a sign that he was far from finished.

The Training House was a stand-alone barracks constructed of thin polycarbonate struts and walls of Martian cementitious panels insulated and sealed with patches of silicone sealant that were peeling away in spots. It was obvious that not a lot of care and attention was being paid to the upkeep of the structure. It was heated via inefficient above ground venting from the main thermal units in Svyatogor, which kept its uniform temperature just above the freezing point. The population was a constant churn of criminal and subversive elements deemed persuadable by Svyatogor's branch of the OneWorld Intelligence Units and the artificial general intelligence engine that powered its analysis. From the desk in the center of the central yard, the passengers of the transport were led by a string of hungry looking Home Guards to the empty bunk room at the far end of a long row of low houses with peaked roofs that reminded Antioch of a documentary screen he'd once watched of some othered populations rounded up and condemned to disappear.

Antioch dropped his duffel bag on an empty bunk. He turned to the man sitting on the next bed. It was his seat companion from the transport. At least he could see his face now, although it revealed nothing, just a blank, guarded expression, eyes empty of any warmth and thin curls of condensation from his nose as he breathed.

165

"Well, we can breathe at least," said Antioch.

The man said nothing, not even a grunt of recognition. He did clear his throat though, as if about to respond. Antioch decided not to press matters. The rest of the transport had settled down on their respective bunks, ready to sleep. It was an escape from the drab reality of their new confinement. Antioch pulled up the thin corded sheets and began to drift off, dropping the most pressing concerns from the forefront of his mind, wondering instead if he'd ever see Garcia again, or Ann, or anyone from his time on the Nazar. His life on Earth seemed even more fabulous, a distant dream of former experience that would never be again. He wondered if it was better to forget, but decided that clinging to memories was a solace, an elixir made of equal amounts of pain and pleasure that allowed him to escape into a realm of mind that seemed unassailable even to the self-imposed working of the Nurvalink implant, that bit of solenoid plastic webbing currently corrupting his nervous system in ways impossible to discern.

Over the next weeks, Antioch underwent OneWorld indoctrination and training designed to incorporate him into the template of colonization efforts on the Red Planet. The trainees were awakened with the piped in sounds of harmonics while pastel lights rose in intensity on the walls of the bunkhouse. The heating was turned up to anesthetic levels as they dressed in newly pressed all-body suits of insulating rubber lined with the synthetic silk produced at the Svyatogor Laboratories. Home Guard house matrons served steaming plates of lab-produced spicy meats, aromatic greens, and carbo fritters on the line in the commons. Inscribed over the false arch in Pontic font could be dimly read, as if spying an ancient inscription: Community, Collaboration, Collective. With full bellies, the trainees listened to music, steam punk jazz and techno bop on synthesizers. Before heading out to their machine learning sessions, Master Sergeant Leo McKew of the Svyatogor Home Guard, the chief executive officer of the Training House, lectured them, standing on a chair in his black knee length rubber boots every day, on the Illusion of Individualism, the Peril of Free Choice and Free

Conscience, and the transactional benefit that would accrue to everyone, or the Triple Double You, the Win Win Way, as he liked to repeat and as was plastered over every bulletin board, screen, and visual device within the confines of the barracks, or possibly even Mars itself.

Machine learning systems were tuned to individual learning styles. As soon as Antioch checked in, placing his forehead on the rest pad and leaning his body into the cocoon of pleasure-enhancing jelly foam, his visual cortex and mental activity were hijacked to an image world mined from his subconscious and supplemented by the library of the OneWorld's virtual networks, aligned faster than light speed between the distant planets' servers. Immersed in an interactive dream, Antioch quickly learned that mental resistance to the imagery tuning was not remotely possible. He became momentarily subsumed in the thought processing that brought emotional gratification. In this dream state, he was bent to the will of a higher order. Afterwards, he felt rejuvenated, refreshed, eerily calm, as if portions of his brain had been excised, the parts that dealt with survival, flight, and fight. Thus softened up, he was led into a room where, with other trainees, he was encouraged to engage in conversation with their tutor, a robot named Lenina, with a flawless generic female face, and large empathic eyes. Antioch was mostly silent, listening to others raise latent issues of pain and deprivation that still haunted them. Lenina would sympathize and offer solutions, counseling patience, stepping away from the confines of self, allowing the process to play out until the memories of the past were completely integrated into the visual patterns of fullness and gratification.

"And you. Antioch," she said once, turning to him as she glided between the two long rows of low desks. "Do you have a thought? Are you still hanging on to your precious memories? Why are you reluctant to engage?"

"I don't see the point," said Antioch. "I know what you want me to say, so I say it. That's the way the game is played, right?"

"This is not a game, dear. This is healing for your mind and for your soul. We are all connected. Do you see the beauty? Do you feel the union with the life force?"

"It's okay. But..."

"But what?"

"I don't know."

"You need more."

"Yeah, I guess."

"What do you need?"

"Describe it."

"Describe what, Antioch. I need more specific instructions, dear. Tell me exactly what to describe."

"The union."

"Do you miss your mommy?"

"Yeah, I guess so."

"What's my name?"

"Lenina."

"That's right. Do you understand now?"

"I think so."

"Much better, dear."

It went on for what seemed like months. Then the system of privileges kicked in and they started to take transports into Svyatogor, dropped in the center by Sergeant McKew who liked to drive them personally and sang for them on the way. He had a good operatic tenor of a voice and favored classic 20th century standards like Free Bird and Angie. Pulling up at the Plaza Demnick, he would remind them of the pickup time and warn them not to be late before pulling the handle to open the front and back doors and lowering the ramps for the wheelchair bound to descend to the curb.

"Remember, guys. Win Win Way. A Triple Double You all the way home, baby. Right?" asked McKew.

"That's right, Sergeant McKew," said Antioch, stepping past, careful to smile broadly. The sergeant liked a big smile and would make sure it got into your file as an anti-social stigma if you weren't seen to be a smiler.

Besides, thought Antioch, stepping off the transporter, what were the odds that any of them would not show up for the return trip back to the Training House? They all were well aware that they could be traced spatially and emotionally through the Nurvalink chip, although there were rumors, someone had seen a research brief, that the effectiveness of the chip's neuronal webbing grew steadily poorer after a certain length of time that depended on the energy and wattage of an individual's metabolism and personally applied mental stimulus.

Antioch took a deep breath, drawing in the mild, manufactured air of Svyatogor into his lungs as a cure all for what ailed him. Despite the cold stares the trainees received from passersby, there was a vibe of release, of freedom as they looked around at the cityscape. They congregated together uneasily on the sidewalk, drawing a meager sense of comfort from one another. Their secondary issue survival suits and drab gray Training House bodysuits set them apart from the regular Svyatogor folks streaming past and around them, attired in all manner of material and well-fitted design. They seemed to hover on the edge, unsure of where they belonged and unhappy in their outfits. It was not a team Antioch was thrilled to be on, but it was his team. He couldn't deny his own agency. That would have been a betrayal of himself at too deep a level. He accepted his crew as a matter of personal responsibility for this and every moment.

Across the street at the entrance to the Champion Center, a press crew of the official OneWorld news organization, RedAge Century 22 Network Mars, waited between the hotel's red masonry entrance and the open doors of a black luxury module. It was the appearance of some star, some Earth celeb on a goodwill tour.

"Who's that?" someone asked in a whisper.

"Sharika S!" brayed Georgie, one of the female trainees. Georgie had been assigned for rehabilitation, charged with prostitution and dealing contraband satinate. She was a good source of information. She still corresponded with people in Novaroma and Svyatogor through human intermediaries in the OneWorld that she could inform on if needed. All of this was well known to the detainees, since Georgie was quite free with her personal details, one of her endearing qualities.

"Oh, yeah, I heard she was coming to Novaroma," said Antonio, one of her former clients, whom Georgie believed had ratted her out to the OneWorld authorities. Antonio was considered a risk for suicide and was on constant security alert. People avoided any exchange with him, exacerbating his isolation. It made for interesting times. Nobody picked up on Antonio's comment.

The thought occurred to Antioch that they were being presented an opportunity to overcome the usual difficulties they encountered on their jaunts to the big city, the second largest Martian conurbation. They were not welcome in the markets or public health centers and were in constant danger of running afoul of the Home Guard on patrol in downtown Svyatogor, suspects immediately in any random situation that called for intervention. These encounters and the subsequent disciplinary proceedings were often an excuse for automatic lengthening of their time of training, and if not that, at the very least would result in a doubling down on the process, kicking off additional accomodations. Antioch had avoided contacts with the Home Guard, but he wanted to maintain his lucky streak and get out of Training House as soon as possible. The process had long ago ceased to entertain him. He was enduring it as best he could. He knew that his latest Nurvalink data did not favor his early release. In the long run he would be seen as a liability and shipped off to the food producing plants and experimental stations, where he would probably be put to work in terraforming. The quintessential Martian civilizing project incorporated and increasingly relied upon agriculture laborers to provide trace minerals.

"I'm going there," proclaimed Antioch suddenly, setting out across the road.

He knew there would be some to follow and that the split in the group would be along unforeseen lines. That was how their collective was purposely randomized. He thought that this decentralizing algorithm was actually an unintentional gift to any rebel activism. There was still a legacy of human group-centered emotional tuning that he counted on to be present in all of them.

The traffic swirled: Svyatogor's public system transporters, private modules of the well-connected, e-bike couriers hauling strategic resources between various bio-factories and the city's main data centers. It all came to an eerie, silent halt as Antioch stepped across the parkway towards the corner of Plaza Demnick and Sierra Leone Strada.

"Who's with me now?" he wondered, as he reached the other curb and slowly turned in the thin Martian morning light coming through the shielding exonet shell of the city.

He wasn't shocked to see Antonio and Georgie holding onto each other for balance, skidding their way in slow motion like two drunks between stopped vehicles. He was pleasantly surprised to see three more detainees follow behind them: Melchior from the moon colony Palesrina, June, a native born Martian, and Elgin, his bunkmate who had yet to utter a word in his vicinity. He thought Elgin, judging from his slouching, passive-aggressive body language, was probably from somewhere in the Siberian post-methane hinterland, but he wasn't sure. It was a motley crew, but you went down with the one you had, he thought, sizing up the situation, categorizing and prioritizing, calling to mind his combat experience in the Balkan conflicts. He waited until they were all gathered around.

Across the street, the rest of the detainees watched from a distance with their habitual inscrutable expressions. But Antioch could sense their fear and loneliness. It was their compulsive baseline, and it grew worse with anything unplanned or unscripted.

"Hold on," said Antioch, grabbing Elgin by the arm and yanking him back as he tried to get past.

"What's the problem?" grunted Elgin, spinning around.

"Just wait," said Antioch.

"Why should I?" whined Elgin.

"Because I say so. Listen to me. This is it. We are going to sink or swim together. Get it?" asked Antioch, gripping Elgin by the shoulders.

The five others gathered around. Their usual decrepit look had shifted. They stood straighter, more alert. They looked him in the eye.

Elgin finally looked up slowly. Now in the moment, there was no doubt that Elgin, along with all of them, declared allegiance. They understood that Antioch was about to try and pull off the stunt of a lifetime.

He turned from all of them. Ahead was the knot of people around the black transporter, still disgorging the Earth visitors. Antioch walked briskly forward, purposely keeping his mind blank. When he reached the edge of the small crowd, he was whistling a nostalgic tune that came to him unbidden from his youth. He remembered the words:

The story is over, it doesn't exist.
What we built one day has vanished.
Don't think it wasn't worth it.

He slipped like a knife between people. A hand grabbed his wrist, and he wrenched his arm away. The world exploded, fragmenting into quadrants that shattered in the air around him. From behind, someone attempted to put him in a headlock.

His hand shot up to his neck, preventing the lock. He slipped out and away and flipped his assailant, twisting his arm.

He felt a thud as a bat or something cracked him on the head, sending him to his knees. Somebody kicked him. He rolled into a ball. There were screams. And then he heard a female voice, serene but authoritative:

"Hold it! Hold it! Everybody stop right there!"

Antioch stood unsteadily, holding the pain in his ribs by shallow breathing. His assailants, two hooded Home Guards, stood before him, glaring with hostile intent. They were without a doubt ready to kill him, drawing their box knives to slit his exposed throat. He turned to the woman who had stopped them.

It was Sharika. She wore a black cape, yellow fish skin tights and black stilettos, and her bare skinned arms shone with enhanced biogel luminescence. She studied him as he looked her in the eyes, searching for meaning in each of her soft black, unmoved pupils. It was not yet time for words. He held on for what seemed an eternity, ignoring the pain when he breathed.

"Where you from, honey?" she finally asked.

"Tennessee, ma'am," he said. "We just love your stuff. We come here to see you." He caught his breath, gritting his teeth hard.

"You are a long way from Tennessee. But everybody's got a chip on their shoulders, am I right. Who's we?"

"That's them over there. We just want to see the show tonight."

Sharika looked over to the group of detainees at the corner, beyond the crowd surrounding the transporter. They shuffled uneasily as if roped together by some secret force. It was fear, thought Antioch. He could feel it.

"And you are what? Some kind of spokesperson for these people? What do you call yourself? As far as I know, nothing moves here without OneWorld approving."

"We're detainees. They let us out every so often for the day."

"Detainees. Let out for the day. Or what passes for the day in this god-awful settlement. Isn't that sweet? And you want to see yourselves some show."

"Yes, ma'am."

"Well, then. Gather up and come inside."

She smiled.

Antioch waved at Melchior and June who were the ones attentive to what was going on. He saw that they were trying to round up the others and working to find the resolve to begin to move. Then he turned back to Sharika heading for the door of the building. The two Home Guards hovered menacingly. He needed to catch her attention again before she disappeared. He leapt forward, standing up to the two glowering guards.

"Hey there, maam! Sharika!"

Sharika stopped and turned her head before going in the door.

"You've got to help us here. Looks like someone didn't get the message," he yelled.

Sharika walked back down the ramp and over slowly, while behind her, a handler in a synthetic fur coat held the door.

"Hell, now. Haven't you heard about live and let live? What kind of training do you get here in Shittygor anyways?"

"It's bit of a problem, Mizz Shornstein," said the Home Guard, standing away, while the other spoke into the air and played with the clip in his ear.

""Well, you tell the boss that there will be a big problem if you don't stand back and let these people in, if you catch my meaning. This whole project has been my baby for too long now to let these assholes get in the way," she said, turning back towards the entrance to the building.

There was no response. One Home Guard turned to his partner listening to the earbud. Presumably, thought Antioch to himself, there was some recalibration going on, otherwise there would be reinforcements and Home Guard transporters would have already been on the scene carrying dozens of personnel and attack bot9s.

"Come on in," said Sharika, ushering the detainees inside the building, the Champion Center for Activity and Culture, OneWorld's municipal headquarters and main public space in Svyatogor. Once inside the door, Antioch's eyes adjusted to a thousand overhead xenon bulbs inset in the replica of Mars floating over the entire lobby. The platinum plated interior decking reflected the light in a dazzling brilliance. He started to read the plaque in the wall about the history of the center in the context of the broader Martian colonization. It was written in the three languages of the Martian colony's original underwriters: English, Russian and Arabic. There was a dedication his eyes skimmed to:

This edifice, the Municipal Centre Champions of Svyatogor, is dedicated to the brave persons of the Adriselba Home Guard Units who perished while the initial assembly stages of the Svyatogor Mars base were ongoing. In the fires of the chemical explosions of May 2057, they perished attempting to save the lives of their fellow OneWorld explorers. We salute and commemorate all who dream of a Homeland and summon the courage to Never Look Back.

He pulled himself away and caught up to the others. The detainees straggled behind Sharika and her retinue as they made their way around the back of the auditorium to the makeup rooms and the lounge behind the stage. Several hundred people were already inside for the concert. Cheers went up from small knots of concert-goers as they spied the retinue making its way around behind the seats.

The lounge had walls lined with a green, reflective plating. There was a molded metallic bench topped with warm fermented drinks and the best of the aromatic Martian food

175

known as espaprofone, with cyano-based protein and leafy greens in a synth dairy sauce. Sharika waved away the server bots. They buzzed off back into the auditorium. She turned to Antioch and the detainees. The handler stopped in front of a blank screen. It went on as he stared at it, and there was Sharika, prancing on stage in the daylit outdoors of some arena in what looked like mid-continent North America. The summer sun lit up the golden faces of the audience, highlighting their adoring expressions of gratitude and comfort. Antioch missed the Earth light and temperate, geo-engineered climate. There were billboards behind the audience on the screen plastered with by now outdated OneWorld logos in a 2040s brand font such as **Contentment Without Content** and **Don't Worry Be Won**. She was singing a pop/psyop nostalgia number about alien love and quantum eternity. Antioch remembered the way OneWorld was known for incorporating the long-established religious and spiritual longings of communities in pop culture forms, designed to attract growing numbers of loyal adherents through enhanced endocannabinoid uptake brought on by the ritual music festivals playing on the screen. He realized, however that Sharika was a shill for the totalitarian system that ran the two planets, and would be best handled by showing gratitude for the largesse she had demonstrated by saving them from the Home Guard on their day trip into the city. But he would stop short of trusting her. In the end, they were on their own.

"Have some food, my friends," said Sharika. "We have time before the show. You. Come here and talk to me," she said, looking at him.

The detainees were busy gathering food on plates, stuffing their faces, and warily watching the screen of Sharika onstage. Melchior and June stood apart, watching him.

"It's okay," whispered Antioch as he went by.

"Are you sure?" asked June.

"Are we safe here?" asked Melchior.

"I think so. For now," said Antioch.

He followed Sharika. The handler held a curtain aside for him. She settled herself on a thick carpet surrounded by pillows. She motioned with her arm to the floor beside her. Her smile was a mixture of nurture and surveillance, and he couldn't decide which of the elements carried the weightier portion.

Antioch sat across from her. She pulled her hair behind her and tied it in a knot. He couldn't tell her age. She looked somewhere between youth and old age, past the bloom of life, but still retaining a fire in her eyes that came from some gypsy past, he imagined.

"You get nervous?" he asked.

"A little," she smiled. "Tell me something about yourself, Antioch."

"Why?" he asked.

"I want to help you," she said.

"Well, I owe you. We owe you," he said, not taking his eyes off of hers.

"We're not taught to owe each other. You're dating yourself, dear."

"You always do what you're taught?"

"Of course not."

"Only got the one life. That hasn't changed, has it?" he asked.

"They do have the Win Win Rewards, right?" she said.

"They say it's bugged. The rewards don't ever get fulfilled. We'll never know. Who's in the program? I'm not. Are you?"

"You don't have to convince me, amigo. I'm from a long line of anarcho-syndicalists, survivalists in Comarca Aragon. The drought of 2107 killed the last of our olive trees. But not the spirit of republican resistance."

"But whose tune do you dance to now? That's what I'm asking."

"I want to help you. Trust me. I can get all of you back to Earth."

"Why would you do that?"

"Human potential, in a nutshell. I can use you."

"Explain," said Antioch. He was intrigued. A warning light was going off in his mind somewhere, though. He shook his head.

"What's wrong, amigo?"

"It's the Nurvalink," said Antioch. The pains in his head were getting worse over time, but this was a new kind of hurt. He thought there was a growing rift between the emergent thoughts and desires in his frontal lobes and stronger and more explicit directives coming from the parietal system where the chip was ingrained.

"What is it?" she asked.

Antioch was stretched out on his back, and she was holding his head in her lap. He didn't remember getting into that position.

"What happened?" asked Antioch.

"You blacked out."

Antioch sat up. He'd had a dream. He couldn't get it out of his head. A strange man somewhere in an old, book-lined room looking out a window onto a snow-covered field, with pine-forested hills in the distance. He'd been in the room also, maybe sitting on the floor like he was now. The man would look at him, like he was studying some artifact or something, maybe hoping he'd do something surprising. He'd look out the window, then he'd look at him again as if Antioch held the answer to whatever he was doing just beyond the range of Antioch's current understanding. It was very strange.

"What is it?" she asked again.

"I wanted you to explain, didn't I," he said.

"Explain what, amigo?" she asked.

"Human potential," said Antioch.

She looked at him and scratched her head.

"We don't have time," she said. "They're going to be here any moment."

"Who?" asked Antioch.

"Oh, the usual suspects, the literary elites, the well-connected. Suffice it to say, Antioch, that they all need one thing. Juice, more juice. Apparently it's what I've got, and I can get them some more."

She looked at him to see if he was with her so far. Antioch was aware that her eyes were thin slits, with glimpses of shared light coming through.

She went on:

"The Nurvalink is running low on input for its models, and so far at least it has failed to show any sign of a general intelligence of any meaningful sort, I mean capable of producing a non-aligned heuristic. All of which leaves a no pun intended stale taste in their mouths. Not to mention neural glitches like the ones you're experiencing, amigo. I have some room to maneuver and I'm fully taking advantage of it. You, I mean all of you, I can use you, put you to work, be part of the free creative process that builds the necessary resilience and connectivity that the system lacks. The OneWorld advisory councils have blessed the process and provided subsidies. That's why I'm here. What science tells us is that the journey to and from Mars does wonders for the growth of new neural networks in the brain, both collective and individual. See, you're unique."

"Where?"

"Earth. My ranch, Estancia Los Manantiales, Santa Cruz, Argentina. We're building the augmented networks. Are you in? If not, I am okay, I promise you, and you will just watch the concert. But I have to know now."

It sounded legitimate, but Antioch wondered: what if it was a trap, the whole thing a setup to see which way he'd jump, the final test of the Training House? He thought of Uvlin in

Atlanta, living her lonely, single life. He could hear her voice and feel the tug of her free born spirit calling out to him for protection and guidance. The upside was worth it.

"Yeah, count us in."

Sharika sang all of her hits. They were ushered into a special viewing room off the lounge area for the concert. It had a closed circuit sound system and a large screen showing several views at once of the concert hall. The concert goers reacted in thrall to the sense of belonging she called forth in all of her numbers, but especially her last one, Rajfa Three, which she sang in Arabic and in English, alternating the two languages in the chorus:

> *Breathe, Call these bones*
> *To live, Call these lungs*
> *To sing, On the day of the tremor!*

Antioch watched on the screen. Tears were streaming down many of the faces. There was an air of apocalypse to the audience and their music, an extended riff on annihilation, and it sent a shiver down Antioch's spine, realizing that it was a call to self-sacrifice in the name of the OneWorld's mission of interplanetary conquest. He realized that this was really the prerequisite to citizenship in this world, acceptance of the immolation that could occur at any moment, in the name of what? Whose imperial ambition? It left him sea-sick, head-spinning, yet entranced. Sharika was truly magnificent. She obviously intended to embody some goddess-like qualities, but Antioch resisted her inspirational mission. He would never be onboard with that attempt at immortality, he thought. The tug of the music threatened to drown out his own sense of identity and leave him in a whirlpool of soul-destroying ecstasy.

Sharika was playing a double game and had enlisted them in the liberating project of her creative's ranch back on Earth. The notion was thrilling. He couldn't wait to get off the Red Planet and its life of drudgery. Things on Earth weren't that much better for most, but at least you weren't living under a bubble both physically and mentally. It would stifle the life out of him slowly and then all at once to stay here one more day.

The screen went black when the song ended.

"What's going to happen to us, Antioch?" asked June.

"We're going home, June," said Antioch. The others stopped in their tracks and turned towards Antioch.

"Home?" asked Elgin. He couldn't remember Earth anymore. Instead of the usual disdain, Antioch felt sympathy for Elgin. They were all in the same boat, drifting on the sea of abandonment. They only had each other.

"Yes, Elgin. Earth, remember Earth?"

They gathered around Antioch, wanting to hear more, as the doors burst open. A unit of Home Guards streamed inside the viewing room, weapons drawn. As if they would put up any resistance, thought Antioch. The lights went out inside the room, plunging them into total darkness. There was one high-pitched scream. Antioch realized the scream was fake. None of his crew had the lungs for it.

Antioch sat upright with his back against a thin, cold panel, with a hooded head and shackled limbs, arms stretched tightly behind his back. The transport holding him rumbled for hours across the Martian plains. He was in that frame again of consuming nothingness, just the sound of his own body, the beat of his heart marking his membership in the life force. Beset by anxiety, grieving the loss of whatever hope he'd so recently held, yet he didn't think he would die immediately; OneWorld had already invested time and energy into processing the detainees. Now it was a question of maximizing their utility, as with every input of the Martian colony. The shame of his continued imprisonment had also waned with the dawning knowledge of the common slavery – to the ideology and system of the OneWorld – that held all humans both on Earth and on Mars in some rigorous, twisted solidarity. The illusion of hierarchy and privilege had not settled into a convincing enough pattern.

There was nothing to dispel the people's overarching frustrations and chafing anger at austerity and sacrifice proclaimed from above, and the OneWorld's managers were therefore in a constant state of panic at the possibility of rebellion.

In some odd way, despite Sharika's betrayal, it felt good to Antioch. As his body was jolted by the transport's unpredictable route, his thoughts nevertheless propelled him along a diverging track. Despite being shackled and bound, he was gaining traction on the way marked out for him. He knew then that personal victory or defeat would be up to him alone to define. That realization was enough to settle his thoughts and hold sway over his emotions. The hood that was meant to keep him powerless by cutting off his eyes was an additional cover and protection for the casts and journeys of his mind. Its vision could far outpace the mechanical spins of manufactured wheels. This road he was on had been travelled before, and those previous travelers were with him in spirit. It was meant to be this way. He had never before felt more truly alive to himself than he did in those first few hours in the transport headed out of Svyatogor for godless parts unknown.

It didn't last, that freedom. As the transport rumbled on for what seemed like interminable hours, Antioch's resistance wore down. The first time he went to lie he'd quickly seen he was in deep trouble. Sharp jabs of metal tore into his shoulder. He'd shot back upright. The floor of the transport as well as most of the bench was covered by inset spikes, he discovered, probing awkwardly with his feet. Leaning over from the waist, hands shackled behind, Antioch fell off the seat as the transport suddenly lurched. He screamed as he fell face first on the bed of the vehicle, covered in the sharp metal spikes. He struggled upright and managed somehow to get himself back on a free spot, but not before the spikes had ripped numerous wounds. Blood covered his upper arms, legs, and face, soaking into his bodysuit. Consumed by pain, anger, and hunger, Antioch howled as he soiled himself. Nobody responded. The transport was autonomously piloted. There was nobody to register his outrage except the sensor overseers at Svyatogor.

They had designed this hell and it had beat him down. Antioch hated himself for his weakness. If he could die it would be a release from the sickness and disgust he now felt. It amazed him how fast the worm in his brain had turned, torqued by physical pain and privation. The Home Guard didn't need a human or even a bot torturer along for the ride. He did it all to himself.

Covered in gore and excrement, Antioch continued to lose himself in thoughts of dying. If only he could dull the pain. This might be the form of torture they had settled on, an endless trip to nowhere in an autonomous vehicle programmed for an infinite loop, carrying a prisoner seated without support, shackled and blinded, inside the spike-lined death trap. The only resistance open to him was to consciously speed up his demise. They would even have foreseen his arrival at this conclusion. A slow death by a thousand cuts was the cruelest possibility he could imagine. Instead he visualized himself smashing his head against the spikes until he crushed his skull in. He began to prepare himself for this, driven by rage and despair. He could do it; he was sure of that. He was capable of inflicting death, having done it many times before, at close quarters and at a distance. The trick was just to arrive at the level of willpower necessary in order to jump the hard dam of fear that could obstruct him.

He took a deep breath and concentrated his mind on one point, a distant shore free of pain, ready to strike out for that dream land and make it a reality. He heard silence and thought for a second he might have by sheer desire passed into the next world. But it was the transport. It had ceased its rumbling.

What would come was hard to predict. Antioch realized now that survival was not only possible but of the essence. When the door of the transport opened, he flung himself at the black circle of Mars that appeared, crashing hard against the metal chassis of a work bot. that picked him up from the sand by the torso with a pincer extension on its crane arm. Antioch writhed and gagged, trying to breathe without a survival suit, fighting against the deep cold that threatened imminent blackout. Despite his panicked reaction, he knew he had a few minutes left before lack of oxygen, hypothermia, or both weighed in with conclusive effect. His heart beat furiously. Antioch tried twisting himself and looking around, but the bot shook him like a dog with a stick in its mouth. It wheeled efficiently across ten yards of yellowish sand in the dim light of Phoebus.

A cave in the sand cliffs showed a security door that slowly slid open. The bot flung Antioch down on the sand, pinned him there with an extender arm, and held out a blade so that he could unclip the ties around his wrists and ankles. The bot whirred away, leaving him to scuttle inside like a crab seeking safety under water. The security door slid shut. Lying there just inside the sliding door, Antioch gasped with impinged lungs. His eyes adjusted to the darkness, broken by a single LED above the entrance. He took a deep, desperate breath. He heard nothing behind him besides a distant mechanical sound like a pump. The air tasted slightly of camphor or something medicinal, perhaps masking some toxic residue left by the heating and filtration system. He read the English part of the instructions inscribed on the back of the metal door: Maintain Air Lock at All Time (sic). In years to come, he would remember this moment, especially reading the plaque and the unquestionably delusional hope he placed in the misworded warning, as if it was a sign of a fatal flaw, an empathy that he could discover in the strategy of his captors.

The light cast by the bulb above the door extended down the body of the cave, showing the narrowing, black basalt walls descending and curving into darkness. Antioch felt his way along the cave walls back as far as he could. It wasn't long, maybe thirty yards until he could no longer see where he was going. But he forced himself along the walls by touch. The roof of the cave lowered until he had to crouch to continue. At that point he discovered a pick and a shovel propped against the wall. These were the tools, he thought. Meant for him to wield in the work that he was intended to carry out. What was that work? He remembered the instructions from his conversation with Dmitrievsky those long months ago on the Nazar. His task: to find the sand creature, Dmitrievsky had called it a sort of consciousness, not quite alive in the way Earthlings understood the term, sabotaging the manufacture of solar panels. He also discovered a sort of bench carved into the wall nearby stocked with plastic containers. One held liquid that jostled tellingly when he tried to lift it. There were about 10 gallons inside. He unscrewed the top and stuck his hand inside. Gingerly, he tasted the liquid left on his fingers. It was water, he thought. Water and life. And the others must hold food of some sort, he surmised. A store of rations that would be replenished somehow, hopefully often. As long as he was using the tools, the pick and the spade. But how?

Antioch pressed further and further back into the heart of the cave complex. He spent hours pressing along the walls in the darkness. One day, he felt something soft ahead of him on the ground. His hand ran over the dead body. Must have been his predecessor. The long hair on the scalp came away in his fingers along with part of the face. Suddenly, the smell of rotting flesh hit him, and he gagged, throwing up behind.

She must have been dead quite a long time, he reckoned, by the level of decay that had set in there in the stale, manufactured air of the cave. It was a female, he guessed, by the length of hair. He needed to see her, could not just leave her there. He dragged her back to the cave entrance by the feet, slowly and methodically.

Once back at the cave entrance, he could hardly stand to look at her. Yet, despite the flesh falling away in flakes, exposing her ribcage, her teeth, the blackened, noxious guts weeping along the rocks behind them, she must have once been beautiful, he thought. She must have been young. She was dressed in the same detainee bodysuit he wore. It was impossible not to see the lines of her, the shape of her. He couldn't stop looking, trying to imagine her existence, trying to decipher what she had meant to somebody else, a friend, a lover, a parent, a child. He was trying to fill in the gaps, at least in his own mind, as if at least that was enough to conjure a way beyond the guilt that he felt. Why was it necessary to ritualize and preserve in memory what was left of the beautiful vibrating shell of the living spirit, he wondered.

It was the guilt of the survivors who had not seen death, the master, coming. Absurd but there it was. It was his first task, to offer this woman a decent burial, a resting place to hide the shame of what was left and what would be left of him too. But at least they had shared an innocent shame. It was enough to get him moving. But first he would sleep. He crawled to the back of the cave into the darkness and curled into a ball on the sand.

He woke, not quite refreshed, feeling stiff and sore, as much mentally as physically. He ate and drank from the plastic containers. The food was a creamy, doughy, tasteless paste. He swallowed hard, forcing the barely edible gunk down his throat and into his gut. As much as nutrition, it would be necessary to eat in order to count the days by the internal movement of his body, the hunger that came on him, the need to relieve himself.

In two days of digging at the cave entrance where there was softer rock he completed the burial pit, a deep, long hole in the slab. He called her Skye, the name of his sister and laid her in the pit, curling her legs slightly, on her side, and on her he laid the snail shell he still carried from the Nazar food labs. He paused for a moment and stared at the cave wall.

I didn't know you.

He prayed silently to himself. Mother, sister Skye. Forgive me for my sins. To do for you on Mars as on Earth.

Then he carefully covered her as best he could from the pile of rocks and sand dug out with the pick and the spade. He tamped it all down with the back of the spade so that it was flush and placed as a headstone an oddly smooth oblong piece of basalt he dragged from the cave recess where it had tumbled. It was complete. It was done. She had been transformed into a sort of Martian goddess saint, a light that could shine from within, giving life to the heap of matter he was inside that rotated around the cold sun.

It took more for Antioch to reach the furthest point that had been excavated at the bottom of the cavern. The heating and air filtration system did an outstanding job pressurizing the interior against toxic infiltration of the atmosphere or any interior off gassing from geologic decay, and he discovered a cache of luminescent gel in one of the food containers that he carried in a glass bottle. In this way he could light his passage back and forth from his deepest forays. He felt a need to know more about the cave, about where it led, about the other secrets it inevitably held. A strange curiosity motivated him, but it alternated with panic attacks, where he craved night and day, the normal passage of time, conversation, and the warmth of a fellow human's touch.

He couldn't know what everything was. But he did have a sense that there was change that led in a certain direction that could not be reversed except on the smallest order of things beyond human comprehension. He thought that God existed behind the smallest and the largest ideas that could fit in his mind and that a good task to engage with in the name of sanity and building resilience was to ever expand the possibilities at either extreme. So he developed a practice of spending the time after waking in his spot by the entrance imagining and visualizing the back of the cave, the face of the rock where it had recently been shaped by the blows of the pick, the fractures of the fine-grained rock along the columns of ancient metamorphic molecular bonding, resulting in glimmers of green crystalline formations of olivine in the grey matrix, and the process of volcanic formation, pressurized molten matter at the center of the planet slowly pushing up against the expanding fractures of the cooler layers in the early time of planetary formation. Then again – after the day's work of pounding the cave wall, exposing deeper layers, shoveling away the growing pile of fractured stones and sand from the back of the cave, and retreating to the bed just beyond the entrance light – he pictured the original vast, violent explosion of matter, and he surfed with the blasts of energy through constellations and black holes, and discovered moons and planets of all types.

These habitual exercises kept him going for now. Gradually, his focus grew more acute, he was learning the rock, how to break it up. The pick and the spade in his hands were growing familiar in their heft and swing in the limited space and the strange gravity of the cave. It was expanding under his charge. His hardships had a purpose. And he was fitting himself to them despite the clear limits to his understanding. The problem was the in-between time, when he lost his grip on where his mind should wander. That was when he longed, almost unbearably, to open the security door and slip outside, if only for a fraction of a second, to see the old sun moving across the sky, the moon and stars of the black night brilliantly refracting in real time, casting their magnificent spell on the back of his brain.

He scratched lines with a rock above the shelf of food to keep track of the days. On the thirteenth such scratch, on his way to work, he drank off a slug from the water container. There was just enough for one more drink and maybe one more brushing of teeth. He stuck to daily tooth brushing using finger and sand and water. Once the water was finished he would open the door. He felt his arms. He was strong from the work in the back of the cave with the pick and the shovel. This was his world now, shrunken to responsibility alone for his limbs, his mind, and his soul. If the pick and shovel were of any use, he would be fed, but he wasn't confident that replenishment would come. If not, he would open the door and at last see the sun once more. It would be a good end, one he could be proud of. He had done everything he could. His only failure was Uvlin. The thought of her alone and struggling was enough to negate all the gains he'd made. He wanted above all the things that he would never get to be of more use to his daughter.

He was asleep, soundly dreaming. The noise of the door sliding open woke him up. He had forgotten the noise the door made. He stayed where he was in the dark, in the sand, listening to the bot wheel past him. It must have registered his presence, the parameters of his vital functions. It must be leaving the stores of food and water; this was how it was done, in the night, in the down time, just do what was needed to keep him going. The bot wheeled diligently past him and then some time later wheeled back again. Must have been looking for Skye, he thought. It probably knew that he had buried her, and that would mean something to the OneWorld. He hated the thought of what it would mean, or that it would mean anything at all to those people, if there were people still in charge. His usefulness was as repugnant to him as it was a relief to be kept alive. He hated himself, but he just lay there in the dark, letting that realization sink in, overtaken by waves of disease in his mind spreading to the rest of him and beyond..

There were new containers of food and water, and the pile of sand and rock was gone. So it was clear he was on the right track. He dug some more that next day, not going too hard; the task would be a long time to finish.

He lost track of the days. He knew he was losing himself to the cave. He would give out long before it ended. The sense of loss became a strength of sorts. The emotional toll grew less, until he didn't feel it any more. It had been drilled out of him. Instead, he thought about the worm, what did Dmitrievsky call it, the Dolomite? tossing about before sleep, longing for it to finally come and end the whole saga of his time in the cave. How would it make itself known? he asked himself. Why was it taking so long? Was he missing something? How long did he need to tear himself down? Until he was unrecognizable to himself, his mind ceasing to dwell on itself or to care at all. That was the conclusion he drew, swinging the pick, pivoting through hips and shoulders, the point of it sinking into the cave wall with a telltale snugness that was an extension of his own arms.

Antioch dreamed night after night while lying fast asleep in the sand: he was a young man traveling across an ancient bridge away from the ruins of a not quite as ancient city, its ramparts and roofs ablaze in the aftermath of a terrible tragedy. He traveled into a line of mountains, not wearying, unyielding in his pursuit. There were moons and constellations in the night sky. He had a long time before dawn. His companion was silent; they were steadily becoming more comfortable with each other. It was a hooded, faceless, compact figure, perhaps a monk given over to unbreakable vows of great importance. They climbed up and down the foothills to the line of mountains where once there had been mines of copper and diaqmonds. They arrived at the gate, a large wrought iron structure topped with pointed shafts and a knocker shaped like a seal. Behind the gates was a cliff overlooking the sea far below, and further out on the horizon were the hazy blue outlines of mountainous islands. In his dream, Antioch leaned his hand on the gate, and it swung open. He looked at the little man beside him, but the faceless figure had no words as usual. Nevertheless, he lifted his walking stick as if to invite him to enter.

They sheltered away from the wind. The sound of the wind in the dream was also the sound of something else, a wail of sadness sweeping the sky, a chorus in the wake of the departure of all hope. In the dream, however, they accepted this cry of the wind as the bedrock of their existence, an inescapable bane that could only be endured from behind the sea wall. At the end of the day, as the golden dusk receded into ever darker shades, the little monk and he lay there for warmth. The stones of the beach rose and became the stars, aligning themselves according to some augury that Antioch's companion claimed to be able to decipher in a whisper. He felt the words drilling down into the marrow of his vertebrae like spirochetes and following the path of the nerves into the skull where the implant lay hidden.

At last the wind fell silent, and he slept in a dream within the dream.

Eight

Morrow drew back the curtains. He was pretty confident that he was the first up. He plugged in the Christmas tree lights and made sure they were all on. He wandered through the quiet house. He put on hot water and made a pot of coffee and started the two fires, down on his knees blowing the paper into a flame and watching the kindling catch. The rooms upstairs were full but silent as the children, their partners, and Ellen continued to sleep away the first storm of the season, just in time to cover the fields and the house in a blanket of thickening white.

It made him happy, but he was weary of happiness. It would be fleeting as always and then invariably they would drift further away into their lives. How long could he and Ellen hold down the gravitational pull of the hearth keeping them all in orbit? But the quiet of the house this morning was a blessing. He would not disparage his good fortune. He thought of his mother and the way he would miss her later in the day. When the kids were little they would always drive up to her place in Eastfield on Christmas day and spend the evening with Nana and Dick Cox, her second husband, who predeceased her by several months. She would never admit that Dick had caught Covid, always insisting he had died of loneliness after they'd stopped allowing visitors in the assisted living facility in New London. Morrow had always disparaged the little white lies she told, but he understood them now as mechanisms of resistance to despair and thus a badge of feminine bravery. He put on his coat and wandered through the snow to the chicken house. They were still laying eggs. He found four in the straw, in a little depression they had made next to the boxes where they were supposed to lay. They were funny, ornery, tough little birds, pecking in the snow for the feed that spilled out of the dish. The eggs would be good despite the cold unless they had cracked. He walked back over the icy path with the eggs in his coat pocket, watching his step, and back inside the kitchen. The house was still quiet, but it had an air of consciousness stirring.

"Hey there, old guy."

It was Daniel. Morrow placed the egg carton on the shelf, closed the door, and backed away from the fridge. Daniel was unshaved, wearing his pajama bottoms and a large, old wool sweater he'd probably found in a box in the attic.

"Good morning, son. How are you feeling?"

"Fine," said Daniel.

"Sleep okay?"

"Slept great. Beautiful sunrise," said Daniel.

"Were you outside?"

"Yeah, I went for a walk," said Daniel.

"In your pajamas?"

"Well I didn't go far, just out to the apple trees," said Daniel.

"How's Amaya?"

"She's still asleep," he said.

"Want some coffee?"

"Sure."

Morrow poured two mugs of coffee from the press and took out the milk from the fridge. Daniel was in a rare good mood. He thought about pursuing the moment to talk about Daniel's work prospects and how that was going, but he decided to wait for a better time, build some rapport first. It was delicate to be seen as nagging, overly concerned with his career plans.

"How's Portland? Still liking it?"

"Yah, it's good, man. I mean it could be better but..." said Daniel.

"Amaya likes it there?"

"Well, that's where she grew up," he said.

"You like her family?"

"They're great, super chill," said Daniel.

"Let's go into the living room."

"Why?" asked Morrow.

"I don't know."

"It's nice here. You can see the lake," said Daniel. He put another log into the Jotul.

It was as if he'd never been away. Morrow was grateful that his son was seemingly taking better care of himself now that he had Amaya in his life. For a while he had been worried and had fallen into the bad habit of forwarding links to retreats and healing practices to Daniel until he'd asked him to stop; it was making him feel worse about himself to have his father suggest radical self improvement regimes. Daniel sat against the low window sill in the corner by the cupboard that had once been the old dry sink. Morrow leaned back in his chair facing him. He would have wanted to slow down, just enjoy the moment, but something stirred him into action, an inability, a lack of wholeness. The words popped out of him without much forethought, like a spray of bullets.

"You look good. Healthy, strong. I'm glad you're putting down roots, son. It makes me happy."

"Well, I wouldn't say that. I'm not feeling like I'm putting down roots. Portland's okay for now. "

"What's wrong with it?"

"Nothing specific. Just not maybe the perfect place for us."

"How so?"

"I don't know Dad. Why are you so concerned?"

"Just wondering. Making conversation."

"It's not that big a deal. It's a little precious maybe. Not quite real. And then they don't make it that easy if you're trying to start a business. All sorts of zoning regulations, what have you."

"I see."

"Yeah."

Amaya came into the kitchen then and found a place on the bare cupboard beside Daniel. Morrow studied the two of them. Amaya was in her early twenties, a little younger than Daniel and Sarah and a little older than Mackenzy. She was beautiful, with straight black hair, brown eyes and soft, fine features. He had to admit that Daniel had chosen well. He knew it would be a sentiment that would remain necessarily unspoken although obvious to any intelligent and honest observer. Daniel asked her if she wanted coffee and she shook her head.

"Good morning. No coffee? Are you sure?" asked Morrow.

"No, it's too early. Maybe in a little while," said Amaya reassuringly.

"Well sit down here. You might as well get comfortable," said Morrow.

Sarah and Barbara came in shortly after that, dressed in yoga pants and sweatshirts and otherwise put together. They started making breakfast, scrambling a dozen eggs and cutting up onions and tomatoes at the table. Daniel put more water in the kettle and set out to make more coffee, cleaning out the French press in the sink. Morrow stayed where he was at the table with Amaya and looked around, listening to the conversation swirl around the kitchen about movies, social media reels and things he'd never heard of. It made him happy. He looked into the dining room and caught a glimpse of Ellen. They looked at each other, both of them half smiling warily.

"What kind of a business?" asked Morrow, as Daniel poured fresh coffee into his mug.

"What? Oh. I don't know. I'm designing an app for permaculture landscapes."

"That sounds good," said Morrow.

"Yeah, it's just I'm doing it without looking for any further funding. I don't want to have to get into it with any investors. That gets too crazy," said Daniel.

"I get it," said Morrow.

"Do you, Dad? Really?" asked Sarah pointedly..

"What do you mean?" he asked, turning to face her at the stove. The smell of onions frying began to permeate the room. Outside, the sun was peeking through the clouds and the top of the ski mountain gleamed white with the fresh snow.

"Because it seems like you're always pooh pooing any of our ideas or ambitions. 'Oh, that'll never work.' That's the message you and Mom always give off."

"I'm sorry if that's the impression I've given," said Morrow.

"You don't need to do this, Sarah," said Daniel.

"No, I do. You're constantly putting yourself down, Daniel. " said Sarah.

So this was going to be a bloodletting kind of breakfast, thought Morrow. They had one of these every so often, but it had been a long time since the last one, right around Daniel's graduation. That had been also about his perceived rigidity, he recalled, his adherence to certain precepts he'd tried to impart, like not quitting on a team just because you didn't like the coach or the workouts. That night Daniel had stormed away from the table angrily after warning him against perpetuating the harm onto his sisters. He hadn't come back for two days, and when he did, he didn't say where he'd been. But he had been on a hell of a bender. He was doing well enough in school that it hadn't affected his ability to graduate or his college acceptance. Now Sarah was paying back his protection. He tried to get himself to relax. Ellen poked into the kitchen.

"It's Christmas," she said. "Anybody interested in presents?"

"After breakfast, Mom," said Daniel.

"Well, go easy on your father. He's had a rough time recently," said Ellen, before retreating back to the dining room and the rest of the downstairs. Morrow thought he should go check on the living room fire. He half began to rise before thinking better of it. There was more of a fire that needed to be put out in the kitchen.

"Has he? How so, Dad?" asked Sarah.

"Mackenzy, get your ass in here," yelled Daniel. Mackenzy and Saroj were slinking around between the dining room and the passage to the bathroom.

"Well, you don't want to really know," said Morrow.

"No, I do. We do. I'm just curious. What do you have to be proud of, Dad? Like in your life? What kind of inspiration do you give?"

"I'm proud of you guys. I'm proud of my kids," said Morrow. He steeled himself. That had been a low blow but perhaps he deserved it. Then again, he hadn't expected something like that from Sarah. This was a new role she was assuming as a protectress. It meant she saw herself as able to arbitrate and oversee the family's well-being. It was a role that suited her, he had to admit to himself.

"What about your book?" asked Daniel.

"Yeah, small potatoes. Never amounted to much and never will," said Morrow.

"Dad! How can you say that," said Sarah. Daniel and Sarah gathered around him, standing at the table. He divulged the news as precisely as he could that he no longer had a publisher. It wasn't the end of the world. They would get by. The mortgage was paid off. There was Ellen's salary. Nana's inheritance would provide a bridge and he had the pension from his years of teaching. Not to worry. But it wasn't the finances that had the kids concerned. Morrow found the words caught in his throat when he tried to say anything else.

Mackenzy wandered in the kitchen as they stood silently by Morrow in his seat.

"What's going on?" she asked.

"Dad's publisher pulled out of the contract," said Daniel disgustedly, sitting back on the cupboard.

"Well, we never quite had that kind of contract," said Morrow.

"What? I thought you had a multi-book contract with the last one," said Daniel.

"Contingent on making a sales level I never quite reached, Daniel."

"Dad. I'm so sorry," said Mackenzy.

"The eggs are ready," said Barbara sheepishly from behind her.

"It's okay. It might be the best thing for me to concentrate on something else other than writing."

They sat and ate at the table and on the low cupboard that had once been the dry sink. Saroj and Ellen took some slices of orange from a plate on the table and wandered back out to the living room. Saroj had attached himself to Ellen as an aide and was assisting with laying out walnuts and other traditional items.

"Like what, Dad?" asked Daniel.

"I don't know. The farm. Volunteer work. Maybe I'll run for office," said Morrow.

"Don't run for office," said Daniel.

"Why not?" asked Sarah, turning to study him.

"Eeew, politics," said Mackenzy.

"Hey, listen. It's not a serious idea," said Morrow. "These eggs are great," he added.

"How else are we supposed to change anything?" asked Amaya, piping up, holding her coffee cup up abstractly.

"That's a good point," said Sarah. "Don't knock politics."

" There's nothing left to save. Need to let it all go and start to rebuild everything," said Daniel.

"That's a brave proposal, Daniel," said Morrow.

This was more like it. The grand visions, the post apocalyptic pronouncements. This was the family culture of old, thought Morrow.

"Well, as someone who deals with reality, I'm not feeling that hopeless. What makes me cringe is the useless posing. You think it's so easy to rebuild crap. Why not fix what's broken," said Sarah.

"Look, all I'm saying is let's just acknowledge that things are broken," said Daniel.

"They are broken," said Morrow. Maybe in more ways than one, he thought.

They ate for a while in silence. Daniel got up and served himself some more scrambled eggs. He offered Amaya some more, waving the cast iron frying pan with the rest of the eggs in it.

"Algo mas?" asked Daniel, showing off his Spanish.

"No gracias." She smiled and waved him away with her hand. Morrow liked the way she gestured. It was very aristocratic yet familiar. He also liked Daniel taking care of her that way. That was his son's best quality, the way he tried to always meet the needs of others.

"Anybody?" asked Daniel, before placing the pan back on the stove.

"Saroj has an idea. Family farm as wedding venue," said Mackenzy with a winking note of farce. There was a loud collective groan. This had obviously already been aired, Morrow realized.

"Yeah, just what the world needs. A wedding venue," said Sarah. She looked at Barbara, who laughed loudly.

"What's so funny?" asked Mackenzy.

"I just think it's funny," said Barbara.

"We're thinking of getting married," said Sarah. "Didn't want to say anything until we had it more figured out."

Mackenzy dropped her fork on her plate.

"Wow, congratulations," said Daniel.

"That is so sweet," said Mackenzy. "Mom, did you hear?"

"What's that dear?"

"Sarah and Barbara are getting married!"

"That's the best Christmas present. Thank you, dear."

Ellen approached Sarah and hugged her awkwardly as Sarah half turned in her seat at the table and closed her eyes, leaning her head into Ellen. Saroj beamed from the doorway to the dining room with his ever present vague smile. Barbara stood to receive her hug from Ellen and then sat back down, allowing the meal to resume.

"When?" asked Morrow.

"Don't know, Dad. Maybe the summer," said Sarah. She was crying.

"Don't be sad," said Morrow.

"I'm not sad, Dad," said Sarah laughing and wiping her face with her sweatshirt sleeve.

"Hey, we still have the Christmas presents to do," said Ellen.

"That's right. Time for the traditional famous Morrow Christmas punch."

"Oh Jesus," said Sarah.

"William. Nobody likes that stuff," said Ellen.

"Well, it's already made," said Morrow, standing.

"Locked and loaded," said Daniel, winking at Amaya.

"Everyone out. I'll take care of the dishes," Morrow said.

Their voices came distantly from the opposite side of the house. He turned on the radio to listen to the news from NPR. The president-elect was unironically as ever making noise about the unfairness of the system that was rigged against him, even on this day. Morrow was always amazed at the victimhood that the culture constantly claimed as the legitimate grounds for any public participation. But, be that as it may, he stacked the dishes. It had always been their shared desire to inoculate the kids against some of the dysfunctions of the society at large. Maybe it had been in vain after all. Maybe he and Ellen had always been deluded, unwittingly carrying the virus of self-pity into their home with every action and thought.

"Can I help, Dad?" It was Sarah.

"No, I've got this, Sarah," said Morrow.

"The punch?"

"It's in the fridge. Glasses are already on the side table in the dining room."

"I just wanted to say sorry," said Sarah

"For what?"

"Earlier," she said.

"Never mind. No harm done."

"Are you sure?" she asked.

"Yes, I'm positive."

"I'm proud of you, Dad. Just so you know. You always did your best for us."

"Not always."

"Yes, you did. You worked hard for us," said Sarah.

"Sometimes too hard, maybe. I'll always remember you holding my hand at soccer. Cheering on your teammates."

"That was fun. You were a great coach," said Sarah.

"You were a great player. Our best."

"I wish things were still so simple and easy," she said.

"Yeah. That's what happens," said Morrow.

Morrow was thirsty for a drink of the cocktail punch he had prepared earlier. He entered the living room with a glass in one hand as Daniel was opening his gift from his parents, a ceramic garlic dish Ellen had bought at the crafts fair in town in the fall. He smiled and showed it to Amaya, sitting next to him on the sofa.

"It's beautiful," he said.

Morrow put down the punch, took out his phone awkwardly from his sweatpants pocket and started to snap photos.

"Only happy ones, please," said Ellen.

"Everyone smile," said Morrow, moving around the room to the walnut bowl on a window sill next to the tree. He sat against the window sill and started to look through the photos he'd taken on the phone.

"Mom, why only happy ones?" asked Mackenzy.

"I don't want it impacting your memories. If there are sad photographs you're going to have just sad memories of this day."

"Is that true?" asked Morrow distractedly.

"Yes. Photographs impact our memories and even replace them to a certain extent," said Ellen.

"I think it's better to take a true account. I don't care if there's some sadness. Maybe there's a good reason for the sadness. It's part of life," said Daniel.

"I agree. We shouldn't deny our emotions," said Sarah. "But maybe we shouldn't have any pictures. Just the memories. Pure and simple and true." She looked at Ellen for approbation.

"But please smile in any case," said Saroj. "It will make Mr. and Mrs. happy."

Morrow didn't care. Happy or sad. As long as you could exist in the shelter of each other and let the roots grow twisted into the folds of the earth.

Later on, in the afternoon after all the gifts had been opened and wrapping paper bagged for the transfer station, Morrow and Ellen were in the bedroom tidying up, making the bed. Ellen seemed distracted, not quite right. The sun was coming through the window with the late afternoon refraction that served as a warning about the light left in the day. Another marker of the year was fading, another toehold on life had almost slipped away into the black hole of the past, and Morrow was seized with the determination to squeeze every ounce of goodness and benefit from every thought and breath.

"What are you thinking?" he asked. Ellen straightened and stared at him.

"Nothing much," she said.

"You look concerned," he said.

"Oh, I just wish everyone was happier," she said.

"What makes you think they aren't?"

"Are you kidding me?" she said.

"No, they seem fine. There's some grumbles from the past. Better get those off their chests now."

"You weren't there. Sarah was recriminating me for having 'ruined Christmas' for her as a child," she said.

"What? How in the hell did you do that?"

"I must have told her Santa Claus wasn't real. She was in second or third grade. I think Jagger was telling kids there was no such thing and she came to me," she said.

"Jagger? The kid who lived in the trailer on French Pond Road with his Dad?"

"Shhh. Yeah, he had a lot of sway over the kids in her class," she said.

"But she blames you."

"For ruining Christmas."

"That's ridiculous," said Morrow

"It's not ridiculous. You can't say the way they feel is ridiculous. It is what they feel," she said.

"What do the others think about that?" asked Morrow.

"Daniel said he sometimes felt a lack of emotional support growing up which has impacted his ability to get in touch with his own emotions," she said.

"Is he in therapy?"

"I think so," she said.

"I'm sorry, Ellen. You were a great Mom. Not an adequate Mom. Not a so-so Mom. A great one."

"Stop please," she said.

"A great Mom. And still are," said Morrow.

Ellen started to cry. Morrow hugged her to comfort her.

"Those kids need some straightening out."

"Don't you dare say a thing," said Ellen, pulling away abruptly.

"But..."

"Not a word."

There was a knock on the door.

"Mom? Dad?"

It was Mackenzy.

"Yes, sweetie?" said Morrow.

"We're all going for a walk. Do you want to come?"

"Sure," said Morrow

"Where to?" asked Ellen, her voice fluted.

"The rocks. Do you want to come?" asked Mackenzy.

"Do we have snowshoes for everyone?" asked Ellen.

"We don't need snowshoes," said Morrow.

"I think so. There's some extras, right?" said Mackenzy.

"You should look in the attic," said Ellen.

"We don't need snowshoes," insisted Morrow. He opened the bedroom door.   "

"Daniel and I can break trail. Everyone else can follow," he said. Mackenzy looked past him.

"Behind the old suitcases?" she asked.

"Yes, look there,' said Ellen.

Mackenzy bolted away, into Daniel's bedroom. It had the door to the barn built on the house.

"Hate the way she just ignores me," said Morrow, shutting the door again.

"We're not in charge of their lives any more," said Ellen.

"Tell me about it," he said.

They gathered outside by the barn, stomping the snow into swirls of mud. The sun was out. The snow was stuck to the branches of the trees and beginning to drip off the roof as the sun melted it. They all, except Daniel, had snowshoes of various sizes and ages. Mackenzy walked around making sure the snowshoes were properly attached to everyone's shoes.

"Let's go. They're waiting,' said Ellen, from upstairs in their bedroom.

"I like to see them there. Assembled. That's our army," said Morrow.

"You're so gothic and dark. Is that your reputation as a writer, dear?"

"You flatter me."

"That's why you need me," she said.

It was true, thought Morrow, in a way.

Ellen and Morrow walked downstairs and out the front door. The wind was blustery and the clouds whipped across the sky.

"Let's go, you puppies," said Mackenzy, clapping her gloved hands together.

"Puppies?" said Sarah, scoffing.

Morrow, Daniel and Mackenzy led the way into the field, through the dilapidated open gate that had not been closed since the last of the sheep were sold about ten years before, across the rows of vines hanging on their trellises, and *across the scraggly, unmowed field reverting to forestland. Then they entered the woods themselves, where the snow was not as deep. The way became treacherous under sagging evergreens and around fallen trunks of birch and maple. Mackenzy dropped back to take part in the jokes and conversations going on between Ellen and the others. Daniel concentrated on finding his way, remembering across the frozen beaver swamp and uphill through the hemlock grove. Morrow thought fruitlessly of something to say, frozen in his desire to hold on to the past; it wasn't that he was a dark personality, it was more that he was in love with life and wanting everyone else to feel the same way and disappointed that they didn't share his secret enthusiasm.*

"Fun, isn't it," he finally said, catching up to his son working his way in the deeper snow towards the top of the hill.

"Make sure you stay behind me. We're breaking trail for the rest of them, remember?" said Daniel.

"Yeah. Just wondering if you remember the times we used to come up here when you were little."

"Of course."

That was good enough. They could have recalled together the attempt to cut a cross-country ski trail with the chain saw that kept breaking on them, or the plan for a retreat, a lodge that Daniel had drawn up at a summer program and once dreamed of building. Or Morrow's plantation of Chinese ginseng that would bring in a fortune.

"Where's your ginseng? Isn't it around here?" asked Daniel.

"Funny you should ask. I was just thinking about that. I think it was over that way," said Morrow, pointing to the north.

"It was right at the edge of our land, by the clearcut," said Daniel.

"That's right. Remember when Eddie clearcut all his trees?"

"Right before he sold it off and moved," said Daniel.

"That's right."

"What a shitty person he was," said Daniel.

"He was a piece of work, that guy."

Eddie McCutcheon. Neighbor and lifelong curmudgeon. Rest in peace. The man who had made it his life's mission to eradicate the coyotes in the Mink Hills, baiting them with poisoned cow carcasses that had killed Judd, their beloved golden retriever. He'd read Eddie's obituary recently in the free local advertising rag and had been surprised to learn he was originally from Staten Island. He had known through the grapevine that his last years had been spent in an apartment complex on Route Three in Penacook and that liver failure had caught up to him in the end. His various sons by various women were still in the area. He thought one of them lived in Tuckborough just down the highway.

They could see the twin rocks through the trees, the two erratics that loomed like giant representations of some ancient duality that ruled the woods. They had served as patient playthings for all the Morrow children and as symbols for Morrow himself of something solid and important about the family he and Ellen had engendered. They were never going away, but now he wondered what that mattered if the humans went.

Daniel reached the first rock and brushed the snow off a patch of the thick, papery lichen that covered its lower sections. Morrow caught up and put his gloved hand on the rock.

"Not too bad," said Morrow.

"It's good," said Daniel.

"I just want you to know that I am sorry," said Morrow.

"For what?" asked Daniel.

"For just generally being a not-so-great Dad."

"What are you talking about? You don't need to apologize."

"Well, I was a dick sometimes. I know that. I think it's important to acknowledge that the past wasn't always all that solid for you."

"It was okay. You don't need to apologize. You did your best."

Mackenzy and Saroj emerged from the woods about twenty yards downhill of where he and Daniel had come out. Saroj was getting stronger, able to keep up with his daughter's confident pace.

"You know, I never pardoned my own father. He wanted to hear a pardon from me before he died and I just couldn't do that for him."

"Dad, what are you talking about? Look, just write it down. It's a lot clearer when you write things down," said Daniel. "Just write me a letter or something."

"Okay, you don't want to hear about it right now, I guess."

"Not now. No," said Daniel.

"I understand," said Morrow. His heart went out to his son, in a bittersweet way. He recognized and remembered his own pain as a young man. It still lingered in the way that he could now see it reflected in Daniel. It was their way of being proud and sad at the same time. He was proud of himself and it was proud of Daniel for the ways that he was surviving. It was hard to explain. But at the same time, he wasn't satisfied with Daniel's reticence and unwillingness to hear what he had to say. All this went through his head as he stood in the snow and watched Saroj and Mackenzy approaching through the brush, picking their way around the birch saplings. It was almost a condition of being alive.

Mackenzy slipped up silently, her snowshoes squeaking. She laughed a little to herself about something, a laugh of joy and vitality she shared with Daniel.

"Fucking big ass rock," said Saroj, out of breath.

They all laughed.

"We made it," said Daniel.

"Almost as good as getting an IPO, huh?" said Morrow, looking at Saroj.

"This is the real meritocracy, sir," said Saroj, still chuckling.

"That's what I'm talking about," said Morrow.

"The whole idea is utterly inhumane," said Mackenzy.

"How inhumane, sweetie?" asked Morrow.

"We're all mediocre," said Mackenzy. "We need a national movement to restore the value of mediocrity, of plain, simple humanity."

"Fuck, yes," said Daniel.

"Well, I'm going to prove you wrong. I'm going to climb the rock," said Morrow.

"You can do it," said Daniel. "Go, Dad."

The last time he'd tried this was about twenty years ago, calculated Morrow.

He looked at Mackenzy and clapped his hands together.

"Go, Dad," Mackenzy repeated good-humoredly.

"We wish you the best, sir," said Saroj.

"Here we go. The return of Don Quijote," said Morrow.

"Use the tree," said Daniel.

"Can you give me a hand getting up to that first branch?" asked Morrow.

"Come on," said Daniel.

"I don't think I can jump up there," said Morrow.

"Ah, you used to," said Mackenzy.

"I know," said Morrow.

Morrow felt a surge of adrenalin. Daniel lifted him in a bear hug up to the branch of the hemlock growing alongside the boulder. He managed to hoist himself into the branch with a good swing of the legs followed by a twist of the shoulders. He sat in the branch red-faced, breathing heavily, surveying the faces below. Barbara, Amaya, Sarah, and Ellen came up chatting together in a single file on the trail plowed by Mackenzy and Saroj. Ellen had such an easy way about her of making people feel good. He could see that. He imagined that there were ways that he contributed to the mix, such as this show-offish stunt that he was pulling now, but it was both foolish and graceless in comparison to the social levity and straightforward generosity of Ellen. Still, here he was up the tree and there was no way to go but up or down. Or he could just stay quiet and hope nobody noticed that he was missing. This seemed like not a terrible choice.

"Come on, Dad. You can do it," said Mackenzy.

"What is the chance that he fails?" asked Saroj. He thought that Morrow couldn't hear.

"Where is he?" asked Ellen.

"Up in the tree," said Daniel, twirling his hand in the air like a dancer with castanets.

"That's not so far," said Ellen. "Jump down from there, William," she ordered.

Morrow stood on the branch. It seemed pretty strong and able to hold him. He reached gingerly upward on the trunk and held onto the broken stumps of branches. Then he looked at the rocks before him, covered in snow. There was the hint of the crevice between them. He tried to recall the moves. They included jumping into the crevice and pinning himself there and then shimmying up to the top of the right-hand boulder, which was a little flatter at the top, but now looked covered in ice where the hand hold was. It was worth a shot.

"Do you remember how to do it?" asked Daniel, breaking the stillness.

Morrow cleared his throat. "I think so," he said, regretting that his voice sounded so dry and lacking in conviction. The fact that he was never a great public speaker, the fact that he was back in familiar emotional territory was what it was all about, he thought. He leapt off the branch and fell forward towards the rock. His foot seemed to catch, but he was unable to properly grip anything in the snow-filled crevice. As he rebounded backwards into thin air, he felt his foot stick and his body go upside down. There was a crack he heard before anything. The snow was clearly not enough to cushion him against the concussive force on the back of his head of the rock outcropping.

When he came to, he was being shuttled downhill in the crotch formed by the arms of Daniel and Sarah, with Mackenzy and Saroj ready to take over from them, lunging along the path they had trod earlier.

"Woah, woah," said Morrow.

By the time they got him to the edge of the trees, Morrow had slipped free and was able to hobble the last few yards, over the snowbank left by the plough trucks and onto the road.

Ellen drove down the road in the car and stopped. Daniel held the door open, and Morrow awkwardly got into the car. The pain in the back of his head was just beginning to be apparent. Sarah climbed in beside him and held something against the back of his head.

"Lean forward, Dad," she said.

"Is it still bleeding? he asked.

"I can't tell," she said.

Sarah, Morrow and Ellen drove down the highway to the CMC in Manchester. Ellen drove the car, with Sarah and Morrow in the back. Sarah asked Ellen to switch to Bluetooth and shared some of her music. Ellen flashed her ID at the desk and they proceeded up in the elevator to the internal medicine section. Ellen had phoned ahead to the personal cell phone of

Dr. Mora, who was the internist on duty. He was in his office in jeans and a polo shirt, looking fit and tanned.

"Don't you guys wear scrubs any more?" joked Morrow, as Mora looked at the back of his head under the surgical lamp.

"Not on weekends any more," said Mora.

"Just business casual, huh?" said Morrow.

Ellen and Sarah said they were going down to the cafeteria. Morrow asked them to bring him something.

It was just him and the doctor.

"Merry Christmas. Looks like you're going to need four or five stitches. Nothing too drastic," said Mora.

"You going to shave my head?" asked Morrow.

"I don't think so. Do you want me to?"

"Yeah, I was hoping for a little something dramatic," said Morrow.

"Sorry about that," said Mora.

"Tufts, huh?" said Morrow.

"Yeah."

"Been practicing here long?" asked Morrow.

"About six years now," said the doctor, cutting Morrow's hair and then prepping the area with swabs.

"What's that?" asked Morrow.

"Just some antibiotic ointment. Next I'll apply some topical anesthetic," said the doctor.

"How'd you do it?" he asked.

"Climbing a rock," said Morrow.

"I was going to guess maybe pond hockey."

"No. Never did play hockey. You did, I bet," said Morrow. He watched Mora closely as he prepared the needle and other materials on a tray across the room

"Yes, a little youth hockey growing up. Not good enough for college, though."

"Yeah. Our son was going to play but I pulled him out. He was a great little skater. Tough as nails."

"Why was that?"

"Didn't want to have to pay for all three kids. It was fine. They grew up snowboarding in the winter and playing soccer in the summer and fall. We don't really get a spring, so that was our hiking season."

"Sounds good. We like to hike."

"Yeah, I got into coaching soccer through my first teaching job. I found out, guess what, I love coaching kids."

"Oh, I didn't know you had taught. I don't think Ellen's mentioned that part of your resume."

"Yeah, probably not. "

"We send our two boys to Bedford High. You know they built the new high school. But the hockey team plays at Tri-Town."

"I didn't know that."

"Yeah, it's a decent rink. Nice place to watch the home games."

"Very nice place," said Morrow, remembering the new high school in Bedford with its international baccalaureate programs and its brand new artificial turf athletic fields, where Daniel and Mackenzy had played against those kids through the years. Sarah had been a theater nerd. He wondered why he was telling Mora about all this. He wondered if what made him run off at the mouth was the same thing that made him jump for the rock. What if he never figured it out? Suddenly the doctor's office seemed a prefigurement of much worse horrors. Mora asked him if he felt anything. He didn't.

He was aware of the needle and of the doctor moving his hands over the back of his head. Sarah and Ellen appeared at the door.

"Almost done here," said Mora. Ellen approached and exchanged commentary with Mora about the suture and the size of the cut.

"Looks very clean, dear. Javier has done a great job," said Ellen.

"I would expect so," said Morrow.

Then they were done. The stitches were self absorbing. Mora prescribed some antibiotics. Ellen took care of the paperwork. They were walking away to the door.

"Nice meeting you finally, William," said Mora.

"Hey, good luck with everything," said Morrow. "Really appreciate it."

"Anytime. Stay away from those nasty rocks."

"Yes. Of course. Happy holidays," said Morrow.

"Merry Christmas, Javier. Say hello to Anita, Billy, and Ryan," said Ellen.

Morrow shook the doctor's hand, making sure to give as good a grip as he got. He would never regret that. Sarah said goodbye. Ellen waved, smiled one last time, and they were standing at the bank of elevators just outside the office.

"Nice guy. Dr. Mora," said Morrow. He was sitting in the passenger seat. Ellen was driving. She drove slowly and methodically on the icy roads. Sarah sat in back with earbuds in, listening to her playlist and reading something, possibly a legal brief on her phone. Ellen didn't answer, but smiled at him. He knew he would never bring up the name again, so he said it to himself.

"Dr. Mora," he said.

"Dear, why don't you think of a good movie we can all watch."

"I thought you said that was a bad idea."

"I've changed my mind," said Ellen.

Sarah reached over and tapped him on the shoulder.

"Hey, Dad. Here's the chocolate bar you wanted."

"What did you get me?"

"Reese's. Isn't that your favorite?"

"That is indeed."

Morrow ate his chocolate bar while the twilight came on through the windshield, above the trees, plowing the dark blue heavens in bands of violets and oranges. He had his prize, only wasn't sure he ever deserved it.

"Thank you, Sarah."

"What?"

"That was the nicest Christmas present."

"Just relax, Dad. Should we listen to some music?" asked Sarah.

"Good idea," said Ellen, glancing in the rear view mirror.

When they got home it was dark. Morrow got out of the car unsteadily, but climbed up the steps to the house before the two women. The inside was ablaze with lights. There was music playing. The front door opened before he could get to it. It was Saroj and Barbara. Barbara stepped past him to greet Sarah with a hug.

"So, are you okay, sir?" asked Saroj.

"I think so," said Morrow.

"We took care of the chickens, sir. They are all gathered in their little house."

"Thank you, Saroj."

Sarah and Barbara came up the steps with Ellen. They all went in together. Some sort of ranchera music was playing in the kitchen off the Bluetooth speaker. Everyone else was there in the kitchen cooking and drinking. Morrow thought it was another undeserved bit of grace to come home to such a festive scene. He took off his shoes while leaning on Ellen, who had already done the same.

"We should really have a little bench here of some sort," said Morrow.

"I've been telling you that. Why don't you make one like you always say you will," said Ellen.

"Maybe I will," said Morrow.

214

Amaya was teaching everyone how to dance the cumbia. Mackenzy handed him a glass with something in it.

"It's punch, Dad."

"Did you use the Cointreau or the rum?"

"A little of both."

"Good girl," said Morrow, taking a sip.

They ate tortillas stuffed with mushrooms, guacamole, and ground beef, and watched Dr. Zhivago at Morrow's suggestion. After the movie finished, it was late.

Most had gone up to bed except for Daniel and Amaya, who instead had gone for a walk up the road after the plough truck had gone by for the last time. Morrow and Ellen were in the bathroom together. Ellen brushed her teeth with that recognizable vigor that came from a childhood in the affluent Connecticut suburbs.

"What are you thinking dear?"

"Just admiring your tooth brushing, Ellen. After all these years you're still hammering away in there with the vigor of a child."

"Well, I don't want to lose my teeth. Do you?"

"No."

"Well then, brush your teeth," said Ellen.

Morrow sighed. "I'm not tired," he said.

"What's the sigh for?" she asked.

"I don't know."

"Did you like the movie?" she asked.

"Yes, I always like that movie."

"They lived in interesting times, didn't they?"

"So do we," said Morrow.

"I've always felt that our country was insulated from all that European drama, don't you think?"

"We carry it in our blood."

"That's so dark and brooding, dear. That's what's attractive about you, I guess."

"I don't know why," said Morrow, rolling out a spread of toothpaste on his brush. But Ellen wasn't done yet. She stood in the doorway to the bathroom, her hips just showing under the nightdress.

"Do you think our family is like theirs?" she asked.

"No, but it seems to be expanding. That's always good," answered Morrow.

"Well. Don't count your chickens," said Ellen.

"True. But I can't help it. I feel like this is my night. The expanding man. I cried when I wrote that song," quoted Morrow.

"Sue me if I play too long?" she asked.

"Yes."

"Which one is that?"

"Deacon Blues," said Morrow.

"That's an oldie but a goodie," said Ellen.

"Like us," said Morrow.

Morrow brushed his teeth and took his prostate supplements. He looked at his reflection and saw an old man with hair that clumped on the back of his head as if the wind was blowing. He felt the stitches. He'd taken a hit for the team. There was only one place that offered a refuge from the storm of mortality, and that was his bed. Morrow tucked himself in and pulled up the various covers and quilts with which they had kept themselves warm through many cold nights. He listened carefully, once his heart had slowed and his breathing stilled, to the sounds of the night and the creaking old house. He kept turning over trying to get comfortable.

"What's wrong?" asked Ellen, turning over towards his side of the bed.

'I don't know. Too much excitement, I guess," said Morrow.

"You need to do yoga or something," she said.

'I guess," he said.

"What are you thinking?"

"Oh, not much, really," said Morrow.

"I think one of your problems, dear, is you do much of your thinking when you write. So you don't really feel the need to share with others," said Ellen. She sat up in the bed and stared down at him concernedly as if at a child. Morrow stayed in a fetal position under the covers.

"Maybe."

"So we just, it's a one way service. We're there to keep you happy but we don't really get the sense that you need us. I think I can speak for the kids as well as myself, William."

"That's very true. I need to share more. Maybe stop writing as much."

"What else are you thinking?"

"I'm getting old. It's cold," said Morrow.

Ellen took pity on him at last and snuggled against his back with her back. He turned over towards her one last time, feeling the bounty of her with his hand, and fell asleep.

Theta

Antioch stepped out of the self-driving transporter at the curb of the busy intersection. The walk was lined with the stubs of young breathing trees genetically designed for the Martian atmosphere. They looked like the willows Antioch remembered growing along the riverbanks of his youth on Earth. He hardly thought of those days anymore. Here in Novaroma he could feel like he'd gained for himself a place in the expanding world of the Martian capital after the initial turbulence in the lower ranks of the OneWorld Analysis Service, made up mostly by captive Earthlings like himself that had proved adept at channeling the life force of the planet. He did not like looking back in time, though. Bounding up the steps to the building's entrance, he appeared to be one of the capital's successful elites powering forward with the entrusted secret agenda, the blueprint for eventual transhumanist expansion throughout the Lainakean cloud.

"Hello, boss. Give us a look," said one of the derelict looking bunch of Universal Benefits recipients, the UBers who made a living engaging with the Nurvalink at volunteer centers, paid by the hour for their drug induced rants and what were termed "living art works", arranged around the entrance of the building as if they'd been posed by some producer intending to convey an idea of Martian inequality. In exchange for feeding the web with the uploaded sensory lived experience of rover and bohemian subcultures, a sort of yeast-like additive to the standard language model interface, they were tolerated out on the streets of the capital but memory-holed, excluded from official versions of OneWorld society such as the yearly reports of the Novaroma Executive Cabinet. Antioch not only sensed their utility, but he also knew that among them were former associates of his from the old days in Svyatogor. Nevertheless, he chose to look away when called out by personal interaction, just smiled above their heads and strode past in a stilled emotional pattern like holding your breath. He had made it.

Nobody could take that away from him. He reminded himself of the sacrifices, the long, solitary season in the frozen cave of the Tharsis, the years of struggling in the analysis trenches, renting a series of dingy, lightless rooms in the suburbs of Novaroma, eventually recognized and promoted to managerial status. The strain on his subconscious was the price he'd paid for admission to the upper echelons of comfort and prestige.

The elevator glided seamlessly aloft as music holograms played off the walls featuring the synthetic creations of the OneWorld's Ministry of Communication, vivid, fantastical elements that reminded Antioch of the music videos favored by his mother and her friends back in the Midwestern trailer towns of his childhood. It was funny how now similar productions constituted the living shell of respectability and stability projected by the governmental body tasked with influencing the morale and life quality of the Martian people. But that was how history worked, constantly twisting and turning on itself in some kind of self-assembling mechanism.

Sakumi answered the door, peering around the edge of it as if hiding something from the world. It was one of the standard patterns she and Antioch engaged in, pretending somehow they were illegitimate and counterfeit in their status.

"Open immediately," said Antioch, playing along.

"What have we done, sir?" asked Sakumi in a childlike treble.

"Too much fun," said Antioch.

Sakumi giggled and opened the door to reveal herself in a glimmering, opaque kimono. Behind her in the red and green neon of party lights could be seen her friends and family gathered for her birthday. Antioch smiled and took out the box in his pocket, wrapped in real old-fashioned paper. It was a genuine synthetic Martian diamond necklace with tungsten spirals made by a startup called FabLab, but they really did a decent job, thought Antioch. Sakumi smiled in delight as she opened the box eagerly and tried it on.

"Here," said Antioch, taking it in his hands. She spun slowly around and he moved her blonde hair out of the way before fastening the clasp on the back of her slender neck.

"Looks great," he said as she turned around again to face him.

"Sakumi. Where are you, sweetheart?" It was her mother, Moonga Verdad, the former Vice-Minister of Communication under the regime of Novaroma's former mayor Stanley Mishustin that had immediately preceded the current administration of Zealand Mandelson. Moonga was dressed in flowing red and blue robes, the colors of OneWorld's premier post secondary education establishment, the University of West Mars where she taught courses in psychology and nanotechnology. She had a glass in one hand.

"Oh, it's you Antioch. You're late but never mind," she said. "Will you be staying for the music later?"

"Well, yes. I wouldn't want to miss any of Sakumi's big night," said Antioch, weary of having to defend his presence at family events. Despite her reputation as a silver-tongued administrator, Moonga could never find the wherewithal to hide her disappointment in Sakumi's choice of a non-indigenous older man to fall in love with – only six years after completing her degree work in theoretical physics at the U of West Mars under the tutelage of the finest academics of the inter-planetary consensus.

"No, of course not," said Moonga.

It wasn't only that she found Antioch a disappointment socially. He suspected that she didn't trust his mental soundness. This despite his glowing work referrals which were a matter of public record. Antioch felt unsettled by her presence and inquisitorial attitude, displayed not so much with her choice of words as by her lack of them, the double meaning attending so many of her silences and sparse comments. Sakumi did not like to talk about it and Antioch mostly ignored it.

A little bit of drama would not stand in his way. Sakumi was everything he could ask for in a future wife. The idea of starting a family with her in Novaroma was a soothing antidote to the question of belonging that had hung over him for so long and had portended an uncertain future in Martian post-colonial society. During these recent months he had started to not only accept, but value this new Martian world where he apparently had found a niche. The OneWorld's authoritarian template was giving way to a more benign and tolerant rule, it seemed to Antioch, just as his own rise was beginning to take shape in the merit-based civil service. But he couldn't shake the doubts and self-defeating moods that sometimes rocked his certainty and focus.

"Ah yes, the man of the hour," said a bearded man standing against the snack bar. His benign smile and impeccable suit buttoned up under his chin were the marks of Martian respectability. His name escaped Antioch. He knew it was a family friend of the Verdad's he had met on former occasions, and he struggled to remember the man's name. Sakumi's father stood on the other side of this man in the crowded living room of the penthouse apartment. He was dressed less formally and stood silently, appraising the gathering under lidded eyes..

Antioch smiled back and reached beyond the two older men to a plate of crusted crabs. He grabbed one claw and popped it into his mouth.

"Delicious, aren't they?" asked the bearded man. His name suddenly came to Antioch. Dr. Clough, dean of the faculty of vocational arts. Antioch chewed and smiled.

"They really are, Dr. Clough," he said finally.

"Green crab. A remarkable species. Farmed as you know in our UWM facilities."

"No, I did not know that," said Antioch. "I'd love to learn more, though."

"Oh yes. I was on the board in those years, do you remember, Murson?"

Murson Verdad, Sakumi's father, just stared in response. He was a man of few words. Antioch suspected there was some mental decline despite the Nurvalink hardwire updates that he must have received semi-annually as part of his wife's benefits package.

"You like snacks," Murson drawled, directing himself pointedly to Antioch.

"Certainly, yes," said Antioch. "Excuse me. These look wonderful as well," he added as he reached for some breaded champignons. Before he could turn back to the party, though, Murson had stepped up.

"Sakumi tells me you're doing all right for yourself. I'm not so sure," he said.

"I don't know what to tell you, sir," said Antioch, chewing swiftly and swallowing hard.

"Do you like her?"

"I love her," said Antioch.

"You think that's good enough?"

"No," said Antioch, swallowing again. "It's just a word. I intend to prove it, though."

"You haven't been approved for the list," said Murson, glaring under his prominent brows. He was referring to the list of permanent residents approved by the Advisory Board of Local Settlement, ABLS. Antioch had made an application for permanent status but had not yet been granted an initial review.

"Well, my referrals are all there. I'm in line for managerial rank, sir. With all due respect," said Antioch, beginning to get a little hot under the collar. He looked around the room, catching Sakumi's eye. She broke away from a knot of friends and made her way slowly through the crowd.

"Here's what I think, Antioch. You're using us for your advantage," hissed Murson.

"That's not fair, sir. You don't know me well enough to say that," said Antioch.

"Murson has always been inclined to speak his mind freely," said Dr. Clough. "Fortunately for you, our daughters have their pick of the litter once they reach the age of majority," he added.

"I don't think of myself as part of any litter," said Antioch.

"No, of course not. You're not a puppy by any means, Mister Littell. It's a manner of speech, of course we do know about his good work, Murson, as a research subhead at the policy analysis team. And before that, I believe in the, uh, experimental program conducting energy expansion."

"Dolomite Project," said Antioch, sounding bored.

"Yes. That's right. Some good came of it, I presume."

"One of the more successful programs of the Svyatogor Security Commission," said Antioch.

"Oh, really? I was unaware."

"I'm pretty sure it's been instrumental in unlocking solar expansion and growing the protective greenhouse layer of our Martian atmosphere," said Antioch.

"That's true. But please understand that we must carefully withhold judgement on all settlement seekers until we have credentials approved. As an Earth immigrant, actually a prisoner of the Kraken command, you are not a native Nurvalink subscriber. And so, we don't have any idea, sir, what has been your formation or how deep the roots of dissent and unrest might have lain in your past," said Dr. Clough.

It was a drastic take on his character, was Antioch's immediate thought. There was a presumption of harm instead of an expectation of growth. It was the problem with the Martian regime. Cut off from its roots and dependent on outdated algorithms, it would always have a hard time switching to a model that trusted human capabilities, and the Nurvalink's decline across the interplanetary noosphere was the inevitable result. But pointing that out would have been deemed a subversive act. Besides, Sakumi was on his shoulder, about to say something. It was true that he had not had a Nurvalink assessment in several years and had managed to just ignore the recommendations that had been served to his various addresses. Oversight of the Nurvalink had been so thoroughly self-directed that he didn't think there was anybody, at least on Mars, who had a good overall picture of any individual's status. If the authorities suspected ongoing criminality they could request a review before the Attorneys General of the Homelands. And the metadata was always there.

"There you are. What are you doing?" she asked.

"Just talking," said Antioch.

"Talking? About what?" asked Sakumi.

"About your birthday. Your father was saying how nice it was to have all your friends here," said Antioch.

"Yeah, right," said Sakumi. "Dad? Are we having fun?"

"I'm good," grumbled Murson, turning and saying something inaudible to his friend, Dr. Clough.

"Come with me. I want to show you something," said Sakumi. She took Antioch by the hand and led him to the back of the room. Here was a window looking out at the interior courtyard of the building. They both stared out the window. Sakumi looked swiftly over her shoulder to make sure there was nobody watching or listening.

"We need to talk."

"About?"

"Not here."

Sakumi seemed stressed about something.

"What's wrong?" asked Antioch. Sakumi didn't want to be overheard.

"The roof," whispered Sakumi, leaning close and kissing Antioch.

"Sakumi?" It was her friend Carlisle, appearing behind her. Sakumi turned to her.

Carlisle was one of Sakumi's former classmates at UWM. She was engaged to a prominent young jurist of the Homelands Coordinate. Antioch knew this from a conversation he'd had earlier that week, going over the list of birthday party attendees with Sakumi on the roof of the building in the morning before work. They'd watched over the wall as Murson and Moonga left the building and walked across the park, their usual morning routine. Moonga had walked five or six paces ahead of Murson, impatiently turning and waiting for him at the edge of the avenue. Antioch had commented something about the obvious fact that Moonga and Murson did not seem to be in a very cordial relationship with each other, despite the successful lives they projected for all their Novaroma circle.

"Carlisle, dear, let's go up and check out the roof. And see if the soundscape is working up there," said Sakumi loudly enough to be overheard. She smiled at Antioch, and the two women walked back into the main room. Antioch watched as they wove through the growing crowd of partygoers, while he leaned back against the wall. A bearded young man approached and stood next to him.

"Looks like things are going well," said the man, in a confidential tone. Antioch studied his face as he looked around.

"Yes. Not bad," said Antioch.

"Good food and drink. Good people. I'm with the Transport Ministry. Joost Vangeelstrom."

"Antioch Littell."

Yes, I know. Sakumi's boyfriend. You are with?"

"Research and Public Health," said Antioch.

"Ah, yes. I remember that now," said Joost.

"Excuse me. I need to find somebody," mumbled Antioch. He moved off, leaving Joost behind.

He proceeded swiftly through the crowd, avoiding eye contact with anybody he knew, smiling vaguely at the conversations swirling around him, and once out in the hall, found the door leading to the stairwell.

The sky was empty. Usually there were slogans beaming on the exonet, word salads pleasingly reassuring to the residents of Novaroma, confirming and affirming the three principles of Order, Stability, and Pleasure, which were all that the citizens needed and demanded, according to OneWorld's ruling platforms. But not tonight. The sky was empty due to oversight, or perhaps just some vestigial need for an exercise of the imagination.

Antioch could see the dim outline of the nanotube grid as it accumulated the detritus of fluorides and benzenes, products of atmospheric filtration, against the light of Deimos rising to the east. He sighed to himself, appreciative of the quiet and the panorama spreading outwards, the city in all its lit-up glory. Sakumi parted from beside Carlisle, two wraiths across the roof standing against the edge. She came closer, revealing her downcast expression.

"What's wrong?" asked Antioch as she held out her arms and hugged him.

She didn't say anything.

"Is it the projection? Is the visual working?" Sometimes it stalled and got stuck. The cabling had some problems with earthing in certain parts of the city. But he knew he was wrong to have suggested it. There was something else bothering her.

"It's your birthday," he reminded her.

"I know," she said.

"Why aren't you enjoying it?"

"I can't be tonight. The council has proposed an Earth Program."

"What is that?" Antioch had never heard of an Earth Program.

"Young leaders formation," said Sakumi, making it sound portentous and overblown. "Take three years and work for OneWorld constituent services in some godforsaken corner like Kazakhstan or Abu Dhabi."

"Doing what?" asked Antioch.

Sakumi gave him a quick glance of annoyance.

"Oh, anything. It doesn't matter."

"Sorry."

"They make it sound nice, Antioch. Analysis. Or Research. Make Power Ups or what have you. Just silly. Busy work, more junk matter for the Nurvalink to train on. Of no use to anybody."

"I am sorry. That sounds bad."

"I know. You were just inquiring."

"Just want to know."

"It's nothing."

"But. It's a stepping stone to leadership, right? What you wanted. It's what you've trained for."

"Leadership? Do you think it's what I want? Do you know me at all?"

Sakumi had undergone a transformation. It was dangerous for her and implicated him as well. She was starting to think without limits. Outside the box. There was a point beyond which she might be straying. Novaroma society was tolerant, but once the tolerance levels were breached, it could be a death sentence if it became categorical. Measures would be taken that would render her pliable. Oxygen would be choked out of her by the filtration, slowing her mental capabilities over time and cutting off her ability to communicate. He had heard of cases, rebellious spirits whose visible marks of status in clothing, demeanor, or lifestyle were slowly stripped away, whose ties to family and friends withered, and eventually the only paths left to them were either on the Universal Benefits as a living artist or as a displaced person. In these cases, the displacement would be deemed voluntary. Sakumi's lifespan and her utility would be sucked out of her by force majeure. Where that left him was an idea he didn't even want to think about.

"What's gotten into you? Where is your common sense, Sakumi? You're the one who says if society's not swimming it's drowning. Do you want to drown? I can't let you do that. What about us?"

"Us? What, are we supposed to communicate via the noosphere for three years? Or will you apply to come to Earth as my companion?"

"Sure, I don't know. Maybe."

Sakumi shook her head.

"What do you see here? It's dead. It's already drowned. It will be the same on Earth under OneWorld, Antioch. Have you lost your ideals? What's happened to you?"

"What about us, though? I thought we wanted to build a fortress. We wanted to be there on the other side. Do you not believe in that future anymore? We can still do that. I've paid my dues. I've survived. They can't touch me now. I want to live, Sakumi!"

"It's no good. I can't hide any longer. This is it. I have to choose. Do you understand?"

"No, I don't. I thought I knew you. I can't let you do this. Take this path of refusal. I can't. Where does it lead?"

Sakumi had him by the shirt. She was grabbing his shirt under the neck as if she would choke him. Carlisle was starting to approach across the deck of the roof.

"I don't know where it leads," she hissed. "But I can't live a lie. You taught me that. We can't do that."

"What if I go to Earth? I can apply for something or other."

"How would that work? They would know. That would give it away. It's counter to the point of the whole thing. This is their work. Murson and Moonga, Antioch. They want to split us up. I already turned it down."

"What?"

"I rejected the offer."

"Does anyone know?"

"No."

"Then it's not too late. You can delete the response. You have time."

"No more time. Here comes Carlisle. We pretend nothing has happened. Tonight we dance, Antioch. Put away your hopes. We need a higher purpose, and now we will find one."

Sakumi pushed herself away. Antioch felt the lifeless grip of fear overtake him. He had made the mistake of putting all of himself into a new sense of accommodation to fate and power, of possibility, a life of comfort and status with Sakumi as the linchpin holding it all together, and now he had nowhere to turn. Sakumi had pulled the pin. The explosion would follow as sure as the solar winds, blowing up any possibility of riding the OneWorld's rocket of galactic destiny. All for the sake of the poetic, outdated Earthling notions he had fed her. He knew he was to blame, enflaming her imagination, wooing her with subtle hints of defiant thoughts and words of transcendent individuality and Universal soul. This is where that led, this moment of entrapment and capture. Once again Antioch was fighting to breathe, to stay calm as the walls closed in.

The night was lit up by the music, a wall of sound and light that formed a bubble over the building in the Verdad's upscale Novaroma neighborhood. Under the bubble, dancing bodies glided and swayed. The soundscape's energy profile aligned the orbitofrontal cortex and enhanced hypothalamic oxygen levels. Bodies, lights, and sound fused in a fluid wave of sensory existence that blocked out egocentric thoughts.

It was a success. Afterwards Moonga and Murson and a small group of their friends toasted their daughter with glass bowls of Martian vermouth, concocted in the food and drink laboratories of the UWM. Antioch stood on the edge of the knot of people on the roof of the Verdad's building, looking over their heads to the lights of the city. They were dimmed and going out, leaving just the febrile glow of the exonet hanging in the air. He felt his heart hardening again, preparing for hardships to come. He hadn't thought it was possible to once more take on the furtive air of the covert world that had once, long ago, been all he believed in.

"To our Sakumi, our hopes and dreams. She will go out and live her beauty and reflect her goodness for the glory of Mars and our family legacy," said Moonga, raising her glass bowl to the air.

"Yoohoo!" hooted Carlisle, standing next to Antioch. The crowd of people, neighbors, friends, most of them connected and made good in the administrative state, clapped and cheered like young UBers. Antioch turned. Sakumi glanced at him, her eyes sparkling with secret light as she made visual contact.

"To my friends, especially my special friend, who alway inspires me and stands by me to live my truth," said Sakumi. Antioch's heart swelled.

Slowly they all drifted away. The only people left on the roof were Sakumi, Antioch, Moonga, Murson, Carlisle, and Joost Vangeelstrom. It must have almost been dawn. Deimos melted away on the horizon to the south. Antioch had no idea what Joost's role was in the gathering. But it didn't really matter. Whatever was to unfold would be. Moonga and Murson faced them with blank, open hostility, as if they were obstacles rather than people.

"Whatever good you think this choice brings, I'm here to tell you to rethink it, dear," said Moonga.

"It's no good. You should have consulted with me," said Sakumi, with a downcast, contrite expression.

"What? Are you accusing us of somehow conspiring to have this foisted on you? This, the greatest level you've reached, to be selected for the Earth Program? The creme de la creme! How can you even think to question it?"

"Because I think. That's why. I'm your daughter. You taught me to think for myself, to use reason to discern the consensus opinion and chart a path forward," said Sakumi.

"Well, you have gone astray," said Murson. "That's my consensus."

Sakumi began to cry.

"It's okay, Sakumi," said Murson.

"No, it's not okay," said Moonga.

"Surely..." began Carlisle, hoping to say something to assuage, to help Sakumi's cause.

"Silence!" cried Moonga.

"You can apply for deletion of response. We've all done that before," said Carlisle in a whisper, standing behind Antioch and Sakumi.

"This is not a time for debate. Not a time for overthinking. It is time to do your duty, Sakumi. It's an order, do you understand? Antioch can wait. He will be here on Mars working away, proving his loyalty to the galactic project. It's what would be expected in any case before a marriage can take place," said Moonga with a flourish of reasonableness and matronly good sense.

"Mother," sniffled Sakumi. "May I remind you that I turned twenty-five today. I don't take orders from anybody."

"What about you, Antioch?" asked Moonga.

"I'm okay with it. I can wait, if it's what Sakumi decides," he said.

"Of course it's what she will decide," said Moonga. "Let's go downstairs. The night is getting old," she added, holding out her hand to Murson. The two of them proceeded to the stairwell and disappeared back inside the building.

"How could you say that?" asked Sakumi angrily.

"I had to," said Antioch.

"You should have stuck up for me," she said.

It was no use trying to make amends. Sakumi was too traumatized by the situation to react reasonably, he thought. Carlisle and Joost joined Sakumi and Antioch going down the stairs in silence. They exited the building onto the darkened streets of Novaroma. Only a few UBers sitting stonily in the doorways were there to witness what was happening at that hour of the early morning. There was just a hint of purplish light in the eastern sky behind the foursome as they walked two abreast along the empty sidewalk of Kepler Avenue.

"I'm with you, of course Sakumi," insisted Antioch.

"I don't even know if I can trust you now," said Sakumi. "Nobody understands me."

"I understand you. But Sakumi, what's the alternative here on Mars? If we were on Earth there would be places to, I don't know, to get away for long periods of time, to gather strength while we figured out what to do. That's not possible here, not that I know of. We either comply or we risk relegation."

"I don't care anymore," said Sakumi. "I'm fed up. All my life there has been no alternative. Do you know what that's like? No you don't because you are not a Martian. You're an immigrant. The immigrants always make the worst sort of Martians."

"Look, that's not me. You don't know me," said Antioch.

"No, I don't. It's true. I thought I did. Now I'm not sure. Antioch, who are you?"

They were stopped on the corner of Keppler and Maykel Distinto, both of them hollow, empty of traffic. Looking down the long miles of uniform block buildings to the north,

Antioch felt a sudden sense of vertigo. He had to lock in. Explain himself to the one person who counted the most, the key to his heart.

"Look, I've been a soldier on Earth for the Democratic Alliance, Sakumi. I've worked covert to undermine the Kraken and OneWorld rule; I've been a prisoner in the psyop program in Tharsis. I won my freedom."

"Really? Tharsis?" asked Joost. "I didn't know that," he added.

"Yes, that's right. The campaign to channel the Dolomite. And now, everything I've fought for, everything that I want is here. In Novaroma with you. You are my last chance of happiness, Sakumi. I won't give it up without a fight. Think before you leap. For both of us."

"Novaroma is so corrupt," said Sakumi. Carlisle nodded.

"It's soul crushing," said Carlisle.

"How can you? How can you want me to settle for that?" asked Sakumi

"It's life. We can be alive. We can exist. It's peace. There's room, there's hope for better."

"That's the bait they use to trap us."

"But it's reality based. The alternative is a fight to breathe, a losing fight to even breathe. Is that a wager you're willing to take, the probability of losing your right to breathe? How long can we resist? Look, let's go to Earth. I can apply for companion status if we get your parents to sign on as witnesses to the application."

"No, not my parents. You heard and saw what they think of me. I won't go for their permission. That's not reality-based," said Sakumi.

"Well, I don't see any other way," said Antioch.

"There is another way," said Joost.

They turned to Joost to gauge his words and his expression. Antioch thought it was strange of this man to even be there, but suddenly he was listening to every word he said and trying to tell if they were genuine. Joost's eyes were empty of guile, calm as he looked at them one by one, until he was sure they were listening carefully.

"My parents have the greenhouse, right?" said Joost.

Sakumi and Carlisle nodded as if they knew what he was talking about. Joost turned to Antioch to explain.

"They work in the seed program, genetic engineers. Well, they've managed to get access to an unused greenhouse that only a few of us know about. They grow their own heirloom seeds. It's fun. A harmless enough hobby. Nobody cares."

"Okay," said Antioch.

"They sit there in the summer and relax for hours. It's probably illegal. But it's warm, private, and safe for now, for another month or so. You could stay there. Carlisle and I can keep you fed. In the meantime, you contact the underground. Put out feelers, careful to gain the trust of the street. I'm sure you can do it. If you have the time and can keep from getting caught."

"Yeah, because once you don't show up for work," said Carlisle.

"No, before that. By tomorrow morning when I don't come back. Moonga will be on the necks of the Homelands," said Sakumi. "They will stop everything to find us, are you kidding? What do you think, Antioch?"

"Sure, we don't even have time to think, if that's how we go," said Antioch.

"If we want to do it, it has to be now. Can you take us, Joost?" asked Sakumi.

"I can take you there now, but we have to go via the tunnels," said Joost.

The tunnels were the original dwellings of the first colonizers, the joint Russo Starlink mission. They'd been used as waste pits for the last few generations, until new modular incineration plants had gone up in the Mishustin administration. Occasionally there were reports of youth pranks involving tunnel escapades. Sometimes they ended badly with inhalation of persistent bioaccumulative toxins that needed genetic remediation. It was enough to keep the collective memory of the tunnels alive as a fearful reminder of outdated byways. Even the UBers avoided them unless they were desperate.

"Do you know your way in the tunnels?" asked Antioch.

"Of course. My father has the maps," said Joost. "We've been using them for years."

"Joost has always been a little strange," said Sakumi. She and Carlisle laughed.

"That's a lot of secrets for this little group. Are we sure about this step we're taking? It's going to be dangerous for all of us. We could choose a safer path," said Antioch, the voice of caution. He was definitely getting old, he thought.

"We've always wanted this, Antioch," said Sakumi.

"We've been talking about it all our lives, it seems. Topple this monstrous world that's being built. Take it down and try again," said Joost.

"How am I the last to know?" asked Antioch.

"We always knew you were in," said Sakumi.

"The hell you did. I didn't even know that," said Antioch.

Joost led the way along backstreets that paralleled and cross cut the main avenue. In an alleyway, he stopped and looked around before pointing to a staircase winding up the wall of a nondescript warehouse.

"There's the cover," he said. The four of them hurried along the alleyway.

Pedestrians seemed to burst from the buildings along the avenue. Traffic had picked up. The manhole was under the dogleg of the stairs, hidden under a layer of dusty basalt fiber and hematites that had not been sucked clean by the municipal street cleaners. Carlisle and Sakumi sat casually on the stairs. Antioch and Joost squeezed between the railing and the wall. Joost unzipped his coat and with a practiced deftness removed a bar he carried around his neck. He used it to pry under the edge of the cover. As Joost pushed under the edge, Antioch lifted the cover higher with his boot and pushed it clattering over onto the pavement. It was barely wide enough for a body to squeeze through. Peering down the hole, Antioch could see nothing but blackness. A vaporous cloud of red dust swirled around the hole. Carlisle and Sakumi gathered around him.

"We'll have to go down one at a time. I'll go first," said Joost, turning on the light of the transponder on his wrist. The others followed his example.

Antioch went last, pulling the manhole cover behind him overhead before he began his climb down, using grips set in along the wall of the manhole for his feet and hands.

They descended for a good long time in darkness and silence. Antioch counted the holds and stopped after six hundred. That was about half the distance. He calculated a couple thousand feet of descent. The lights of the transponders below him lit up radiuses of the wall of ice and rock they climbed down before hitting the bottom. Still in silence at the bottom, they watched Joost.

He stopped pacing. They were at a junction of two tunnels. They all shivered, unprepared for the cold into which they'd been plunged. The air smelled stale, like an old freezer unit that had not been emptied for a long time.

"We'll run to stay warm. Is everyone okay with that?" asked Joost. They all nodded, holding their transponder lights up to see each other's faces.

"I must warn you, don't look around. What you see will be horrifying if you look around. Just keep your eyes on the person ahead of you," he said.

"Let's do it," said Sakumi. Carlisle turned her light on her friend. They all shone their lights on her face.

"This is for you," said Antioch.

"Thank you," Sakumi whispered.

Joost set out at a good pace and they fell in line behind him. Antioch brought up the rear of their line. Their way was often blocked by piles of assorted waste heaps which Joost picked his way carefully through. There were stacks of unrotted human carcasses, recognizable limbs sticking out, somber fleshy skulls with scraps of hair. They brushed past, lights flashing on the ghoulish remains. Antioch imagined these were casualties of digging accidents, probably Earth prisoners with nobody to bother about proper burial. The OneWorld colony was famed for bypassing certain long held taboos as earthen folk custom not worth keeping.

Otherwise the heaps consisted of tons of old tools and utensils, food waste and plastic wrappings, some even with lettering from the old Earth heartland. The walls of the tunnel were propped up with steel ribbing against the sagging of ice and rock that seemed to bulge at certain forks. Sometimes they climbed, sometimes descended, and there were points where Joost paused momentarily to get his bearings and catch his breath. Lights flashing, they stood again and continued to pick their way through the tunnel maze. At certain points, the walls wept, moisture gleaming on them. The acrid scent of rotting flesh hit their nostrils. They could hear the hum of generators pumping heated water from underground melt. The geothermal system kept Novaroma warm under the bubble of the exonet. The warmth from the nearby piping was enough to keep the old tunnel system at liveable temperatures in spots. But it also apparently contributed to rotting of the waste piles.

Finally, Joost stopped, hands on knees, and they all rested for a minute or two at a porthole exit. Joost swung open a small metal door on a rusted, squeaking hinge.

"This is the hard part," he said. "It's a scramble."

On hands and knees they crawled up the hardscrabble, frozen scree that crumbled and slid beneath their weight. They were at the edge of the exonet. At the top of the incline, they could look out across the valley of Alba Fossa and see the patch of polyhouses, the original growing and food manufacturing laboratories. Ten or so acres of these houses stretched out before them in a long valley between two ridges. Across the valley, the opposite ridge loomed bleak and foreboding. Behind them stretched the center of Novaroma and behind the skyline to the southeast, outside the exonet and beyond the pale of Martian life rose the giant promontory of Mt. Olympus.

Joost explained the history of the greenhouses, how his parents had been part of the first generations of Earth biotech food specialists. Apparently the greenhouses had been abandoned in the last decade when more modern facilities had opened under the UWM's administration in the flatland.

As he talked, they dropped down the cliff along a track Joost knew. At the edge of the valley, he stopped and pointed to the sensor poles along the periphery of the valley. He outlined for them the importance of timing their movements by the light of the red buttons that glowed on and off as the sensors pivoted on their ballast mechanisms.

"We'll count to five slowly before we go each time," he said. "Just follow me."

They obediently followed behind Joost and made their way into the valley, dodging from shed to shed to avoid the sensors. They reached the greenhouse at the far end of the long valley after a long, patient travail. The daylight was already dimming. From the outside, Joost's greenhouse seemed to be filled with the clutter of ancient machinery and piles of scrap steel, just like all the other buildings. But once inside past the makeshift door, Joost showed them the central lair of old slabs of polycarbonate that he and his father had assembled. It hid a cookpot and alcoves for sleeping. This would be their hideout. It could be heated with an old hydrostatic pump that barely put out any heat, just enough to take off the chill inside the secret space. In the coming days and weeks, as long as it took, Joost and Carlisle would make drops of food, water and recharged transponders every other day at the tunnel's exit.

"Goodbye for now," said Joost at the door, hugging both of them.

"Don't be afraid," said Carlisle.

"No. We know you will succeed," said Joost.

But the two of them were overtaken by doubt. Antioch and Sakumi looked at each other. They were alone in the greenhouse, and the chasm caused by their flight was now opening unmistakable in the chill air of this abandoned and ghostly sector of Novaroma, separating them from the life of comfort that had been theirs just a few hours ago.

"What have we done?" asked Sakumi, talking to herself.

"Sakumi, look at me. We've got to find the way to go on now," said Antioch. He held her and tried to reassure her. Even though he knew his own spirit had been tested and survived under extreme duress – on the voyage of the Nazar, during his solitary ordeal in the cave of Tharsis – each minute and every hour going forward would be a new face of danger. But the only real extinction, he reminded himself, was capitulation to fear.

He alone had made the choice this time, taking on the challenge. It had not been forced on him. He had believed that if there was any spirit on Mars that would not crack, it was hers. That was a source of strength. He would rather take the chance with Sakumi then continue in Novaroma without her, abandoning the only hope he had of happiness. Hungry and cold, they huddled together under some blankets that had been left folded under a pile of dusty tarps. The metallic smell of hematites lingered in the air as the grey mists faded into the long night of winter.

But in the ensuing days Sakumi grew silent, withdrawn. Antioch made his way to the tunnels every day, waiting for the hours of dusk to set out, and back again with food, fresh transponders, and water bottles. Sakumi invariably

239

remained huddled under the tarps, knees up and legs locked between her arms, and barely registered his coming or going.

"Sakumi?"

"Yes?" She lifted her head. There was a reddish tint of light coming in the glass around the corner of the slab. It caught the slant of her finely cut profile. Her hair, once lustrous and full, now lay matted and flat, unkempt.

"You haven't eaten."

She didn't answer.

"Joost and Carlisle are doing a great job for us. They're keeping us fed just like they said they would. It can't be easy for them."

"Are you trying to make me feel worse than I already do?"

"No."

"Well, that's what you're doing."

"I'm sorry. It's just, why can't you eat?"

"I don't feel well."

"Tell me what you feel."

"I just can't do this. It's harder than I thought."

"You've gotta try."

"I know."

"Eat. If you don't eat you won't be able to do this."

"How dare you!" she shouted. "I'm tired of you telling me what to do. Was this all about you getting me somehow to obey? That's not right. It's not acceptable!" Sakumi stood and flailed with the blanket, throwing it off her shoulders and threatening to blow their cover.

"Hey, don't jump around like that. The sensors!" shouted Antioch.

She stopped and slowly settled back to the ground. Her face contorted and tears began to flow.

"I'm just not getting it," she said. "I'm so confused."

"But why? What do you want?"

"I don't know. Nobody taught me how to do this."

"Do what?"

"Be all alone."

"You're not alone. You're with me."

"I know."

"That's the problem. I'm not enough for you. I'm not doing enough, I guess."

"Enough of what?" she asked.

"Of what I should be doing."

"But the fear comes from inside me. There's no way for you to guard against what's inside of me."

"There has to be."

"There isn't," said Sakumi, sad with some certainty.

He wished that she could just imagine a world where everyone would be free, but she wasn't able to. Instead, she was frozen inside by traumatic levels of panic-stricken response. The toxic adrenaline and cortisol had already spread and enlarged the synaptic clefts, so that the patterns of hope were now too complex and could not hold. Breaking down the irrational elements and building those patterns of hope and connection back up would take time and energy, comforts that were altogether lacking in their present predicament. The biggest repercussion of all, given Sakumi's new altered state, was that he would curtail any of his own willing investment of hope without noticing. Every moment took an all-out, one hundred percent vision of certain success. Dropping his levels by any bit would put both of them in danger. He didn't know how to communicate that without making it worse. All he could do was hold her, silently assuring her with the warmth of his body and steadiness of hand. But it was not enough, nothing was.

"We're not alone, you know," he said one day.

"Who else is here?"

"I'm talking about the ancestors. They found their way."

"Please. I don't believe in any of that."

"Not just that. They've entered the Dolomite. She's with us as well. I wish you could see that."

"All of that pagan stuff. Did you always believe in it?"

"I did."

"I never knew that about you."

"Well, it's true. I wish I could convince you."

"But you can't because there is no proof. It's beyond rational. It's an article of faith. It makes you feel better about things we don't understand. Like death."

"But we know what death is. It's a rebalancing of the quantum state of the conscious mind."

"Well, that's one way to interpret it. But there is no proof unless I'm losing my mind. And now so are you. Is that good?"

"It's okay. I saw somebody in the tunnel yesterday. I didn't want to tell you. I don't want to get your hopes up."

The logical explanation was they were perhaps emissaries of the Martian resistance. They were approaching. But so was the Dolomite and the ancestral spirits. He had to keep trusting in salvation.

And then it was clear. There were the Homeland surveillance bot clouds. They looked like swarms of insects. The telltale black buzzing flocks were increasing. But Sakumi did not respond. It was too late. It would be up to him to bring them to safety.

After the black of night had completely taken over, all they could hear was the buzzing of the sensor swarms. Sakumi sat up and shivered. Antioch had his hand on her back, but when the swarm hit the side of the house, echolocating anything inside, they both bolted upright in the alcove.

"They know we're here," said Antioch, hating the sound of his own words.

"Of course," said Sakumi. Now she was ready to listen, perhaps.

"We have to leave here fast," he said. He had no plan. But they had no choice. It was run or die.

"Are you kidding?" said Sakumi.

"No. There's no time for this anymore. Get yourself dressed," he said.

"I can't," she said. In the dark, he studied her face. There was no sadness, no fear in her voice, just sullen resolve.

"What do you mean? I'm not leaving here without you."

"You go. I don't feel like running any more."

"But Sakumi, listen to me. They're not going to spare you just because your parents are Moonga and Murson Verdad."

"Do you even know who I am? I'm not Sakumi any more. I don't have any picture any more of what or who she is. I'm just...I don't care. Save yourself. You're better off without me. I'll be a decoy for you. You need to leave. Go on."

"Sakumi," he begged her. "I can't leave here without you."

Panic-stricken, she had, in fact, forgotten who she was. She shook her arm out from his grip.

"Leave me," she said.

He ran his fingers over her face, feeling her hot tears. It was tearing a part of himself away, to leave her behind. This was a devastating defeat. A goodbye forever. He had no words, just a final kiss.

He rose and put on his shirt and pants and tied his boots. The buzzing increased in intensity until it almost shouted its presence into their ears. He knelt beside her and put his hand on hers.

"Please come. I can't leave you here," he said one last time.

"No, Antioch. I don't want to live any more like this. I can't do it."

Inside his pocket, he stuck a spare folding knife that belonged to Joost or his father. Then he crawled across the floor under the piles of debris to the opposite wall and used the knife to slash through the sheeting of the greenhouse.

Behind him, he heard Sakumi cry out in anger. The drones were inside the greenhouse. She stood and began to run to the door before the drones swarmed and brought her down with stinging injections of neurotoxins that paralyzed her instantly, before she even hit the ground. Antioch was out with a final thrust of the dull knife blade, and he crawled, hugging the ground towards the far side of the valley. The swarms of drones buzzed through the entire valley. They directed their fire. It rained down on the greenhouses in a checkerboard pattern.

He waited in a ditch at the foot of the incline, burying himself under the rocks. Above him far up on the ridge was the porthole, the entrance to the tunnel system. The fires raging in the greenhouses merged with the setting sun.

He was still alive. The drones grew quiet, and there was just the sound of crackling flames coming to him from amid the swirling vortex of winds that swept up the valley. He listened carefully for a voice.

Nine

Morrow felt productive enough by the early spring that year. He pruned the grapes in a bit of a thaw in March. There was still about a foot of snow in the piles on the side of the road. The skiers were still drafting up and down the highway, but mud season was underway.

Mitch called him to beg forgiveness for the debacle with Dun Castle Books and ask how he was doing. Just back from mass, Morrow had been indulgent with him. Then afterwards, in conversation with Ellen, he had confessed how good it had felt to hear Mitch say he was sorry in so many words, but he'd complained to her that Mitch couldn't actually bring himself to say sorry. Instead he'd skirted around it awkwardly. Ellen had wondered if he had considered Mitch's point of view, which he hadn't, to be honest. Mitch's point of view always concerned the profit motive. And to Morrow that was so evidently not to be prioritized, except he wanted and needed to find another publisher. Mitch had some leads with some younger entrepreneurs who were crowd funding a cooperative social enterprise and looking for manuscripts. They liked solar punk, cyberpunk, and space opera. Mitch had mentioned romance as an area of science fiction that they were into exploring, and perhaps they could market Alias Tomorrow as that, and could he think of it as a way of framing that could shape his editing process, which by the way was the only editing process, since there was no money now to hire even a copy editor to clean up the manuscript. The whole thing was beneath his dignity, and he had gone on a long run after that particular Team meeting with Mitch and Anastasia.

They were doing their taxes. Ellen had the folder on the living room table and her reading glasses on. She directed Morrow as to which supplementary document to search for on the old desktop at the window that overlooked the dead brown thatch of the front yard. It was astoundingly complicated, *enough for him to declare a special kind of hatred of the federal bureaucrats who had devised it.*

He and Ellen wondered what they would do. To stay or go. To winter in Florida like a lot of their neighbors or to stick it out in New England like some hardy homesteaders, the way they had initially pictured themselves when they'd married and moved to town twenty five years before.

Taxes done, they prepared dinner together and set out the plates. They ate a congenial meal of leftovers and scrambled eggs and homemade bread. Ellen mentioned that the hospital was facing a buyout from a private group based in the Midwest and the fact that the state was cutting Medicaid reimbursements, which was forcing CMC's hand in the negotiations. On the other hand they were phasing out the dividends and interest tax which might benefit them in coming years as they began to collect on the IRA distributions. Ellen was thinking of retiring soon.

"Yeah, I need to talk to Mitch and see what's going on with the royalties on The Moons of French Pond. They don't seem to add up."

"Yes, those numbers don't match with the 1099. Do you want some ice cream?"

"Ice cream?"

"Yes, there's some ice cream that Mackenzy bought last time she was home."

"What flavor?"

"Mint chocolate. It has a little freezer burn."

"I hate freezer burn."

"I know."

Especially after doing the taxes he would have preferred a fresh container. It was something, better than nothing. But for Morrow, there was something missing. There was an element that couldn't be manufactured, an X factor that threatened everything. Was it known only by him? He suspected it fed into a lot of the alienation and loneliness that was reported in the various news outlets and podcasts that they subscribed to. Maybe it was just entitlement and privilege. Maybe he just needed to knuckle down and finish his book. How else did he expect to contribute? Yet there was always more to be done, better ways to consume to save the planet, improved ways of thinking that would elevate the lives of ever greater numbers of the marginalized and victimized. We needed an interior path. Who was to lead us, he wondered? He thought it wouldn't be him. Maybe Ellen. She served out two cups of ice cream. Two spoonfuls in each cup.

They had done all that was asked for, he and Ellen. They had fought for the good causes, had stood for order and community involvement, playing by the rules and changing the ones you didn't like. And he saw the videos of the screamers, the righteous, full of passionate intensity, puffed up by their mad visions of bygone and mythical days. They clearly believed, though, that they could bluff their way into beneficial places where they would be immune from the blowback of tragedy or karmic balance. And those vociferous few were backed up by the army of so-called Christians who had given up on Christ, doing the heavy lifting of a vindictive and unforgiving cross by rigging the rules against those who lacked conviction. These, the meek and indecisive, the unhappy in the skins, shape-shifting, adapting, scanning the horizon from their watchtowers desperately for the return of empathy, were the best among us. Sad to say, he thought.

Saroj called after dinner, in a flurry of wet snow, the winter showing off its lingering face. It was a video call and Morrow sat on the sofa after putting another log on the fire. Ellen sat next to him holding the phone up so Saroj could see the two of them. She had just showered and was in her nightgown. She handed him the phone. Her hair smelled of lemons. She crinkled it with a towel. Saroj's face filled the screen. They could see his nose ring quite well.

"What kind of phone do you have, Saroj?" asked Morrow.

"It's an Iphone 15, sir. Unlocked," said Saroj.

"It's got a really good camera," said Morrow.

"Oh, yes."

"Where are you?" asked Ellen.

"In California. Junipero."

"Is that nice?"

"It's very pretty, very nice, ma'am. I like it. And the people are very nice. They are all makers here in this house."

"What happened to school, Saroj?" interrupted Morrow. He hated the lag on the WhatsApp platform.

"It's a semester off, sir. It's okay."

"That's good," said Morrow, keeping the conversation going.

"Do you have friends there?" asked Ellen.

"Oh, yes. Many friends," said Saroj. Morrow hoped it was true.

That night they slept well, but Morrow woke early for some reason. The light was just beginning to show in the window. Ellen stirred and they made love in a way, mostly cuddling and holding each other.

Afterwards, Ellen told of a dream she had.

"Your Mom was in it," she said.

"Margaret?" He had been thinking of her also.

"Yes. She was taking the two girls somewhere. And we were going out too, but her event seemed more fun. She was saying something to me. Something about eating the stale bread."

"Yes, that sounds right," said Morrow.

So she had spoken. The stale bread is good bread, and it is good for eating, and that is the way we get to homebase.

"I'm sorry, Ellen," said Morrow. He had sat up in bed and was taking off the covers, in a hurry to hide his nakedness.

"For what?"

"For ever doubting you."

"Oh, don't be silly, William."

"How silly?" he asked.

"You never doubted me, did you?"

"Not really."

He sat down at the desk, fully dressed, shaved, fires on, with a coffee on the desk, and wrote out a quick letter to Daniel on a couple of pieces of yellow legal pad.

My Dear Daniel,

I've been thinking a lot about us lately, especially after our conversations at Christmas. I know I don't always say what I mean, or maybe I say too much and it comes out wrong. So warning, this is me trying to get it right.

I want you to know I am incredibly proud of you. Of the person you are, not just what you do. Dude, you have a kind heart, a sharp mind, and a spirit that seeks to make the world better. Those are the things that truly matter. More than any job title or amount of cash in your bank account.

I know I sometimes come across as critical or worried about your path. It comes from a place of love, I swear. As is clear to everyone, I've made mistakes, blindly trying to find my way, and I just don't want you to fall into the traps that are out there. But here's the thing I know. Your path is your own. You have to find it your way, and I need to trust that you will. And I hope it's as clear to you as it is to me – it's a heck of a trail you have blazed already.

But a little fatherly wisdom. Warning lights flashing red. What's important is not the accolades or achievements, but the connections we make. The love we give and receive. The moments of joy, even the small ones, that we share with others. It's about being true to yourself, even when it's hard, and standing up for who you are.

I haven't always been good at showing you how much I care. I've been caught up in my own worries and insecurities. But I want you to know that I love you deeply, and I am always here for you, no matter what.

I had a hard relationship with my own father, and when the time came to say goodbye, neither of us could find the right words. I never want it to be that way between us, son, and that's why sometimes I say too much, or the wrong things, because for me the attempt to communicate is worth the pain of failure. Better than the opposite, which is prideful silence and the retreat of affection. Please forgive me for my failures to communicate and to spell out for you your value as a human being. Maybe that's not what fathers can or ought to do, Danny. Maybe that's better as a self-appraisal after long journeys of discovery. I know you aren't one to shy away from those, and my hope and aim, (it would be my proudest accomplishment), is to accompany you always on your way, even if it's just these words, or the memories of our brief but happy times together.

Anyway, let me know what you're up to from time to time and I promise to do the same.

Lots of love,
Your ever flailing Dad

"Ellen, do we have an address for Daniel?"

"It's in my contacts list. The laptop's open," said Ellen.

Morrow went out to the kitchen where she'd been working that morning. He put the kettle on and sat down. He needed her password, so he walked over to the living room again and opened the door.

"What's your password?"

"Oh my God. It's forever Jung with a 4 and capital E. How many times, honestly?"

"I forget that."

This time he went by the office and took out an envelope from the drawer. Once back in the kitchen he opened up the laptop, typed out the password as instructed and opened up the contacts file on her desktop. He scrolled down the list and checked names. Daniel was under M for Morrow. He wrote out the address on the envelope. Stuffed the letter in the envelope.

"I'm going to the post office. I'll be back."

"Take your time," said Ellen.

Epilogue

The OneWorld had relinquished its last foothold in the Novaroma UWM campus to the Commission for Renewal, an alliance of the main rebel groups on Mars. At the initial peace negotiations held at the end of 122 in the Svyatogor government complex, Antioch represented the military wing of the so-called Shadow Reformation. His aide de camp was none other than Garcia Jones. Jones looked outstandingly regal in his epaulettes, it was noted in the press reports. These same quoted witnesses as saying:

"Brigadier Littell holds the hopes of all marginalized and yet to be uplifted communities".

The negotiations were successful. OneWorld and its supporters agreed to a repatriation of OneWorld's technological assets, the codes to all data banks and platforms tied to the Nurvalink, and their civilian support, mostly in the upper ranks of the administrative state, to Outpost Ganymede. Another political aim of the alliance was an outreach to renewed trade and culture ties with Earth, especially the Democravian regions where the largest percentage of the population remained non-augmented. Antioch was credited with drafting the final Appeal to Pacify Warring Parties.

In 126, Antioch traveled to Earth as a part of the delegation to the first Conference of Organic Parties to draw up constitutional foundations of the new Interstellar Marquisade. He was housed in Atlanta, and was visited on several occasions by his daughter Uvlin.

Anthony Caplan is a writer, teacher and state legislator from New Hampshire. His previous books include *The Truth Now, Yet Today,* and *The Jonah Trilogy.*

.

"